Meeting the Master

Meeting the Master

ELISSA WALD

GROVE PRESS
New York

Published simultaneously in Canada
Printed in the United States of America

FIRST GROVE PRESS PAPERBACK EDITION

Library of Congress Cataloging-in-Publication Data

Wald, Elissa.
Meeting the master / Elissa Wald.
p. cm.
ISBN 0-8021-3550-1
1. Erotic stories, American. I. Title.
PS3573.A42115M44 1996
813′.54—dc20 96-18200

DESIGN BY LAURA HAMMOND HOUGH

Elissa Wald can be contacted at the following address:
P. O. Box 952
Village Station
New York, NY 10014

Grove Press
841 Broadway
New York, NY 10003

98 99 00 01 10 9 8 7 6 5 4 3 2 1

For Patrick,
my captain

Contents

Author's Note

For years, when asked what it is that I write about, I have responded—by turns flippant, apologetic, and in-your-face—"S&M." What this answer means, though, has only gotten more difficult to clarify. The range and complexity of S&M involvement is as infinite as human sexuality itself. Even the letters *S* and *M* represent many different concepts to different people. As the theme of this book, sadomasochism is probably a misnomer. Here, "S&M" would much more readily stand for "slavery and mastery," not only where it is consciously expressed in bedroom games, but where I see it sublimated and (barely) veiled nearly everywhere I look.

Meeting the Master, therefore, isn't an easy book to categorize. It is wholly erotic—at least to me—but only occasionally very graphic. It is straight, gay, and everything in between. It depicts a dark and little-understood area of sexuality, often outside of what we recognize as a sexual context.

Like anything else that resists a ready pigeonhole, this book will disturb and offend some people, but it is my hope that it will serve many others. Those who, like me, have a perpetual craving for material on this topic; who felt the pull early on, maybe even from early childhood; who have purchased even the most dismal pornography if it promised some kind of a "fix" in this area; who have felt intense frustration at the dearth of quality literature that addresses it in any depth.

It is the aim of this book to sate some of that particular hunger; to explore S&M beyond the stereotypes of leather, whips, and chains; to ask questions and provoke thought; to arouse and entertain.

It is my attempt to tell some of my own truth.

I hope you enjoy it.

Meeting the Master

"Beware the fury of a patient man."
—John Dryden

I dreamed you had the patience of a prayer:
You let me memorize your open hand
Before you closed a fist around my hair.

I read a warning written down somewhere:
"Beware the fury of a patient man."
I dreamed you had the patience of a prayer.

I'll swear to the truth if you'll take a dare,
Plead guilty if you'll force me to the stand,
And close a knowing fist around my hair.

Yours is the rhythm of a rocking chair:
Steady as an hourglass spilling sand.
I dreamed your patience would make saints despair.

I've yearned to cringe beneath your level stare.
My wish has been to be at your command—
To kiss the iron fist around my hair.

I've waited for years, searching everywhere,
But only you have made me understand:
Patience in a slave is itself a prayer,
And answered by your fist around my hair.

Meeting the Master

The Initiation

I.

"You're so sexually inhibited it's unbelievable," Kim told me, in a tone that suggested he had seen much in his eighteen years. "You're the most sexually inhibited person I've ever met."

I was in tenth grade when this fateful judgment was delivered. Fifteen years old and had just broken up with Kim.

Our relationship had begun when I was fourteen, a freshman in high school; he was seventeen, a senior. I fell so hard for him and the crush was so agonizingly sweet that it made up for everything that came afterward, for the lean, hungry years of wanting, of obsessing.

Kim was my first love and the one to initiate me into my own sexuality.

I had always—always—had sexual fantasies. Four, five years old, and lying in bed at night before falling asleep was as lovely as it is now. And the theme has always been the same, involving a confrontation between myself and some authority figure: transgression, punishment, remorse, penance, forgiveness. Even as a small child, I was riveted by men instead of boys: the teachers at school, the counselors at camp, the older brothers of friends. I liked soldiers, firemen, and policemen; I looked at men who wore belts, men who wore boots.

* * *

With Kim, it was fascination at first sight. I had never seen anyone like him. He was half Korean and half British, unmistakably Asian yet pale and full-lipped, with hay-straight dirty-blond hair and slanted green eyes. He was medium height, about five-foot-eight. Lean and sinewy and bristling with barely leashed energy.

I met him during the first week of school. His green eyes glittered with an almost manic brightness and his hair was, literally, standing on end. He was clad in a sleeveless Union Jack T-shirt, torn jeans belted with a chain and a pair of handcuffs, and several bracelets as spiky as his head on each wrist. I had seen him before in the halls—he was hard to miss—but we had never spoken. A friend of mine, Montgomery, introduced us in the cafeteria.

"Delilah, this is Kim," he said, nodding at what I had begun to think of as "the creature."

"Hello," said the creature, sounding strangely articulate.

"Nice to meet you," I said, with a slightly condescending smile. And that was it. I didn't see him again until the next week, again in the cafeteria. I had forgotten my lunch money, and I still knew very few people at school. Forlorn and hungry, I worked up the nerve to approach him, and he gave me a dollar so I could eat. By the time I got to the lunch line, though, it had already shut down, and the only thing left to buy was ice cream. I exchanged a quarter for a stale vanilla cone topped with a frozen cluster of nuts. I knew from experience that it wouldn't taste much different from the paper it was wrapped in, but it was better than nothing.

"You wasted my money on that?" Kim asked when I returned.

"I have to eat something. It was all that was left," I defended myself, and bit in. The almonds were bitter; I spat them into my palm.

"Hey," he protested. "That's the best part."

"Well, you can have it," I said snidely, opening my hand. He startled me by seizing my wrist and bending to take the chewed, spit-ridden contents in his mouth.

"Oh God," I cringed. "I can't believe you just did that."

"It's just spit. No worse than kissing," he said, and smiled. It was then that I felt the first twinge. It was a brand-new thought—kissing the creature. Brand-new and not altogether off-putting. But it was only a twinge. It took what happened to Daniel River to make me fall in love with him.

It happened in early October. I was sitting with Kim and my best friend Cheryl on the lawn in front of the school. Everyone hung out on the lawn after school, often for hours. The Frisbee Club, which was actually a motley group of sixties throwbacks, stayed the latest—they played Frisbee until it got dark or someone cut open a foot.

Cheryl and Kim were arguing about whether it reflected badly on an upperclassman to associate with bratty freshman girls. He was teasing her and she was arguing back sharply—far too seriously. I realized that Cheryl liked Kim as much as I did, and I filed this knowledge away along with a secret and resolute disregard. I stayed quiet while she got more and more worked up, thinking it was setting me in a good light. Quiet and—I hoped—enigmatic. Once in a while, Kim's eyes met mine and it seemed as if we were sharing a glimmer of a silent laugh.

The day was cold and golden and beautiful. The leaves were changing and falling from the trees. My crush was a tender swelling beneath my ribs: tense, fluttering, happy.

The argument between Kim and Cheryl was winding down. She was abandoning her fury and coaxing him for a piggyback ride to the pay phone, which was in the parking lot behind the school.

I felt more than a little jealousy at the sight of her draped across his back. I was somehow wearing his sweatshirt, though, and walking beside him. We rounded the corner and there, by the wall, was a tight circle of leather-jacketed backs. From within it, someone was screaming.

"What's going on?" Cheryl said, then, "Oh God!"

"They're just playing," I said, but even as I heard myself I could see a slight, blond-haired boy pressed to the wall with a mask of blood where his face should have been.

I was barely aware of Kim shaking Cheryl off. I went weak in the knees at the sight of that blood, at the sight of the boy sliding, as if he'd been shot, down the wall to the ground.

The next part is seared into my memory in languorous slow motion, and I replay it often, even now. As Cheryl and I backed away, Kim lunged forward. I watched his receding back, his tawny hair flying behind him, and as he ran toward the scene I could see the glint of a razor from within the ring. Kim never hesitated. He hurled himself into the pack the way, as a child, I flung myself against the arms locked against me in Red Rover. He did not speak; he did not glance at the attackers. He reached the boy and hauled him swiftly to his feet.

The ranks pressed in and Kim turned, shielding the boy with his own body. He blocked two punches in quick succession and I remembered that he knew karate. A third caught him hard on the side of his face. He did not flinch or make a sound, or do anything else to acknowledge the blow. His leg snapped out in a kick which caught one of the assailants in the stomach, causing him to stagger backward. Then all of them moved backward, and suddenly they were gone. Cheryl and I ran over, and I recognized the boy. His name was Daniel; he was a junior. The four of us returned together to the front lawn of the school.

We were immediately surrounded by what was left of the Frisbee Club. Daniel's eyelid had been slashed; most of the blood seemed to be coming from there. A dark stain had spread on the front of his jeans where he'd wet himself. I noticed blood spattered on my own clothing, on my own arms. I was trembling slightly, and cold.

Daniel was shepherded to the school nurse and the police were called. Cheryl, Kim, and I were repeatedly asked to describe what happened. For me, only one thing mattered: Kim's part in it all. Kim had seen someone being beaten by a pack of boys much larger than himself, and without thinking about the danger, without thinking at all, he had thrown himself into the middle. For me, he had swiftly and irrevocably become a hero. And the whole time I sat there demurely and told the police the facts and tried to seem quietly traumatized, I was exploding inside. Kim was a hero!

Eventually I was allowed to leave. I went straight home to my room and lay down on the floor. I was so wild with excitement I didn't know what to do with myself. And I was slightly ashamed as well, for despite the horror of the afternoon—the violence and the cruelty, the slashed eyelid and the blood—I had never felt such joy.

From this afternoon on, I began to worship Kim in earnest. I had never been so passionately absorbed in anyone. I watched him constantly and furtively; I prayed to have him, I lingered on the lawn after school whenever he did, thrilled just to be in his presence. Becoming increasingly bold, and increasingly drastic in my measures, I stole his camel-colored suede jacket from the boys' locker room and slept with it nightly, inhaling his barely detectable scent from its interior.

I look back at him as if through a kaleidoscope; I see him in a fragmented, firecracker-bright burst of images. Patiently, tirelessly explaining algebra to a very slow, very obese girl he barely knew. Climbing a tree to get a stranded cat. Sitting on the front steps of the school, strumming his guitar, with a cluster of admirers around his feet, gazing up at him with rapt attention. Unself-consciously singing:

I want to be like him
I want to think like him
I want to know all of his secrets
Want to feel life through his skin . . .

His voice was low and sweet; his eyes smiled with the irony of his lyrics; his mouth was gently curved, sensual and kindly. I watched his hands on the strings. There was an uncompromising knot in my gut, tight and hard, hungry.

He paid some attention to me. I had never had a boyfriend, was unfamiliar with the courtship ritual, and as such could not interpret his actions. We talked from time to time after school, and he often allowed himself to be coaxed into gymnastic displays when I was around. He was a proficient acrobat and a passionate show-off, climbing the columns in front of the school, walking on the fence, turning handsprings on the lawn.

Once he was teasing me. I was standing on the grass watching Frisbee practice when I felt something smack the back of my head. Upon turning around I could see, among the people nearby who might have done it, Kim looking quite innocent, if a bit too bright-eyed. By the third cuff, his misty stare into the distance was shading into a smirk, and I retaliated suddenly, bringing the back of my own hand into sharp contact with his left cheekbone.

"Hey," he said, startled. "What'd you have to hit me so hard for?"

"You did it to me," I answered, thoroughly unconcerned.

"What do you mean, I did it to you?"

"You hit me first."

"I hit you like this," he said, tapping me with a fraction of his former force, "not like *this*." And he slapped me hard across the face.

I heard it before I felt it. A few seconds passed before I felt a shape like a handprint burning where he had struck. Humiliation left me expressionless.

We stared at each other for a moment, equally startled by what he had done. Then I turned away mutely, not knowing what else to do. Some of my friends were drawing on the blacktop with colored chalk. I went over and sat down with them. My whole body hurt.

After a few minutes I sensed Kim hovering on the periphery of this activity—it was probably his chalk. I kept my head down. It was all I could do to look at him out of the corner of my eye. We didn't speak for the rest of the day.

That night I lay in bed, looking out into the dark, thrilling to the memory of it. I had roused him to action and emotion. A transaction had taken place that included only myself and him; he had acted upon me, left an imprint. I lay savoring it, as if it had been a kiss.

Sex and violence are, for me, inextricably linked. And I can't remember a time when this wasn't the case. It was a sense I always had, before I could put it into words. No matter how crude, unseemly, or even grotesque the forms this combination might take.

I was twelve years old and in a motel room with my family when I first saw studio wrestling on TV. And I could neither believe what I was seeing nor tear my eyes away. One wrestler lay defeated on his back while another knelt beside him to inflict the slow, deliberate, proprietary damage. Picking his head up by the hair and slamming it into the floor. Rising to grind a casual heel into his groin.

"What is this?" I cried. "Is he allowed to do those things?"

"It's all staged," my brother assured me. "*Studio* wrestling, you get it? None of it's real."

"You shouldn't be watching this trash anyway," my mother put in, without looking up from her book.

The match was ending; another was beginning. A black man was entering the ring with a white opponent. It was announced that the loser would have his head shaved.

Growing up, my brother and I were allowed to watch very little television. It took special circumstances for the four of us to be grouped around the tube, unusual situations like this one, in which a heavy rain was foiling our ski trip. It wasn't the fighting itself that I found so riveting; my father liked to watch boxing, and I was familiar enough with the blood, the twisted grimaces of pain. But this. This was something different.

The black wrestler had lost the match and was being dragged into the center of the ring. The victor was brandishing an electric razor. "I can't believe this is happening," I said. "I can't watch." But of course I did watch, through the cracks of my fingers. It was an awful sight. The victim was bucking and writhing. Three or four men held him in place as the razor plowed through his Afro and great chunks of hair fell to the floor. They were doing an erratic job, so that he looked grotesque until all his hair was gone. Once completely shorn, he looked all right again; he had a strong, clean jawline and carried baldness very well. But I wasn't to be consoled.

"That had to be real, didn't it?" I demanded of my brother. "They can't fake shaving someone's head. Why do they do it? Just to humiliate the loser? Isn't it humiliating enough to lose?"

"Christ, would you relax?" my brother said. "Who cares why? They're Neanderthals."

"They're still people," I argued. "They're human beings, being degraded in the name of entertainment."

"He's getting paid a lot of money for this nonsense," my father said dismissively, reaching for the newspaper. "He probably grew hair for the match."

I had never seen anything like that before. And yet it was as if it had always been there; it hadn't really startled me as much as I pretended. I thought I understood this spectacle, with a secret and unspeakable understanding. I saw what my mother and father and brother did not: the urge to take part in a perverse drama, inflict punishment in a public game of humiliation. They did not see this, or would not acknowledge it. It bewildered me: how did these sensible people produce a creature of such depravity?

I had to wonder: whence had I sprung?

II.

I got Kim. I don't know what I would have done if I hadn't, but perhaps this was a possibility I couldn't allow myself to consider. I had to have him, so I got him, and I have never been happier than I was then.

It was as wonderful as a first love could be. He was a senior in high school, all-knowing and worldly; I was a starry-eyed freshman, tender and impressionable. He was a coveted figure at school; I was queen groupie, suddenly turned queen. And I was exactly what my wonder and naïveté suggested: untouched. I had made it all the way to high school without anyone so much as groping under my T-shirt. Therein lay much of Kim's power: he knew my body far better than I did.

Years later, when I was in college, I met a woman who belonged to the gym I had just joined. She first came to my attention when she was lifting an unbelievable stack of weights with her ankles. She was exquisitely muscled; I couldn't stop looking at her. She also seemed very irritated all the time, as if undecided about whether she wanted to lift the weights or hurl them through the gym window. One evening she turned on me.

"What the fuck are you always *staring* at?"

It took a moment for me to be able to answer. "It's just that—well, that you have a very beautiful body."

She softened, but just slightly. "Look, do you know what you're doing in here? Or are you just fucking around? Because if you don't have a real plan, you know, you're never going to get anywhere."

I told her I had a routine I'd made up but didn't really know how efficient it was.

She offered to tell me a few things: "Let's start with your upper body. Come here and let me look at you. Take off your shirt and let me see your back." I pulled off my tank top and turned around, overcome by a heady sense of peril. And then when she put her hands on me, touched me the way you would an apple for bruises, a tremor ran through me from crown to toe.

She mapped out a regimen for my metamorphosis and started me off right then and there. She'd tell me to lift a certain amount of weight ten times, and just as I was nearly done, as I was lowering it for the ninth time and nearly beside myself with pain, she'd order me to "go for twelve." Physical agony had never been so sweet.

She drove me home that night.

"By the way," she asked casually in the car, "are you straight or gay?"

With some reluctance, I said straight.

"You got a boyfriend?"

I said I was seeing my karate instructor.

She snorted. "You fall in love with anyone who has some sort of didactic position toward you. It's such an obvious element of your personality."

She had known me all of an hour and a half. And yet she was undeniably right.

I wanted to learn, and Kim showed me. But the way he showed me was surprising, and surprises me still whenever I think about it. He moved slowly. So slowly. He made it painfully slow; he filled me with an agony of longing. I was amazed, disbelieving—and frightened of my own insatiability. For a long time we did nothing but kiss—thrilling kisses. I had never really been kissed before. There had been quick, awkward, spin-the-bottle kisses in grade school, and the detached, experimental kisses that were obligatory at parties throughout middle school, but nothing like this, this exultant pressing together against the columns in front of the school, on street corners amidst falling autumn leaves, in his bedroom on rainy afternoons. He was gentle. And slow. I wanted, I waited, I waited desperately for him to touch me. For his hand, at long last, tender on my rib cage, over my bra, under my bra. I was passive. I didn't know how to be encouraging, let alone aggressive. I gloried in the giving of myself; it was all I knew.

Looking back, there seems an unbelievable sweetness in not knowing what to do. After the first love comes a certain confidence. You know, or think you know, what men like; you're in a position to coolly appraise; you know what to do with your hands and your mouth and you know what you want.

I was far from any of this. I was wide-eyed and amazed, vulnerable and open. I followed where he led; I moaned under his hand; I filled out, as if for him, in less than a year: from a nearly flat chest—unworthy of a bra—to full, firm convexities I couldn't believe were mine. I learned all my erogenous zones, and consequently how to masturbate: a mixed blessing. For a long time after Kim and I were history, I was in a sticky situation where nothing could stack up to my own hand. Kim came before my hand; Kim might as well have stuck a British-Korean flag in my cunt. For years I compared every boy to come along with him, and all were doomed to pale. In his wake, finding no one to satisfy my newfound need, I could only do it myself, often several times a day.

Kim never pushed me to do anything. Not so much as a suggestion ever passed his lips. He wasn't in a hurry, and he was wholly uninterested in intercourse. Whether he was saving his own virginity, and for what, was unclear, but fucking me was not his goal. He was ever slow and gentle, apparently satisfied with what others called foreplay as an end in itself. He revealed none of the frantic gluttony or agitation of boyfriends to come; tenderness was enough for him. And for this he was an exquisite lover.

* * *

Kim had two heroes, Gandhi and Martin Luther King. He admired gentleness, said he wished he were gentle himself.

"You are, Kim," I told him, and believed it. We were sitting on the lawn in front of school.

"No, I'm not, not really. Not like them. Not even, say, like any of *them,*" and he nodded at the Frisbee Club scattered over the grass, sailing their disks through the autumn air. I studied them dubiously. They were a strange and skinny bunch, whose pacifism and bell-bottoms always made them an immediate target for anyone who wanted trouble.

"Then again"—Kim's tone changed suddenly, taking on a flat edge—"other people make me feel like a saint. Certain individuals . . . make me feel like the gentlest guy on the face of the earth." He was staring pointedly in front of him and I followed his gaze to Guy Bryant, a leather-clad, mohawked young man who was now approaching the lawn. In many ways, although they were arch-enemies, Guy was a wayward counterpart to Kim. They were both very distinctive figures at school, each liking to be the center of attention. They were similarly built, both lithe and lean and clean-muscled—and both had reputations as skilled fighters. But Guy was a bully where Kim was a knee-jerk defender of the oppressed, and they had consequently locked horns on several occasions. It remained unclear which of them would come out on top if a fight between them were ever allowed to run its course. They had always been separated before anything decisive could happen.

Guy leaned on the fence and stared at the Frisbee Club as if their very existence were an affront to him. I could see by their skittish glances in his direction that his singular presence was unsettling the whole group. In another moment, he was joined by Joe Ritts, his sallow little sidekick. They lit cigarettes and stood in silence for a while.

"Y'know," Guy suddenly announced loudly to Joe. "The lice epidemic is back in the public schools."

"Is that right, Guy?" the smaller boy said.

"Yeah, ain't it a bitch? My sister got sent home from school yesterday; she got 'em from someone. They say longhaired people are the most likely to carry 'em and spread 'em around." He glared meaningfully at the hippies. "That's how come my sister got 'em right away. She's got long hair. But then, she's a girl, *girls* are supposed to—"

"She probably got them from your greasy Mohawk," Kim shouted across the lawn.

Guy turned, startled, and saw Kim for the first time. A look of frustration crossed his face. He threw down his cigarette and ground it angrily underfoot. "Suck my dick, Kim," he said, turning away.

"Wouldn't want to cheat little Joey there out of a job," Kim returned.

"Did you hear that, Guy?" Joe whined. But Guy was already stalking away. Joe wavered in indecision a moment, then flipped Kim the bird and took off after Guy.

Several members of the Frisbee Club turned to Kim and made elaborate, sardonic bows in his direction. He laughed with pleasure.

"Look at them," I said, resuming our discussion. "There's a difference between gentleness and defenselessness. It's not that they *won't* fight so much as that they *can't*. I think pacifism is mostly cowardice."

"Do you think Gandhi was a coward?" he asked.

This brought me up short. "I don't know anything about Gandhi," I said.

"That's certainly clear."

I didn't respond.

"And what about Martin Luther King?"

I fell silent for a while. "They're different," I said at last. "You can't compare them to the Frisbee Club, for Christ's sake."

I was irritated with the whole conversation. I was being ridiculous and I knew it. But I also knew we were concerned about two different things, while Kim did not. And I could see no way to show him.

"Don't you think violence ever has its place?" I asked.

"I don't think it ever accomplishes anything," he answered.

"Sometimes," I said haltingly, "sometimes it's just exciting."

"Not to me," he said.

Therein lay the problem. Kim would never understand if I told him what I wanted. My desires, which made no sense even to me, would seem even crazier to someone like him. Not that I ever got over my shyness in his bed anyway. If I couldn't say "touch me" I certainly couldn't say "hit me." I couldn't say: tie my hands, hold me down, spit in my mouth. If I could have, everything might have been different. I wouldn't have had to really get him angry.

We played a game.

It was about reflexes. Kim would hold his hands out palms up. I would place mine over his, palms down, and he would then try to slap at them before I could pull them away. Then we'd reverse it.

Kim was far better at this than me. When we played, he would go untouched for long minutes while my knuckles reddened and my fury mounted. Eventually I'd become incensed and after a painful volley of blows I would often, only half-jokingly, slap his face. The first time this happened he laughed. Every time after that, it pissed him off. Sometimes he would hit me back, sometimes not. Whenever he did, a tingling flash of ecstasy would split my body.

It mystified him that I wanted to play the game so often.

And once, we were in my room after having watched a rerun of *Batman.* In the episode, burglars had bound Commissioner Gordon to a chair and gagged him. The gag consisted only of a piece of cloth placed between his teeth and he was able to mutter loudly, if incoherently, from behind it at the villains.

"What good does a gag do?" I remarked to Kim afterward. "The person can still make all the noise he wants."

"Not the way I'd gag 'em," Kim stated flatly.

"What do you mean?"

"If I gagged you, you wouldn't be able to make a sound."

"Sure I could," I said, knowing Kim could never resist a challenge.

"Get me two socks," he said. "And a bandanna."

I produced these items and perched on the edge of the bed.

"Open your mouth," he said.

My lips parted as if for a kiss.

"Wider." His voice had taken on a strange edge.

I obeyed silently. He folded one sock into a compact square and pushed it to the back of my throat. Above this invasion we stared at each other. His gaze was steady and impersonal.

I closed my eyes and tried to control my breathing.

"Wider," he repeated curtly. I stretched my jaw still farther and felt him push the other sock into my mouth. I could barely hold both. He then placed the middle of the bandanna between my teeth and knotted the two ends tightly behind my head.

"Now," he said. "Scream."

I tried. It sounded like the wheeze of a broken accordion. Helpless.

"Go ahead," he said smugly. "Make some noise."

I gave it everything I had, to no further avail.

"I think I like you better this way," he said.

I could feel my pulse racing wildly, and cast my eyes down lest he detect my excitement. I wanted him to keep talking to me, wanted to remain in the position of being able only to register, not answer, what he had to say. And when he was done talking I wanted him to push me down on the bed, hold my wrists above my head with one hand, and set me to writhing with the other. . . .

From within my reverie I heard him go on, "Yes, you seem to have become docile very quickly; I should have tried this a long time ago."

I looked up at him hopefully, searching for some hint of seriousness in his expression, but could find none. There was nothing but teasing affection in his smile.

"Maybe I'll leave you like this all night," he was saying, but his hands were already on my shoulders, turning me around so he could undo his handiwork.

One evening in the last chill of March, Cheryl and I went skating at the Schenley Park ice rink. The skaters had been asked to leave the ice while workers smoothed it over with their trucks. We were sitting in the locker room when two older girls came in. I recognized them as seniors at school.

One of them was crying. "What's he so mad about?" she protested to the other. "I wasn't lookin' at that stupid kid. He makes this shit up inside his own head."

Guy Bryant appeared in the doorway with two of his buddies. "Get your fuckin' skates off and get in the van," he roared. Everyone turned to stare at him. "You got three minutes," he added, then disappeared.

The girl bent clumsily to unlace her skates. "Why does he have to be like that?" she wept.

Her friend dropped an arm around her shoulders. "What are you lookin' at?" she snarled at us. Cheryl and I dropped our eyes.

In another minute they were gone. I was afraid to follow them out, but I wanted to badly. I ached to know what was going to happen next. At that moment I wanted to be Guy's girlfriend. The dismal reality of such a situation did not occur to me. I wanted to be the object of such irrational jealousy, to feel male rage breaking over me like thunder.

I recounted the incident to Kim later. He snorted. "That doesn't surprise me in the least," he said. "When the miserable fucker gets tired of hippie baiting and fag bashing, naturally he starts in on his girlfriend. And until a position in a used car lot opens up to provide him with his true mission in life, I guess we've all got to deal with him."

I began to challenge Kim at every opportunity. His anger was deeply arousing to me. I loved the sense of danger, of unleashing something I couldn't control. Something to which I would have to surrender.

My provocation took many forms. I was always late whenever we were supposed to meet. I would openly flirt with other boys in his presence. In our play wrestling, I kicked below the belt. But it was difficult to get Kim really upset. He was easygoing and tolerant by nature, and wasn't one to hold a grudge. He took to asking me to meet him twenty minutes earlier than he really wanted, so that for his intents and purposes, I'd be on time. He had a remarkable lack of jealousy, and if he noticed my flirtatiousness, he didn't care. And the more points I scored in our wrestling, the more I pleased him. Kim knew karate and judo and thought everyone should know at least some self-defense. He showed me the most vulnerable parts of the body and how to go for them. If I managed to land a particularly painful kick or punch, he'd howl cheerfully and clap my shoulder in appreciation.

"I'm creating a monster," he'd gloat. "A little monster."

It frustrated me that he so rarely retaliated. Soon I was upping the ante; it became like a game. I took his favorite pair of biking gloves without asking, and "lost" them on an excursion with friends. That got him angry all right, but only for about half an hour.

"It's not so much that you lost them," he repeated several times. "It's more that you didn't even ask if you could *take* them."

We were in his room. I was sitting at his desk, staring out the window at the rain and pretending to be much unhappier than I really was. This was the most delicious part of any confrontation: the charade of regret. I loved having to work at placating Kim. It was only satisfying if he was considerably upset and if I was undeniably in the wrong.

"I didn't think you would mind," I said softly.

"'Then why didn't you just ask me and make sure?"

"I guess I didn't really think about it."

"You never think about it. You have absolutely no respect for other people's property. It's like when you stole my jacket. I mean, it's very touching that you wanted this relic of me to sleep with. But what was I supposed to tell my dad when he asked me where it was?" A righteous pause. "Here I am thinking I'd lost it somehow, this expensive suede jacket. Didn't you think that was going to cause trouble for me? The gloves were expensive too," he added.

His bringing up the jacket was a sign that he was softening. He pretended gruffness, but he loved the fact that I had taken it. He was not immune to worship.

I gave him my most imploring look. "Kim . . . I'm going to save my money and get you another pair. . . ."

He regarded me for a moment, then relented.

"I don't want you to do that. I just want you to *think* about things. . . ."

And it was over, too quickly. Why didn't he ever milk an advantage? Why didn't he brood? More alarmingly, why was I able to bring him around so easily? Was he so taken with me that he couldn't hold his own?

Another time, during an argument about whether males were inherently smarter at math than females—"It's not chauvinism,

Del, just a fact"—I hurled his calculus book through his bedroom window, which fortunately was open. Still, it landed in a patch of mud and broke at the spine. Kim was incredulous.

"Look at this! Look what you did," he said, lifting the ruined text from the mire and showing me the damage. "This isn't even my book, it's the school's. What the hell was the point?"

It was hailing lightly. We stood shivering in his backyard; I waited to see what he was going to do. When I didn't answer, he said, "Why don't you just go home?"

"Maybe I don't want to."

"Maybe I want you to. So maybe you should get the fuck out of here." He turned abruptly and went into his house, slamming the door.

A little thrill of pleasure ran through me. I didn't go after him for fear that he'd relent. I walked home slowly, replaying his last words over and over. They gave me a glow inside, like wine.

"Hey there," my father greeted me as I came in the back door. "Looks like you got caught in the hail. Couldn't Kim drive you home?"

"He's mad at me," I reported, delighted with the sound of it.

"Ah, well," my father said, in a mock-dreamy voice. "Young lovers' quarrels are soon mended."

As if on cue, the phone rang. "I'll get it," I said, heading upstairs.

It was Kim. He'd wanted to make sure I'd gotten home all right. "I should have driven you," he said. "You really pissed me off, though. I don't understand why you do these things."

I didn't understand either. Such a short time ago, I'd wanted Kim with what I'd thought was hopeless longing. It had been a miracle that he'd wanted me back. And at times I was dazzled by the perfection of our moments together. There were afternoons at his house where we made cocoa, built a fire, and spent long hours in front of it while snow fell outside the window. He would brush my hair, gently working the tangles out, while his cat curled on my lap and firelight flickered on the walls.

I couldn't say exactly when it all started to make me restless. I do know it happened a lot sooner than it should have. I had found at fourteen what most people search for all their lives and I threw it away with both hands out of sheer perversity.

By spring we were fighting all the time. I created at least one major confrontation a week. I searched for the perfect fight like a surfer for the perfect wave. It always eluded me. If anything, Kim became less excitable; I was wearing him down.

In the face of his passivity, I began to feel what I never thought I could feel for him: contempt. How could he let me walk all over him like this? Where was his self-respect?

Frustration changed my tactics. Where before I had been intractable, I became cruel. Where I'd been capricious, I became destructive. Whenever he did retaliate, I fought harder, wanting him to overpower me, to prove himself.

I realized that he loved me at his own expense. His love made him weak, and I was making him miserable. This occasionally caused me regret, but much more often I found it infuriating. I needed someone strong. Couldn't he see that?

Everything finally came to a head at the end of the school year. It was a warm night in May and I was sitting in the Hounds of Hell, a little Pittsburgh dive where the Others had finally gotten a gig. The Others were a pathetic high school band which the student body regarded with a kindly scorn; in some ways they were like a cult. Maybe fifty kids had turned out to hear them; many wore paper bags over their heads.

I was there alone; Kim and I were in another fight. Several of his friends were there and they asked where he was. I curtly replied that I wasn't his keeper. I was feeling particularly bitter and decided to get drunk. This was not difficult since I rarely drank. It took little more than a single beer to trash me, and beer was everywhere. A lot of people had brought their own, and someone gave me a bottle of Amstel.

I downed it slowly and right away felt different. The noise dulled and even the band started to sound okay. I felt someone sit down next to me. It was Guy.

"Hello," I said. I smiled at him.

"Well, hey there," he said. "What's your name? No, wait, wait just a minute, I know who you are. You're Kim's girlfriend, ain't you?"

"Please," I said. "Don't mention that name just now. I'm ready to kill him."

"Yeah? Well, honey, I know that feeling well." He laughed as he ripped the cap off a bottle of Bud. Then, glancing over at my empty Amstel, he said, "You want another beer, darlin'?"

"Sure," I said. "Thank you." He handed me the Bud and got one for himself. I took another long drink.

"So tell me," he said, "what's a girl like you doing running around with someone like him anyway?"

"To be honest," I said, speaking slowly so as not to slur my words, "I couldn't say." This struck me as funny and I started laughing.

Guy grinned broadly and put an arm around the back of my chair. I not only allowed this, I delighted in it. I was not attracted to him in the least—despite the scene at the ice rink—but we weren't going unnoticed by a single one of Kim's friends.

We exchanged further small talk and I finished my second beer. Guy's arm dropped from the back of the chair to my shoulders and his other hand found my left thigh. "You should find yourself a better man, honey," he told me. "If I didn't already have me a steady I'd be glad to take you on."

Suddenly George Wallace and Arthur Kane, two of Kim's friends, materialized in front of us.

"Delilah, we're leaving now," George said coldly. "You look like you could use a ride."

This proposal seemed like an amazing piece of good luck. If they took me home, they could hardly fail to mention the situation to Kim. And I really didn't want things to go any further with Guy.

"Well, look at that!" I said brightly. "My ride's here!" And I got a little unsteadily to my feet.

"Leavin' so soon?" Guy drawled. "Well, ain't that a shame. But don't I get a kiss good night?"

I laughed, leaned over, and there in front of everyone, I gave Guy Bryant a lengthy kiss good night.

* * *

I awakened at maybe three o'clock in the morning to the sound of gravel hitting my window. I could barely get out of bed; a bad hangover had already set in. I stumbled across the room in the dark and jerked the blind. It snapped up to reveal Kim standing on the front porch.

I opened the window and leaned out. "Everything you heard is true," I called down to him. "Now go home and leave me alone."

"Come outside," he said.

"No."

"Del! "

"I said no."

"How can you do this to me?" he said, and his voice broke.

"It's easy," I said, my head aching. "I want out of this, Kim. We're not right for each other and you know it."

"Come outside," he pleaded.

"I'm going back to sleep," I said.

He started to cry. He made no sound at all. The tears coursed down his face and onto the ground. I found this unbearable.

"Kim, I'm sorry, but there's nothing to say. It's over."

There was a pause while we stared at each other. Only the cicadas filled the silence.

"It's over," I repeated. "Good-bye."

And I closed the window.

III.

Kim did not just give up the night I said it was over. Getting him out of my life was a drawn-out, messy, vicious process. But once he went away, he never looked back. And after the first few weeks of our separation, I realized he was just fine without me. In fact, he was much better.

He had found his own apartment, had begun Carnegie-Mellon University with its summer semester. He'd made a lot of new friends at school already, and everyone seemed to see him around, saying he looked like he was having fun. Now that he was no longer there for the taking, I decided I missed him. He had filled every day of my life for nearly a year, and I felt his absence sharply.

I was also uncomfortably aware that I had behaved badly and wanted to see if I could set things right. I wanted to see if we could be friends.

Understandably, he didn't seem to think so. Whenever I called, he was cold and unreceptive. Now that he was no longer in love with me, and was in a position to be as cruel as I had been, he let me know, in full measure, about all my shortcomings and flaws, which were apparently numerous. It was during this period that we had the phone conversation where he informed me that I was sexually inhibited—repressed, even. This was the first time he had said anything of the kind, and I found the information worrisome. Very worrisome. I knew he was seeing another girl—Julia—who was even younger than me, a fourteen-year-old blonde who attended a Catholic school near his apartment. She was no doubt a tigress in bed. Any Catholic schoolgirl had to be: put her through confirmation class every morning with a nun, refuse to acknowledge the existence of premarital sex, force a girl way past puberty to wear the same clothes as her six-year-old sister, and the inevitable result was heated frenzy in the backseat of a parked car, the blue and green plaid thrust up and out of the way, her firm and lovely flanks naked and open to instruction—his instruction—to which she would prove herself a model apprentice, where I was already a lost cause.

It was right about this time that Madonna came out. Madonna with her triumphant, Catholic-school-veteran's smirk and her dangling crucifixes. She aroused an intense mixture of hatred and fascination in me; I couldn't take my eyes off her. And whenever I watched one of her videos or listened to her album, I would follow it up in the same way. I would go through my closet and spend about thirty minutes making myself over. I would get dressed up in some black, tattered, lacy thing and paint my mouth with hot pink lipstick. Then, if nobody else was home, I would go downstairs to the foyer—her helium voice still blasting from the stereo—flutter my lashes in the full-length glass, gyrate a couple of times on the white marble tiles, and stare at myself with hurt, half-lidded eyes. I would end these sessions by stretching out on the cool stone surface, pulling up my trashy skirt, and getting myself off, often three or four times in succession. The record would end and in the ringing silence the only sound was my own harsh breathing.

I was about six years older than the average Madonna fan, and it was a closet affair.

I also became obsessed with Kim's girlfriend. Quite separate from my misery about Kim, even, was my lust for knowledge about Julia. She was an incredible presence, living with me night and day. I probably spent no more than about three hours, collectively, in her presence over the year, but from these glimpses and fragments I constructed a fragile and golden perfection that would have tortured the Venus de Milo. Faithfully, lovingly, I fashioned her anew each day, using all my insecurities and the best of my imagination. I melted her down from the stained-glass windows of the church and cast her up again in demure brilliance, giving her eyes the mystic blue of the Virgin's cloak, her hair the warm gold of the sunstruck cathedral floor. All the dignity and finality of Catholicism were contained in her slow, mysterious smile. And she had at once the skill of a whore and the purity of a saint, like Mary Magdalene.

She was willowy, she was supple. Whenever I saw her, she seemed to be adjusting her clothing—throwing a light overcoat around her shoulders, buttoning a strap on her dress, pulling at her green kneesocks.

Her voice was low and resolute. Serenity draped her like Rapunzel's hair, heavy and golden and enigmatic. Serenity, in fact, seemed to be her overriding characteristic, and I wanted it. I—with my ferocity and fierce tears, my sweatiness and my melodrama—I coveted that regal peace. (It was not to be mine.)

Beyond all this, she was good. She was clearly a good person; she was good to Kim as I had not been. She stroked him, she caressed him, she kissed his cheek in greeting whenever they met. (Why hadn't I done that?) They never fought, Kim told me. She was kind and considerate to everyone; she ingratiated herself with his friends. She was, altogether, a completely golden girl—as golden, through and through, as her halo of hair. And I was as dark and full of tangles as my own.

* * *

I took it into my head that I wanted to go to confession. I felt it would be an appropriate step toward amending my life. To this end, I sought out my friend Jim, who attended Central Catholic and would be able to tell me how to go about it.

"Jim, tell me the procedure for a confession. I've decided I want to confess."

"Don't," he said.

"Why not?"

"Because it's ridiculous."

"No it's not. Why do you say that?"

"Because it is. You should be glad you've never been forced to do it. What do you think you're going to get out of it? That entire world is on a whole different plane from yours. Trust me, it's not going to give you anything you can use."

"Well, just fill me in anyway. What do I do?"

Jim sighed. "You go into the confessional booth and kneel down."

"All right, then what?"

"Haven't you ever seen any Italian movies? You say, 'Bless me father, for I have sinned.'"

"Do I say, 'It's been fifteen years since my last confession'?"

"No, you'd better say it's your first confession."

"Will he know I'm not a Catholic?" I asked.

"Probably."

"Then what?"

"He'll ask what your sins are. And what are you going to tell him?"

"Oh, I'll say I was cruel to a lover," I said, with light self-mockery.

"You realize it's a sin for you to have had a lover at all, by their standards?"

"It is?"

"Yes. Any sexual activity before marriage is a sin. Most sexual activity in general is a sin. Even masturbation is a sin." Jim paused to let his point sink in. "Your whole life is one long sin, Delilah."

I decided to abandon the plan.

* * *

I would call Kim maybe once every six weeks. I usually made these calls late at night, from the basement, with the lights off.

"Hello?"

"Kim?"

"Yeah."

"Kim, it's Del."

"I know who it is."

"How are you?"

"Never been better."

"Uh . . . how's Julia?"

"Never been better."

"Oh . . . well, listen, I was talking to Mark Kelly the other day," I would venture. "He told me I came up in conversation with you, and you called me a bitch. Is that true?"

"Yep."

"Well, why did you say that?"

"Because you are a bitch."

"Kim," I'd say, and I could hear my voice get high and anxious, "Kim, I wish you didn't hate me."

"I don't hate you."

"Then why do you say I'm a bitch?"

"Just stating a fact."

"You hate me," I'd repeat. Tears would be on the way.

"No," he'd say thoughtfully. "No, I really don't. Hate requires at least some degree of enthusiasm. And that's something I don't have."

"Kim," I'd whimper. "Kim, I love you."

A pause. Then: "Good."

"Why is that good?"

"It ought to be a valuable experience for you."

The months dragged on and so did my ambition to become a sex goddess. I amassed an extensive collection of lingerie: garter belts, fishnet stockings, fingerless gloves, stiletto heels. Black leather miniskirts and black leather jackets. I experimented with boys I had little or no interest in. I started to walk differently, laugh differently.

Throughout the rest of high school I tried out my charms on a number of men, but I slept alone. Nightly I repaired the past; fantasia warmed my bed. I repeated my resolve to myself over and over, as if on the beads of an invisible rosary. *I'll have his affection again. I'll win back his love. No matter what it takes. If it takes forever. If I have to crawl every inch of the way. I'll do what I have to; I'll pay any price.* With this litany I would put myself to sleep.

IV.

With daylight came a different world. Stretches of several weeks or even months could go by where Kim and I didn't run into each other, and it was easier not to think of him. If he had become the most sacred thing in my life, he still didn't take up much more space than any god will, when all is going well. When I didn't see him, I could almost forget about him.

But I couldn't control what happened when I did see him. I couldn't control the painful pang, the rush of adrenaline that accompanied the first sight of his slight frame, his strange gait. I usually saw him at concerts or outdoor events that included a band. On these occasions, a crowd of people grouped around some spectacle was a sure indication that he was in the middle. Kim loved to dance, and he was a wild dancer, often seeming frenzied, abandoned, when in actuality every move was tightly controlled. I would always push my way through the tight ring, until I was on the innermost fringe but camouflaged among what I knew was to him a faceless crowd. And I would watch. Hopelessly and miserably mesmerized, I would watch him dance until he was bathed in a sheen of sweat, until his clothes were plastered to his body with it.

One evening, during the fall of my senior year in high school, I found myself in one of these crowds. It was at the Carnegie-Mellon carnival, and Kim was near the radio van putting on quite a show. As I stood watching, a girl broke into the hollow space that was his and began to dance with him. She wore a black tank bra and a brilliantly colored short skirt, which rode up her legs as she gyrated in perfect rhythm with him. She had streaked dirty-blonde hair and was wearing dark glasses. She moved seductively close to him, lifting her skirt even higher with her hands, teasing him. Her legs were fleshy and feminine, too thick to be considered good legs, but unbelievably white and smooth.

Kim was dancing like a robot. His motions were tight and deliberately mechanical against her confident, unbridled movement. He stared straight ahead of him with a frozen expression—past her, ignoring her—but I could feel, agonizingly, the stricken excitement he clenched inside his jaw.

When I could stand it no longer I broke away from the scene. It was about ten o'clock at night. I walked alone across the football field with sparks from the fireworks showering down around me, not bothering to wipe away the tears streaking silently out of my eyes.

The next afternoon I went to his apartment with no idea what I meant to do. His roommate answered the door, and told me he was taking a nap. I went into his bedroom without knocking, silently climbed the ladder into his loft, and saw his sleeping form. Trying not to wake him, I stretched out beside him on the mattress, about three feet away. I felt a small shock when he said "Hi" and tossed part of the blanket in my direction. For a crazy moment I had the idea that he didn't recognize me.

I moved closer to him and closed my eyes. I had absolutely no expectations; this small gesture of his was already outside of what I had considered the realm of possibility. But then I felt his arm encircle me and pull me to him. Startled, mute, I held my breath and stared at the opposite wall, trying not to feel, trying not to really be happy, feeling that he would soon ground me swiftly and without regret, perhaps tomorrow, perhaps in another hour. And then he was kissing me, kissing my mouth; he was on top of me, his body stretched along the length of mine, and I was trying to remember if *this* is what it had felt like, back *then*.

I had no idea why he was doing this and I didn't care. My overriding thought was that I had waited three years to be in his bed again, and here was my chance to show him how far I had come. If he still thought I was so sexually inhibited, he was in for a surprise.

As if to eradicate that scared fourteen-year-old girl from his memory forever, I slid down between his legs and began sucking him for all I was worth. I felt fierce satisfaction at his sharp intake of breath, his whimper of pleasure. I sucked him hungrily, fervently, as if his cock were something nourishing or comforting, and was rewarded by his harsh panting and his hands in my hair.

It didn't take long. Not at all. It was, in fact, one of the least demanding blow jobs of my experience. Smooth and rhythmic for about five minutes, before a few sudden, vehement thrusts; then his body shuddered, he seemed to be trying to hold back, and he came. And I swallowed.

We did not exchange a word. I understood that I was not supposed to question his motives, and further, that this event did not represent any change in my status with him. What did happen was that I replaced my occasional, piteous phone calls with these silent and, to me, infinitely more dignified visits. His house was on my way home from school. Once every five or six weeks I let myself in (he never locked the door if he was home) and sat down somewhere near him. He might be practicing guitar, working at the computer, fixing his skateboard. I'd wait for a while; sometimes he wouldn't reach for me, but usually he would. If he didn't, if he wasn't going to, I could mostly discern that sooner rather than later, and once I had, I would quietly take my leave.

The third time I came over, I brought a box of Trojans. All through high school I had deliberately and dramatically saved my virginity. I wanted to emerge intact from that long dark tunnel of adolescent lust—the experimentation, the pawing, the locker room betrayals, the greed—pure and half-visible through an imaginary cascade of white lace. And give it all over to Kim, lay it at his feet.

In his loft that afternoon, when he grasped me by the shoulders and thrust me onto my back, it occurred to me for the first time that he had no way of knowing this. He doesn't even realize I'm a virgin, I thought as he penetrated.

My flesh gave way immediately but the pain was incredible. He stopped in mid-thrust to stare at me and I smiled up at him triumphantly through soundless tears. He closed his eyes and shook his head, but almost as if it belonged to someone else, his body resumed its motion. I moved with him, wanting him to go on and finish, and he did just that, without opening his eyes again.

I always did whatever he wanted. I reveled in doing whatever he wanted, in serving him to the last detail. It was of absolutely no import to me that I had a boyfriend at the time. He remained as ignorant as everyone else about my afternoons with Kim; losing my virginity did not even lead to intercourse with him.

I started to think of myself as Kim's sex slave. The rest of my life was not altered by this. In fact, in my day-to-day interactions with other people, I felt wrapped in an immense and dazzling calm; it seemed I'd found the peace of mind I'd wanted for so long. I felt split into two selves, one which remained wholly pleasant and unruffled in the dailiness of school and friends. And then the other one—burning, intense, bent only on the hard-edged, resolute encounters with Kim that made serenity possible. Those wordless transactions where I felt understood in my body and my soul, in my sorrow and my atonement. Recognized, transported, absolved.

It was with my boyfriend at this time, however, that I finally confessed my real fantasies. Billy. The first time I saw him, he was carrying a riding crop—an intricately woven, beautiful thing—though there was nothing in his attire to suggest that he had been or would be riding. I followed him for forty-five minutes through the streets of downtown Pittsburgh and finally into a dilapidated little coffee shop, where I seated myself across from him at his table.

"Hello?" he said inquiringly. And suddenly smiled. He had deep blue eyes and maybe a day's worth of stubble on his jaw.

"Why are you carrying a whip?"

"Why are you so interested, darling?"

We sat there for hours, till well after nightfall. I listened, transfixed, while he told me all about it. Told me I was only one of millions. And that it was everywhere.

For my birthday that March, he gave me the very quirt he'd been carrying that day, and on my final visit to Kim, I brought it with me. Within days, I would be leaving for school in New York, and somehow I was sure Kim knew this. I placed the whip suggestively by the side of the bed, as I had done long before with the package of condoms. Kim ignored it completely until afterward. Then, as I was getting dressed, he picked it up, held it out to me, and broke the silence of many months.

"Here," he said. "You can remember me as the one who didn't need any props."

V.

I didn't see him again for almost two years, until the last day of Christmas break during my second year of school. I had been on an errand for my father and Kim's street was on my way home. To be honest, I had chosen the route which would include it. As I neared the house—the desolate porch with the battered sofa, the tired lawn, a cat on the walk—my old lust, wild and insistent, took me up the front steps.

I opened the door without knocking and walked in, making no sound. There was a light on in the kitchen, the sound of dishes being done. I approached the entrance silently, and saw him. For a moment I was overwhelmed by the sight. His sinewy compact figure—familiar as my reflection and still unspeakably precious—standing at the sink, his back to me. I could always tell in the first glance how he was feeling. I could read misery in the set of his shoulders and the tilt of his head, hostility in his gait, exhaustion in the color of his skin. Standing at the kitchen threshold before speaking, I decided he was feeling fine.

"Hi," I was finally able to say, and he turned.

"Hey-y," he said. "How are you?"

He seemed glad to see me.

"I'm all right," I told him. "What about you?"

"Getting by," he said agreeably. "What are you up to these days?"

I still dream about you, I thought of saying. I still worship you.

He probably knew; in any case, there was no need to tell him. I could see now how I'd set the whole thing up and played it out; if it hadn't been completely my own fantasy before, it certainly was by now, and I hardly needed more from him than an occasional appearance. A cameo.

"I can't stay; I've got to get home and pack," I said. "I just wanted to see you for a minute."

"I'll walk out with you," he said. "I've got to go downtown." He set the last dish in the rack on the counter and picked his jacket up from the back of a chair. We left the house together and began walking toward his bus stop. There was a light wind. I wanted to lie down in the moment and let the leaves blow over me. It was an exquisite day, as cold and golden as the autumn he'd received me. Four o'clock in the afternoon and the moon was already in the sky.

"This is where I get my bus," Kim said when we had reached the corner.

"Okay," I said. I turned to look at him one last time and in that look was all my bewildered passion, all the homesickness in my gut.

He held out his arms; I went into them. And for one priceless moment I was against his heart, felt it beating, strong and steady, against my ear.

Ruby and the Bull

July 18, 1990

I've become so bored with Bull. Our little domestic arrangement is starting to irritate me beyond description. He's slipped into this *reasonable, responsible* Big Daddy / house husband role, feeling indispensable whenever he changes a lightbulb and lecturing me about buying in bulk—it makes my teeth ache. I can't remember the last time we had a good conversation, or when he challenged me in any real way. At this point, I feel like I'm with him out of convenience—convenience and inertia. What worries me is how I'm going to untangle myself. He's still so in love.

Ruby called him Bull. Animal names were a thing with her; she gave them to all her boyfriends. The last one, whose real name was Charles, had been Goat. Sometimes he still called the apartment. "Oh, hello, Goat," she would say into the telephone.

Judd was powerfully and squarely built, with black hair kept in a crew cut, narrow bruised-looking blue eyes, and a thunderous brow. He had a bad temper when provoked, and grew clumsy when tired. So he was Bull, sometimes embellished to Big Bull, and, when she was especially happy with him, Big Bully. "You! Big! *Bully*," she would crow beneath him.

The pet name was not always used with affection. "Out! Out of my kitchen this minute!" Ruby had yelled just the night before, when he'd accidentally knocked a bag of flour to the floor. "How can I get dinner together with a bull wrecking the room?"

"Well, maybe you shouldn't be running such a china shop," he'd defended himself, retreating.

Ruby was beautiful, and difficult. Her body was small, lithe, and softly curved despite considerable muscle from years of competitive track. Raven-black hair fell straight to her shoulders, streaked with a red-wine color she mixed herself from several jars of henna. She was full-lipped, sleepy-eyed, heavy-lidded, dreamy—her face had such a dreamy innocence that it was easy to be startled by her quick, scathing judgments and sly wit.

She waited tables at night and had little to do during her days, most of which were apparently spent sleeping late, running at the reservoir in Central Park, and lounging in the apartment until she had to go to work. Eating Wheaties with yogurt and reading gay male porn. Judd had been bewildered when she'd first started buying *Drummer* magazine and books with titles like *Sex Behind Bars*. She had long ago drawn him into what she called her "S&M thing," and their bedroom activities consisted mainly of inventing scenarios in which she could submit to him. Judd had never ventured very far in this direction before meeting Ruby. He once tied a girlfriend to the bed, but she became frightened and he'd abandoned the idea. Nothing he did appeared to make Ruby uneasy. He had been afraid, in the beginning, to hit her very hard. "Come *on*," she'd said early on, exasperated, even verging on insulted. "I can take it harder than *that*."

It took a few times before he felt the thrill. And it *was* a thrill—one he couldn't see himself doing without anymore. It scared him a little to realize how it excited him to strike her. "What does this say about me?" he brooded aloud one night.

"It says nothing," Ruby declared, all authoritative finality. "Porn is a place you visit, not a place you live. Anne Rice said that," she added.

He stopped questioning it. Still, he felt no desire to read about it. Especially two men doing it.

"Why do you look at this stuff?" he asked her once after leafing through her latest purchases from Christopher Street.

"Because," she explained impatiently, "there isn't any worthwhile straight S&M material out there. Gay men have sexier minds. I wish I was a gay boy."

"Oh for Christ's sake," Judd said. He felt slightly affronted for no reason he could name. That was Ruby, though. She often said things just to shock or unsettle her audience—Ruby never tired of converting those around her into an audience—or because she imagined it lent her some kind of perverse glamour.

Judd wasn't sure why he picked up her journal in the first place. It had been before him on her desk for months, and he'd never even been tempted to look at it. When they'd first started seeing each other, she used to lock it in a drawer, a habit which wounded him to the quick.

"Don't you trust me?" he asked her reproachfully. "There's no way I'd ever touch your diary, Ru." And at the time, he'd meant it. Judd had never been the suspicious type. Hell, he never even read her postcards.

So he couldn't say, even to himself, what took hold of him that evening. Things between them were somewhat strained at the moment, but this had been the case many times before. They were sharing a small apartment; occasional tension had to be expected. And he'd had no confrontation with Ruby at all.

She was on her way out the door as he was coming in.

"You're going to work already?" Judd asked in surprise.

"I have to be there an hour early to fill in for Tiana," she explained, referring to another waitress.

"You rumpled little thing."

"Don't even talk about it. She called me begging at the last minute. I didn't even have time to iron my blouse. Boris is going to love that." Boris was her boss.

"I wouldn't worry about it. I'm sure he's too happy with what's *under* the blouse to care."

"I hope."

They kissed briefly at the door and she was gone. Judd changed into jeans and a T-shirt and wondered what to do about dinner.

There was a cold slice of pizza in the fridge from the night before. He decided that would be enough; he wasn't that hungry. It occurred to him that for the first time in a long while, he didn't have to do any work to catch up at the office. He'd already read the *New York Times* in its entirety as well. Judd heated his pizza, polished it off, and washed his dish. Then he considered the evening before him. It was a rare luxury, and he didn't know what to do with it. He liked to read, but wasn't one who, like Ruby, would go to a bookstore with no idea what he meant to buy. Nor was he a man to go to the movies alone. Though it wasn't his turn, he did the rest of the dishes. When the sink was clear and he turned off the jet, a forlorn silence settled over the apartment.

He wandered into the bedroom. There it was, on Ruby's night table. Judd looked at it carefully for the first time. The book had been a present from her closest girlfriend; it was beautifully bound in soft gray suede and had probably been quite expensive. Judd wished he himself had given it to her. He mostly gave her things she pointed out to him beforehand, and they were usually of a childish nature: a rag doll with a cat's face, dressed in a green petticoat; boxes of candy; pink pajamas with feet. Judd loved buying these presents for Ruby, maybe because they rendered a wholly different side of her, made her silky and shy as surely as her pale jade chemise made her eyes green. She changed from the dazzlingly self-confident, caustic creature he knew (and in some terrible part of himself feared) into the soft, tender-eyed pet she looked like and should have been. She actually took the cat doll to bed with her, wore the pajamas.

Judd picked up the journal. It was lovely in his hands, having at once the satisfying weight of a hardback and the broken-in softness of his old suede jacket. He sat down on the bed and flipped the pages with his thumb, the way he would a deck of cards. The paper was as fine as the binding, bluish-white and delicate, like the inside of an eggshell.

What are you doing, he asked himself. His heart had begun to pound as soon as he'd touched the book, although Ruby was gone for the evening and there was no chance of her surprising him. He would put it back exactly where he had found it, and she would never know. So why was he so afraid?

"If I cheated on you once, and it was never going to happen again, and there was no chance of me giving you some dread disease, would you want to know?" Ruby had once asked him.

"*Yes,*" Judd answered immediately, glaring at the mere thought of it.

"I wouldn't. I don't think I'd want to know. What would be the point?" Ruby said thoughtfully.

"I'd never cheat on you," he assured her. "I've never cheated on any girl, ever. When I'm serious about someone, I'm not looking to see what else is out there."

"You looked at me when you were still going out with Maryanne," Ruby pointed out.

"I didn't have much of a choice, did I, with the way you kept getting in my face," Judd said. "And anyway, I broke it off with her before I started anything with you. That's not cheating."

"I've cheated on all my boyfriends," Ruby reflected, no hint of apology in her tone. She had said this before.

"It's nothing to brag about." Judd was suddenly cold.

"I'm not bragging. I'm just saying. But not you, Bull. I've never cheated on you."

"I'd leave you," he said flatly.

"So you say." Ruby spoke with a secret little smile. The smile infuriated Judd. She didn't believe him. She didn't think he would ever leave her. Then she saw his face and her smile vanished. "Oh, stop scowling, Bull. I really wouldn't cheat on you. Why would I? You're very good to me and sex with you is wonderful." She came over and stroked his short, bristly hair. "Look, I know it's not exactly wise to sit here and tell you I've cheated on everyone I've gone out with. But see, that's the point. That's not something I would have told someone else. I want to be completely honest with you."

Is that what he was afraid of? That he would read about an infidelity? It was easy for her to do whatever she wanted, with all her afternoons free. But no, that had never really been a threatening possibility. He believed what she said, about his being different.

But still. Something else. He was afraid of something he might find in her journal in the same way that he was a little afraid of her. He didn't want to think of what it could be; he didn't want to acknowledge it.

Judd decided to open the book to someplace in the middle. Perfectly at random. He would read a single entry. Then he would close it, forever. He was too tantalized by the thought of such an intimate glimpse into Ruby's mind to let go of the idea. But he wouldn't violate her diary any further than that.

Judd closed his eyes and opened the book. He sat on the bed for a moment without moving. Blood was pounding almost painfully in his ears. His mouth was dry and it was an effort to breathe.

He opened his eyes. The top of the left page was dated July 18, about six weeks back. Ruby's familiar handwriting covered the paper in magenta ink. He gingerly flattened the page to read.

"I've become so bored with Bull. . . ."

"Why are you sleeping out here?" Ruby asked, upon coming home to find Judd stretched out on the living room couch.

"I'm not asleep."

"Well, why are you lying in the dark?"

He didn't answer. She snapped on the overhead light and emptied her apron onto the coffee table.

"Tips were great tonight, Bull. I walked with a hundred and ten bucks. That's more than I've made in weeks."

She seated herself beside him, on the edge of the sofa. Each night, she liked to tell him about that evening's customers, the more eccentric the better. Tonight was no exception, and she chattered happily, separating the bills out by denomination, oblivious to his silence. After sorting them, she folded the money neatly and replaced it in her apron.

"Why are you so quiet, Bull? Don't you feel well? *God*, my feet hurt." She leaned down and briefly massaged them, working from heel to toe and back again. Her toenails were painted a faded, dusty plum. "We've got some beer left in the fridge, don't we? I think I need one." She released her feet and moved to stand. Judd reached over and took a fistful of her hair, jerking her back down. Startled, she cried out, and twisted, with some effort, to face him.

"What—Judd—"

"Take your clothes off."

She stared at him for a moment, then smiled. Judd could see she thought this was one of their games. Maybe she was right; Judd wasn't sure himself what he was up to yet. As in all their most successful games, however, she was believing him enough to be a little frightened. Her calling him Judd was a sure sign that he'd caught her off guard. He watched with satisfaction as her fingers—trembling slightly(!)—found the top button of her blouse and unhooked it. He felt the familiar rush of power that came with these scenes, the sweetest aphrodisiac.

Ruby stripped slowly down to her underwear, studying her reflection in one of the faded brass panels which flanked the fireplace. She was vain about her body, there was no denying it. She drew her clothes off lovingly, caressing her arms and legs in the process and looking at herself with an almost mournful appreciation.

"You really think you're something, don't you? Something fine." Judd's voice was a dangerous murmur. He circled her with slow deliberation. If she felt vulnerable in her nakedness she didn't show it. She put her hands behind her back and smiled faintly, proudly.

"Too dazzling for mortal eyes," he continued.

"You could go blind," Ruby said, picking it up.

"Too beautiful to be true."

She was still and watchful as he moved around her. Beneath her diligent expression, which suggested an actress waiting for a crucial cue, there lurked a subtle amusement.

"Your real name isn't even Ruby. It's Rebecca. But that didn't fit your precious little self, did it? Anybody else would be calling herself Becky, but not my little girl, oh no, she's calling herself *Ruby*. Because she thinks she's such a *gem* . . . isn't that it?"

"You got it," she purred, goading him.

"What are we going to do about that?"

Ruby said nothing.

"What are we going to do about this attitude of yours?"

She regarded him with interest, remaining silent.

"Go get me my belt."

Ruby turned and went into the bedroom, to the closet, where his black leather belt hung from a nail on the door. She returned, doubling it for its use on her body, and offered it to him.

Judd went to the drafting table in the corner of the room and pulled the chair, an old barstool, from under it. He placed it in the center of the floor. "Come on over here."

Ruby approached and, without having to be told, bent over it. The seat came up to just under her rib cage, so that she had to stand on tiptoe and her arms dangled down in front of her. "Good. Stay like that."

Judd left the room and returned with handcuffs, which he used to secure her wrists to the rung of the chair. Then he stepped back to admire his handiwork. She was well positioned, stretched taut in an upside-down *U*, both for beating and fucking. He stepped up close on her left and resumed his hold on her hair, wrapping his hand in it tight enough to hurt, then closing it into a fist at the nape of her neck. With his other hand, he eased her underwear down.

"You have it coming tonight, bitch," he hissed in her ear. "I'm gonna work you over like you've never had it. I've spoiled you rotten, but this is the end of that." He drew his arm back and watched her set her teeth for the blow. Then he brought it swiftly down, whistling cleanly through the air to meet the back of her thighs.

Beating Ruby was a consummate pleasure. He often thought it bordered on an art. Every move was as choreographed, as tightly controlled as a dance, and more intimate. It was more intimate, even, than what came next. Because anybody could fuck Ruby, but what act could approach the intimacy of punishment, the *deliberation* of it, the careful administration of blows to the smooth, copper flesh? It was practiced and essentially professional by now. He knew how to strike her. It was a priceless knowledge, hard-won and indispensable—Ruby demanded expertise. It was about so much more than simply pain; it was about intimidation, it was about timing. He knew what would elicit a whimper from her, what would bring a moan. What would make her howl. He beat her this night as long and as hard as he dared, and afterward, after he'd let the belt drop to the floor, plunged into her from behind, and taken her ruthlessly; after withdrawing, spent, and running his palm over the welts he'd raised; after releasing her wrists from the rung and helping her to slowly straighten up, she turned to him, smiling, her tears still drying in their tracks, and told him it had never been better. Never.

The second time was easier.

> May 31, 1990
> I got a job today. At the Blue Lagoon, a bar and grill on the upper west side. I went in around lunchtime and was directed to the owner, who was sitting at the bar. I asked if he was hiring. He looked me up and down, lingering on my tits, then said yes. And sent me home to change. Every time I start at a new place, having said I have experience, I feel like a fraud. I'm always sure I'm going to get found out immediately—as being afraid of the hot oven and hot plates, afraid of the cappuccino machine, unable to carry trays, incapable of standing up against more than eight tables' pressure, clumsy with the American Express apparatus, etc., etc. And of course, there's always that period of about five days where none of the other waitresses are going to say one nice word until you prove yourself. It's such a cold, lonely time—I hate it. But then, the kitchen people are nice to me, they call me Mama. "Put some marijuana on it, Mama," they say whenever they hand me a plate. Marijuana means parsley. And the hostess called me "sweetheart." I felt so grateful to her. Being new somewhere can make you grateful for the littlest things.

Judd read that entry several times. He couldn't quite believe it. He'd been there that day, when Ruby got her job, and she hadn't seemed the least bit nervous to him. She'd bragged about being hired on the spot, on sight, and said she'd rather wait tables in the summertime than work any other job. "In an office, you're stuck with nine to five, and the same boring people forty hours a week.

Waitressing is more flexible, more social, better money, and you eat for free. Get a group of guys in on a Friday night and keep bringing them drinks—by the time you leave you'll have all their paychecks in your pocket. I wouldn't do anything else."

She hadn't revealed even a hint of insecurity.

Judd loved her after reading this confession, loved her utterly, loved her more. She was vulnerable after all. He remembered her going off to the Blue Lagoon that first day, in her black skirt and white blouse and the old waitressing apron unearthed from the back of a dresser drawer. He tried to imagine her struggling with the trays and gingerly testing the plates for heat. Committing the specials to memory, ingratiating herself to customers, and smiling hopefully, uncertainly, at everyone she met. He could almost see it.

June 1, 1990

Whenever Bull and I have a fight, I always keep my cool. I'm sly and mean, mocking him, cutting him recklessly to shreds, while he flusters and stutters and tries to answer me as reasonably and honestly and *earnestly* as he can. I can't put it into words. He doesn't know how to hide his pain. He has a nakedness, a stubborn *sincerity*, that's truly amazing to behold. He's a truly good man, maybe the best man I know. Too good for me.

June 7, 1990

There are times when I love waitressing. I love standing in for Jackie once in a while and working the graveyard shift, from midnight till eight in the morning.

The most amazing people come to the restaurant in the middle of the night—writers with their manuscripts in stacks all over the table, guzzling endless cups of espresso; strippers from nearby clubs; insomniacs, night owls. It's strange to serve dinner food all night, and then all of a sudden the sky's turning blue, then pink, then yellow, and I'm pouring coffee and serving breakfast.

And then, of course, waiting tables undeniably taps into all my serving-wench fantasies. I love giving men their breakfast and calling them sir. "Can I bring you some more coffee, sir?"

June 18, 1990

I have to admit that I stay with Bull almost entirely for the sex. We have such a fantastic sex life. In a game where nearly everyone wants to submit, Bull wants only to dominate. In every relationship I've ever had before him, I've had to take turns—what a drag. Bull says the thought of being dominated makes his skin crawl, and that's fine with me.

It's a good arrangement that we have. I know that without these segments where I feel afraid of him, in awe of him, we never would have lasted more than a couple of months. Sometimes it occurs to me that I'm in control all the time. That I give him his nightly power as surely as I withdraw it in the morning. That he's mostly a pawn in my whole fantasia, a magazine image—brought into three dimensions, and all the better to masturbate with. And it doesn't bother me. Why should I let it bother me? I don't want to give it up. It's getting me off. I want it waiting for me at the end of the day. Never mind how it gets there.

After that last entry, Judd climbed out onto the fire escape. The night was hot. Salsa music floated from a window across the street, and below him on the sidewalk, men were setting up little foldout tables for dominoes.

He hadn't known his girlfriend and he still didn't know her. Except now he understood a little better just how much he had not known. And did not know.

He understood for the first time that her sexuality wasn't something he had any kind of hold on. It was nothing she kept in any kind of compartment. It ran all through her, through everything she did. Right at this minute she was pouring it out with the coffee.

He hated her now.

She lived alone. He had never touched her. She didn't care about the truth; she was an unapologetic liar. A manipulator. Judd marveled at the way everything had changed. In his mind, she even looked different. She looked lonely. A lonely puppeteer.

Below him, men laid out their dominoes. Young punks rode their skateboards in lazy circles and girls were jumping rope. Communion was everywhere. People got together. They worked things out. Little rituals, little rules. Pecking orders and alliances. Even children knew how to do it. He felt himself newly dazzled by the faith it took, the tender trust. He felt dazzled by Ruby's solitude.

And he loved her more.

A hand on his shoulder. His eyes opened in darkness. He struggled to orient himself. A light was snapped on and Ruby was standing in front of him. In her uniform. She must have just gotten home.

"What—what time is it?" he asked, wincing in the sudden brightness.

"It's like two-thirty. I had to work until the band left. Judd," she said, speaking quietly in a tone he'd never heard, staring hard into his face, "Judd, have you been reading my journal?"

He looked at her dumbly. It took a moment for the question to register. She was wide-eyed and white-knuckled, clutching her apron. Her hair was loosing itself from its raggedy ponytail.

"Judd, it was sitting on the coffee table. When I left, it was on my desk," she continued, in the same urgent hush. "Were you looking at it?"

"I was going to tell you tonight," he said truthfully.

Ruby backed up a few steps and pressed her fist against her mouth. They stared at each other for a long moment. Then she shrieked and started to cry.

"Ruby . . ." He put his hand on her shoulder. She tore away from him.

"Don't you fucking touch me, you sleazy motherfucking son of a bitch! How dare you do this to me, how dare you violate me like this when I've trusted you with everything! When I've let you fucking move *in* with me! You better get the fuck out of here right now, get out tonight, you aren't sleeping in this apartment another fucking night!" She paused for breath and stood panting in the impotence of her rage. His heart contracted. Again he reached out and again she darted out of reach. But when she spoke again, it was low and controlled, each word bitten out through her teeth.

"I want you out of here tonight, Judd. Find someone whose floor you can sleep on, because you're not staying here. You know I'm going to Philadelphia this weekend. You can come back then and get your stuff."

Judd got up and stood wordlessly for a moment before pulling on his jeans. He waited for Ruby to resume her attack, but she only stood glaring at him with grief-stricken eyes. Finally he said quietly, as a mere statement of fact, "I would have left you anyway."

"You! You would have left *me*?!"

"I know you'd like to think you're the only one who feels betrayed. But there is also the chump here."

"I don't know what the fuck you're talking about."

"I think you do." Judd picked his belt up off the floor, and, smiling at it ironically, slid it through the denim loops of his jeans.

"It's *my* goddamn journal," she nearly screamed. "I can write whatever I want in it. That's the whole *point* of it. My God, don't I have the right to my feelings? What, you never have a malicious thought? Don't you ever get disgusted? Ever get bored? What are you, the fucking Thought Police?"

"You're right," he said. "You're right, there's no question about that. I wish I'd never picked it up." He opened his hands and held them out in a gesture of futility. "But I did pick it up."

Ruby stood perfectly still, silent, as if she needed to concentrate hard to make sense of this information. Then she said, in an almost conversational tone, "I am never going to forgive you for this. Never."

Judd nodded and walked to the door. She darted ahead and opened it. As he walked through, she tried to slam it after him, careless, as always, about the neighbors. He caught it before it reached the jamb and shut it softly. It made an assertive sound.

The Resolution

I was sitting on the curb across the street when Jorgé emerged from the clinic. I had been there a long time. That didn't have to mean the news was bad, I'd been telling myself for the last hour and a half. Doctors keep you waiting all the time. . . .

But there was no way to misinterpret what I saw on his face. His almond skin was splotched with grief, the black eyes bloodshot. I stopped breathing.

He stood leaning against the scaffolding that flanked the building. I was frozen, feet rooted into the gutter. He still hadn't seen me, was as unaware of my presence as he had been all morning, when I'd followed him here. We were still for several minutes.

When he finally turned in the direction of the train, I found the strength to stand.

"Jorgé," I called. My voice broke on his name.

He looked over, shiny-eyed, and for half a second a startled grin played around his mouth.

"Hey, whore." He answered with our old joke even now. I knew he wasn't surprised to see me there.

We came together in the middle of the empty street. I entwined myself around him, pressed my body full-length against his. My fingers dug into the ravine of his back.

I clung like a cat on the trunk of a tree. For the first time in years, his mouth sought mine. And my lips, teeth, all of me parted as hungrily as ever to receive him.

I met Jorgé in the circus when I was fifteen. From the very beginning I couldn't take my eyes off him. He was a liquid-eyed Puerto Rican dream, with black ringlets spilling down his back, a nose that looked as if it had been broken more than once, and a wide and beautiful face I longed to hold in my hands.

The Arabs who worked on the concession wagon with me were amused to see how I stared. "Jorgé doesn't go for your kind, honey," they laughed. I was wounded; I thought they were referring to my being an orphan. Having run away from the St. Mary Magdalen's Home for Girls less than two weeks before, I still saw the world as cleanly split into those with families and those without. I had yet to realize that circus people were nearly always as rootless as me. And to learn that by "your kind" the Arabs had meant women.

Still, the minute I saw Jorgé, I knew he was special; it was around him like an aura, and I wasn't wrong. He wore an ironic expression much of the time, intelligent and resigned. He was seventeen, had been with the circus for two years. The first look at him was enough to let you know he could go somewhere better anytime he chose; by the second, you knew he wasn't going anywhere, not anytime soon. Everything about him suggested he was there for a long haul. His eyes were as still and quiet as two stones on the ocean floor. Like everyone else whose life was tied up with that tent and caravan, he had suffered and was suffering still. But almost immediately I could see that in his case, no one wanted to touch it. His pain held the threat and pull of some inaudible siren song. But our daily lives provided all the storm most of us could weather.

I didn't know I was beautiful until I got to the circus. The nuns had made sure of that. I'd reached adolescence in the same heavy, burlap-colored shifts, thick stockings, and rubber-soled shoes we'd all worn since childhood. We washed with hard cakes of yellow laundry soap, and used a blue, medicinal shampoo each week against lice. My hair was always wound tight against my head, fastened painfully with jabbing pins.

The stuff of nymph-hood—the baubles, rhinestone-studded combs, heart-shaped sunglasses, flavored lip gloss—never fell into our hands. We didn't have our mothers' clothes to dress up in, makeup to play with on the sly, so we didn't experiment or preen. We didn't think about our looks. Not much, anyway.

When I joined the circus, I was still wearing the Home uniform. The boss, Hale, must have known I'd run away from somewhere, but couldn't have known where and couldn't have cared less. When I stepped into his trailer office, his eyes lit up in vulturous delight.

"So you want to work here? Well, how old are you? And don't you lie to me, girl."

"Seventeen," I quavered.

"Eighteen, baby. You're eighteen. And don't forget it." He leaned back in his seat and appraised me coolly. "You know how to work hard. I can see that. You don't cross me, you can turn gray and die here if you want. Sleeper 15 will be empty by this afternoon. I'm chasing that crackhead punk off my lot as soon as the morning show is over. He's been taking money from the wagon, has been for weeks. You can have his rack." He paused to stroke his mustache. "You're not a day over fourteen, are you, girl?"

"Eighteen, sir."

"Good! Good, good. You'll be fine here. All right, go walk around, strut your stuff for the stable boys or something till that junkie scum's cleaned out of here."

As I reached the door, he added, as an afterthought, "And get out of those rags. Tell Augustine to give you something to wear."

Augustine was the costume lady. The inside of her trailer was like a gypsy wagon. The only light in the room burned from within a fuchsia lampshade, bathing everything in a pink glow. Bits of material were strewn on every surface, and sequins littered the floor.

Augustine herself was wearing only a kimono and clogs. She had fire-colored hair with gray roots, penciled-in eyebrows, hard lines around her mouth. Upon hearing Hale's decree, she disappeared into a back room, commanding me over her shoulder to strip. I took off the Home uniform and did not see it again until the following evening, when the cook had me bring the cat man his supper. It was lining the lion's cage.

Augustine returned with a drawstring sack. "You're just a baby, aren't you?" she mused.

"I'm eighteen," I countered meekly.

She roared with laughter. "Yeah, and I'm twenty-one."

She began pulling clothes out of the bag. "That Hale doesn't miss a beat, does he? Well, he pulls it off. Now, how are we going to dress you up?"

She glanced up at where I was shivering in worn grayish underclothes. "You're a pretty little thing. With your face, you should be in the show."

I gaped at her.

"What's the matter? Don't you know you're a looker? I don't know where it is you came from, and around here we don't tend to ask, but I can guess there couldn't have been many mens around, and not many mirrors either."

She came over and pulled the pins from my hair. It tumbled down my back. She ran her hands through it softly, murmuring in appreciation. "Do you have any talents?" she asked.

I didn't know what to say.

"I mean, can you dance, ride a trapeze, walk on the wire?"

I shook my head.

"Too bad. You're too old to train."

I caught sight of a shimmering, sea-green garment that had spilled out of the sack. I had never imagined a color like that. It lay glinting on the trailer floor like something marvelous washed up on a beach. Without thinking, I knelt to touch it.

"You like that? It belonged to Mamie—she did the elephant act. Cut out of here in September; they say she married the tattooed man from the Coney Island show. She was about your size. You can try it if you want."

I hung back, shy, but she picked it up and shook it out: "Come on, it's all right." I let her help me into it and fasten two dozen little hooks in the back. I felt as naked inside it as I had before; it was the slightest thing I'd ever worn.

"There!" she said. "Now look at yourself." She turned me toward the vanity. I looked. And I saw what I had never seen before: a delicate young girl, smooth-shouldered, milk-skinned, with fragile collarbones jutting out over the blossoming promise of breasts.

Augustine was delighted with my wonder. "Sit down," she insisted, indicating the vanity seat, and began pulling her works out of a drawer: a palette of eyeshadows in every shade, colored pencils and tubes of glue and pots of rouge with little brushes. I must have been there for most of the day. She curled my hair and piled it on top of my head, dusted my eyelids and painted my lips. By the time she was done, my body hurt from sitting still so long, my left foot had fallen asleep, and she was as excited as a child with her first doll.

I will never forget the girl in the mirror that afternoon. She was like something in a storybook: raven-haired, red-lipped, head tilted dreamily to one side. Stars in her eyes, and something else too: bewilderment, gratitude, disbelief.

When I come across a picture of myself in a magazine, or on a billboard, I can see that this look has never left me. That's what made you, my manager tells me. That's what they're paying for. It's one in a million can hold on to that, and it's the real thing. You can manufacture everything else.

I stared at Jorgé all the time because he was beautiful but mostly, I have to admit, because he looked so much like Christa. His midnight hair was blue in the water, red in the sunlight, long and tangled as a pirate's, just as hers had been. His black eyes were as deep and direct, and he moved with her indolent grace. She had radiated heat and sure enough, Jorgé was never cold. His body by itself was enough to warm a double bed.

Jorgé was Puerto Rican while Christa had been American Indian; he was a man where she'd been a girl. But he had her lovely, languid angel face; her competent, long-fingered, strong-fingered hands; and the hollow of his neck was home to me as only hers had been before.

It didn't start out that way. Jorgé had hated me at first. This was because I was as ignorant as I was naïve, speaking too freely with the wrong people, and never thinking of who might overhear.

Hale put me on one of the two concessions wagons the first day, where I had to learn to spin cotton candy. My three coworkers were known by everyone else as simply "the Arabs." One of them, Abdul, was almost as new as me. He had joined the company just a week before.

"Have you noticed, Abdul," asked Mohammed, the wagon master, "that only faggots don't have to work hard during load-out?"

"I noticed," Abdul answered. "I should pretend to be a faggot so I won't have to lift any stringers."

"That shouldn't be hard for you," Ashish put in, and he and Abdul began a mock scuffle.

"What's a faggot?" I asked.

Everyone burst out laughing.

"Where did she come from?" Mohammed demanded. "How can she not know what a faggot is?"

"Maybe there's still a place in the world where men are men," said Ashish.

I didn't understand what they meant but I felt myself coloring. I decided from now on I would stay quiet when I didn't know something.

"A faggot," Abdul bit out, "is a man who sucks dick."

"Or fucks another man up the ass," Mohammed added.

"Or *takes* it in the ass," said Ashish. "Look at her! She really didn't know."

I hadn't. Sex, even between a man and woman, had never been talked about at the Home. The things they were saying were unthinkable, the crude words appalling. I stood dumbly looking around at them, incredulous and strangely ashamed. My face burned.

"What's the matter?" Abdul hooted. "You look sick!"

"She's a normal girl, that's all," Mohammed said. "It makes her sick to think about faggots. Doesn't it?"

"Yes," I managed to say. What I really felt was scared. This new world was too raw. I wanted to shake off their terrible words, make them have nothing to do with me. "That's the sickest thing I ever heard."

"Well," said Abdul, "it's sick to you and me, but faggots get special privileges around here when the work gets rough. Maybe if I act like one," and he flapped a loose-wristed hand in my direction, "I can take it nice and easy during the next load-out."

"Let me know if you need help practicing, Abdul."

We all turned in the direction of the voice, which came low and cold from just outside the open window. Jorgé stood beside the wagon, his face expressionless except for his eyes, which were snapping like a turtle's.

"Hey, no offense, man," Abdul said. "But it's true, isn't it?"

I looked from Jorgé to Abdul and back again. Sudden comprehension dawned. In the startled moment I met his gaze, I understood that he had been standing there for some time, had heard all the Arabs had said, had heard what *I* had said. And why he cared. The anger and contempt in those eyes turned my stomach to ice. I'd gotten Christa back after all these years only to lose her again without warning. Before she—he—had even recognized me.

I stared at him, stricken. He looked back at me coolly, then turned and began walking away. I followed without thinking, leaving the wagon without permission.

"Jorgé," I called to his back.

He stopped and let me approach. But when I stood before him I couldn't think of what to do.

"Jorgé, I'm sorry," I said. "I didn't know."

"Didn't know what?" he asked.

"Didn't know . . . what you were."

"What am I?"

I was silent, sensing that I should not repeat the word they had used. And yet I didn't know any other.

"Well? What am I?" he insisted.

"A faggot," I said softly.

"That's okay," he said. "I didn't know you were a bitch." And he was gone.

I stood motionless at that spot for what seemed like many minutes, my heart swelling huge and painful in my chest. From a distance I could hear the Arabs shouting at me to get my ass back on the wagon. And when I could move again, I went.

All through the afternoon show, I rehearsed what I might say to Jorgé at dinner, when the crew convened in the cookhouse. How to explain that I wasn't really sickened by anything he did, it was only the words and the tone of the Arabs that had frightened me. How to tell him I wanted to be his friend; that I was sure, in fact, that I already knew him. It sounded crazy even in my own mind.

As it turned out, he didn't give me a chance to say any of this. When I took an empty seat beside him, he made a sound of exasperation that drove all the words from my head. We were quiet throughout dinner while the rest of the table laughed and joked. Although I cast several furtive glances in his direction, he did not look at me once. He ate steadily and silently, his body turned away from me. I was too miserable to eat at all. After he finished two plates of food, he left without ceremony, and I stared after him through the cookhouse window. When I saw him enter his sleeper alone, I went after him.

I was standing outside the metal door trying to find the courage to knock when it jerked open.

"What do you *want*?" he snapped upon seeing me.

"I—I just—I just wanted to talk to you for a minute."

"Well, I'm not interested. Leave me alone." And he took off across the lot toward the main tent.

All evening I moved around as if crippled and did my work without speaking, so that even the Arabs noticed.

"What's the matter, are you brokenhearted over your loverboy? Because we pissed him so much off this morning? Don't worry about it—he was never going to like you anyway; we told you what he wants and you don't have it. Besides, he is angry no matter what because he has to do the garbage in the morning."

I looked up from where I was boxing popcorn. "What?"

"Yes, don't you know? If you are late for a call—and you should keep this in your mind, girl—you must get up at five o'clock in the morning and empty all the trash cans on the circus lot into the Dumpsters. It is a disgusting job—the smell all by itself could kill a pig. And now that it is summer, it is even much more worse."

"And Jorgé was late to a call?"

"He was forty minutes late. So they make him do this tomorrow."

I went back to the popcorn, turning this information over in my mind. Actions speak louder than words, Christa was always telling me. And it came to me what I could do.

The next morning I woke at quarter to five. It was black outside; everything was quiet. Across the lot, I saw Jorgé emerge from his sleeper and disappear behind the band shell. I crossed the dew-soaked grass and found him emptying the first few trash cans. Even in the dark, the muscles of his back were visible, rippling through his shirt. I watched him for a moment before speaking quietly. "Jorgé."

He whirled around, startled. "What—who—"

"It's me."

He peered through the gloom. "You. Again. What are you doing here?"

"I came to help you."

"Help me?"

"With the trash." Even as I spoke, I was gathering the edges of a garbage bag from the rim of its can.

"What? Are you crazy? Why would you want to do that?"

I knotted the top of the bag and lifted it out. Maggots swarmed over the rusted tin in the bottom of the empty can. This time when I spoke the words were certain and resolute. "Because I want you to accept my apology."

He regarded me for a long moment, and I held his gaze. Then his face relaxed, and he nodded, once. "The white Dumpsters are for biological waste," he stated. "This trash here goes in the green ones." This was all he said, but his tone had changed. I began tying up another garbage bag, shaky with relief. For the next two hours, we worked in tandem, speaking little—tying, lifting, and hauling the remains of the day before. It was hard, heavy, filthy work, but I felt the first flutter of happiness since he'd become angry.

When all the Dumpsters were filled and every trash can on the lot relined with fresh plastic, Jorgé met my eyes and said, briefly but deliberately, "Thank you."

It was a precious moment. He was telling me it was all right. Gratitude welled up inside me, coupled with a strange grace. "Thank you too," I said, almost in a whisper.

He gave me just the trace of a smile. "Now go take a shower."

Christa had been two years older than me and I'd slept in her bed for years, curling against her body like a kitten before a hearth. Looking at her spare and sinewy frame, no one would guess the warmth, the perfume, the voluptuousness she exuded in sleep. The beds were narrow and I was bony, but she was supple, tender and yielding. Knees and elbows melted beneath her sheets. It never felt like a tight fit.

By day, she charged the atmosphere; she tampered with the air and sunlight. The Home was a different place when she was within its walls or on its grounds. She knew how to create luxury, and with every step she took it lingered in her wake. She stole things from the rich lady whose house she cleaned, the summer she was thirteen and I was eleven. Silk stockings we wore all fall beneath our wool ones, jasmine-scented oil we rubbed into our skin secretly each night. She smoked pink cigarettes and melted chocolate bars into her coffee.

"Did you know," she told us all after coming back from her maid's job in town, "that all the rich little kids on the block play Orphans the way we play House?" She had pure orphan glamour, and she spread it around us like a cloak.

Christa liked girls, and she loved me. Of course, growing up as we did—almost never seeing boys—it was sometimes hard to know what we really were. A lot of us turned to each other, and it worked for the time being. But Christa never wavered, inside the Home or out. Men might try to speak with her when she went into town, but none of them ever caught her attention, or even made her think about how she looked.

She loved girls and Jorgé loved men and I never loved anything but the two of them. Or the one, depending on how you see it.

After the morning I helped Jorgé with the trash, we went back to the way we had been before. Neither friends nor enemies, we saw each other at a distance each workday and had little occasion to speak. He sold novelties—T-shirts and stuffed elephants, clown makeup and balloons. I squirted colored juice onto Sno-Kones and grilled hot dogs, gazed at him across the lot and ached to know him.

Then Katja, the contortionist, had a party the night of the Fourth of July. It was after the evening show. A grill smoked outside her trailer, where the chicken wings and back ribs she herself would starve before touching charred and sizzled for the rest of the company. Her guests brought everything else. There were Russian and Moroccan and Mongolian concoctions, as well as candied ham, potato salad, pigs' feet, and mince pie. Still, when Spike arrived with a plate of very unremarkable-looking brownies, a whoop went up from the gathering and there was a stampede to take them.

"Spike's magic squares!" was the rallying cry.

I took a couple after the mayhem had cleared, mostly to see what was magic about them. They tasted strange, almost mildewed. Hardly worth the excitement, as far as I could tell.

Twenty minutes later I couldn't walk in a straight line. I saw Augustine from across the lot, then in what seemed like less than a second, she was at my side. Everything around me was wavering like the heat off the grill. My heart rose up ready to explode in my throat; I tried to swallow it back down but my mouth was too dry.

Terrified, I reached out and plucked at Augustine's sleeve. "Augustine," I said. "Help me."

"Lottie? What's the matter, precious?"

"I—I—oh God, *help* me, Augustine!"

She peered into my face and then burst out laughing.

"Who gave the baby a brownie? Spike, how could you?"

Her mirth unhinged me. I began to howl and cry.

"Lottie, come on now, it's all right. The brownies were laced—I'm as zonked as you are. Don't fight it, baby, just ride it." She patted me affectionately, distractedly, on the shoulder. "Ride it!"

"I don't want to! I don't like it!"

Spike appeared suddenly, looming before me. "Lottie, honey, it don't get much finer than this. You're experiencing some of my holiday hash. It's special stuff, baby, you gotta try and appreciate it, you know what I mean?"

"When—when will it stop?"

"With this stuff? A couple of hours."

"A couple of—no, no, I want it to stop now, make it stop *now*," and I trailed off into sobs.

The others were gathering around us.

"Lottie's freaking out," Augustine explained between chuckles. "It's her first time, she didn't know."

"Give her some Scotch," someone said. "It'll help bring her down."

"No, don't give her any booze, idiot, that's only gone make it worse."

"Give her some milk. . . ."

"Give her to me." It was Bo, the snake man. There was general laughter. "Naw, I ain't jokin' now. Lottie baby, why don't you come on with me. I'll make it real nice for you." He wrapped his arm around me. "Make it your first time for everything. Right? We'll ride it together, honey, me and you; you'll see how good you feel in a few minutes."

"You're slimier than your snakes, Bo. Get the fuck away from her."

It was Jorgé.

I broke away from Bo and went to him, clutching his body like driftwood in a flood.

"Oho, it's Jorgé to the rescue, is it? Could Jorgé be going bi-bi?"

"Ah, cool out, Bo. Take her, Jorgé," Augustine directed. "I know she'll be safe in *your* bed!"

Raucous laughter.

Jorgé took me away from there. He took me back to his sleeper, his arm around my waist, my head on his shoulder.

"I'm scared," I whispered once we were inside.

"I know you are. But there's nothing to be scared of."

"I mean, I just . . . I can't . . . think right."

"That's the point." He pushed back the batiked sheets that draped his bunk and I crawled in.

"What's the point?"

"People do it because they don't want to think at all."

"Do you do it too?"

"Every day of my life."

"Every day of your life," I repeated.

"Every chance I get."

"Oh." I made an effort to consider this. "Did you eat any brownies tonight?"

"I brought some back with me," he said. "I would have had them before. If I hadn't got caught up in saving your virginity."

"But—you're not going to eat them now, are you? I don't want you to eat them now."

"You wouldn't know the difference," he said. "I act pretty much the same."

"You do?" I marveled at this. "How can you?"

"Oh, practice. Many years' worth of practice."

"Well, don't. Anyway, don't. Please not tonight. All right?"

"All right, Lottie."

"You promise?"

"Yes." He leaned back against the wall, sitting Indian style. I was suddenly seized with panic.

"You're going to."

"No, I'm not. I said I wouldn't and I won't."

"How could anyone like this?"

"You're just scared, that's all."

"Yes I am. So scared. And I can't wait for it to end."

"Well," he said reasonably, "nothing bad has happened to you so far. Right? And nothing bad is going to happen."

I thought this over. It seemed true.

"But I hate how it feels," I said. "Like . . . my mind . . . feels split in half. I want to walk myself through it, hold my own hand . . . but I can't. I just can't."

He was looking at me with amusement and concern. He had the eyes of a watchdog, tireless and tired. "Well, I'll hold your hand. I'm holding you now, you can let go. That's what you're here for, isn't it?" He spoke softly, drawing my head down onto his lap. "I've got you, it's all right."

I put both arms around him and rested my cheek against his thigh. His shirt was unbuttoned to the navel, baring his hard brown chest. I never wanted to move again. His fingertips were grazing my back, ever so lightly stroking my hair. My tears began again silently, of their own accord.

"Lottie. Why don't you go to sleep. When you wake up it'll have worn off."

"Will you stay here?"

"I will."

"Jorgé."

"What."

"Did this ever happen to you?"

"What, you mean did I ever get wasted? Get paranoid? Sure, of course. I still freak out once in a while, even now. It can happen to anyone. It happens around here all the time."

"It does?"

"Oh yeah. It's great. Afterward they're all so mortified, wondering just how stupid they got and what they did. And I always look at them the next day as if to say, *I know.* I *saw* you. . . . I know who you are." Jorgé laughed softly into the near dark.

I watched the last of my tears stain the denim of his cutoff shorts a darker blue before looking up at him.

"I know who you are," he repeated.

I hesitated. Then: "I love who you are," I whispered.

He glanced down at me, a genuine smile of surprise lighting his face. For a moment, even his eyes were in it. "You're *sweet*," he laughed, all gentle indulgence. And lifting my head, he slid down beside me, slipping an arm beneath my neck.

As I lay against his chest, my trembling subsided. He held me close against him, staring at the ceiling. I was suddenly and deliciously drowsy, and no longer afraid.

He cradled me, crooning almost inaudibly, murmuring like a mother, wordless and low. And grateful as a slave, I finally slept.

This incident altered my relationship with Jorgé, brought it into the realm it had been waiting to enter since I'd identified him, on day one, as Christa come back to me. From that night on, he continued to look after me, and let me share his rack whenever I was particularly lonely or forlorn. He had the role of caretaker, in general, in the circus, though his was a casual, incidental kind of caretaking, involving no production, no heroics. And no martyrdom. He was known to drop by with coffee, and aspirin, whenever someone was hungover and couldn't get up in the morning. He was there to massage pulled muscles, rub Tiger Balm into aching temples. He doted especially on the men, who were more gruff than grateful, at least in the light of day. But women came to him too, tearfully seeking advice about their love lives, asking if an outfit "worked," begging him to salvage a bad haircut, or just craving his sensitive attention.

I wasn't territorial. There was no need to be. His passion was reserved for men, his lust for their bodies and beds. But beyond all that, I knew, as I had with Christa, that he loved me best. And I needed nothing more.

I was there for him always. I gave my body and my soul to him early, as an ongoing consolation prize. This made me the slave of a slave, and I was proud to be. Men took him when they'd gone too long without a woman, and he took me when he had gone too long without a man. But he was never unkind.

For a while, before anyone was used to my belonging to him, he was an object of jealousy for the first time in his circus career. I reveled in giving him that, since his was an otherwise hard and unyielding lot. I lost track of the number of times I glimpsed him on his knees—head flanked by denimed thighs, a careless grip somewhere in his blue-black tresses—under the bleachers, behind the stables, in the sawdust. Prone on his belly in the hay. Or thrust up against the wall. Much as he craved them, these encounters usually left him without relief. And when he was hard up enough, I was there for the taking.

His circumstances set the tone of our sex, determined whether it would be sweet and unhurried or hard and desperate. Most often it was wordless, melancholy, candlelit, and tinged with brooding. I received him each time with equanimity, with a serenity born of quiet and fathomless adoration. There was nothing I would not do and he knew it and didn't make too much of it. We were casual, the edges of our encounters soft with wear. We sat on the metal steps of his sleeper and looked at the stars, we smiled at each other across his pillow, we walked places with our arms around each other and laughed often.

That was the last real happiness I ever knew.

I understand that people envy me. Or think they do. Maybe I should try harder to enjoy what I have, but there's too much I can't forget. When I was little, I imagined that one day Christa and I would have our own house—with a clothesline and a cat and a fireplace like in picture books. Later I fantasized about Jorgé and I sharing a trailer—not just a section of the sleeper car, but our own trailer like the performers. With curtains made out of material donated by Augustine and strings of glass beads veiling the doorway. He could have his lovers and I would give him children.

Now one was dead and the other dying. My nights were spent in sterile hotel rooms and my days with oily people I didn't know. The rest of the world was cozy beneath patchwork quilts with rain drumming on the roof and I had to wonder—shake my head in wonder—who could ever be jealous of me?

I remember everything. Not one detail escapes my memory. The images swirl in my head like confetti in a paperweight, sealed in and unchanging.

Quarantine. I thought it was a beautiful word, probably because it sounded like quarry, like sunlight glinting off clean-edged, quartz-colored rocks. There was a quarantine when rubella invaded the St. Mary Magdalen Home for Girls. Christa had it and I didn't so we were separated. She slept in the west wing while the healthy were confined to the east.

It was a mystery why she had this thing and I didn't. We'd had everything else together: colds and fever, influenza, lice. Maybe there had been a mistake. There was no knowing and it didn't matter.

East wing. Well after midnight. Alone in bed for the first time in years, I couldn't sleep and knew I wouldn't be able to. Not without her.

The window slid open as silently as if in a dream. Snow was falling, slow and ponderous. Me in a white nightgown, an angel darting barefoot across the courtyard. Climbing in through the west wing window where the infected slept.

Christa's face was flushed, her black hair in damp tendrils against the pillow. Heat emanated from her like a halo. I slid into my place at her side, letting the ice water from my feet bleed into the sheets. She murmured and sighed and gathered me in without once opening her eyes.

Once I was in, I was there to stay. It took the sisters a day and a half to realize what I had done and by that time the contagion had claimed me. I wore the roses, as we called them, proudly, like battle scars—evidence of my own daring and subterfuge. Christa was only slightly less horrified than the nuns.

"You're crazy, Lottie," she said softly into the dark. It sounded like an endearment.

"Why? For coming over here? I would have *gone* crazy, staying in the east wing with Emma and Mary Agnes and Sister Thomasina. . . ."

"We could die," she whispered. But it was the "we" that dissolved my fear into the air like smoke.

What happened was that three girls died. And Christa was the second. The days following her death were the most interminable I have ever known, but I didn't weep; I just waited to go. It never occurred to me that I mightn't.

But sleep didn't come. And didn't come. And when it finally did, it was so fitful, the dreams so agonizing, that it was worse than being awake.

And then I heard the doctor tell the nuns I was getting better. It wasn't my constitution he was worried about, I heard him confide to them; I had the strength of an ox. But an air of dementia. He sensed there was something not quite right about me. This tapered into a whispered conference they imagined I couldn't hear, and in fact, I couldn't catch much of it, but I absorbed the tone. The nuns were reassuring him that my oddness was circumstantial. The result of recent tragedy. I heard the words "grief," "inordinate attachment," and "loss" amid the rustling of habits. It seemed to have nothing to do with me. Let them speculate, conjecture, and explain; I was floating. I was mute. I was gone, or should have been gone: another mistake. As with the rubella, I waited for it to rectify itself. But this time my body didn't comply.

The truth asserted itself slowly, insidiously, as the days passed without taking me in their wake: I had let her go without me. How had it happened? What hadn't I done?

She was fourteen and I was twelve. Jorgé was exactly the same age she would have been: another sign. I wasn't going to let it happen again, no, not this time.

I understood that this was more than a coincidence. The parallels were too strong. More than uncanny. It was a test, one I would not fail twice, and I was grateful, so grateful, for the chance to put it right.

Not long ago, I saw a picture in the paper: a funeral scene. The wife of the dead man trying to throw herself into the coffin with her husband. She was being restrained by several others. I sympathized with her, but I couldn't help thinking: Too late. All wrong. You should have thought of that before.

From the clinic we went uptown, to the apartment of Jorgé's mother, who was away for the weekend. I'd been there before, many times over the years. It was the place I'd taken my first bath, pouring nearly a whole vial of her rose-scented crystals into the water, ignoring Jorgé's sardonic remarks about being baptized in style. Now we lay together on her bed in our old position, with me in the crook of his arm, my lips against his throat.

"I knew it going in," he said several times. "It would have taken a miracle for me to be negative. They offered to help me inform my sexual partners. They might as well announce it on the radio." He twisted suddenly to look down at me. "Are you worried about it, Charlotte? I don't think you need to be. It's been almost eight years since you and I . . . and I'm sure I got it after that."

"I'm not worried," I said. I was, though. I worried that I might not have it. And that he wouldn't allow me to get it. From him, anyway. But then, I could work on him. Bring him around. He believed in things like this. Love without limits, suicide pacts . . .

"I wonder if I should quit the circus. How long could I keep it a secret there? It's so homophobic as it is. But what else would I do? What do people do when they get news like this? Travel, right? I should do Europe, now that this is in my face."

"Do Europe?"

"You know, go to Paris, Venice . . . but with what, what money? And who would I go with?"

"You know I'd pay for that," I said. "And you could take anyone you wanted. Or I'd go with you."

"I don't want to take any more of your money."

"Oh, Jorgé, what are you thinking? You know how much I make. What have you ever let me buy you, anyway, besides designer underwear and drugs? And what am I going to do with it, anyway? I can't take it with me."

"No," he said, "but you're not going anytime soon."

Wait and see, I thought.

"I'll do what I want" is what I said.

Jorgé brightened for a moment. "Hey, why don't you get Brian Morgan to go with me? Tell him you'd consider it a personal favor. I read somewhere that he's after you—is it true?"

He was referring to the actor, with whom I'd done a recent shoot. "I guess so," I said.

"Ow! You lucky bitch. What's he like in person?"

"Oh, Jorgé. I don't know. And you know I don't care."

He was quiet at this. My apathy toward everyone but him was a topic we usually avoided. Today was not a usual day, however.

"I love you," I said now. "Only you."

"You're going to have a hard time, then," he replied acidly.

"I'm already having a hard time."

"I don't get it. You know? I really don't. You have the universe at your feet. An army of beautiful men pounding at your door. You have everything the rest of the world can only dream about: beauty, fame, wealth, glamour. None of it means anything to you. You continue to hunger, pathologically, for some *faggot* you met in the *circus* when you were fif*teen*!" This last was almost a shout.

"That's correct." I tried to sound defiant, but my voice was shaking.

"You're a freak," he said, spent.

I didn't argue. I knew Jorgé would consider anyone who loved him a freak.

As always when I was lying with him, I didn't want to ever get up. Here I was safe from the assault of flashbulbs and microphones, the slick pack of dark-clothed cameramen that seemed to be everywhere, and no one understood how they frightened me, except Jorgé. And, according to him, my manager.

He works it, that bastard, Jorgé often told me. Your confusion and fright. It's the Marilyn thing: the orphan catapulted into the limelight, unable to fathom the attention, or to adjust. My poor little Lottie.

I hated when he talked like that, tender and pitying. I didn't want him feeling sorry for me. I didn't want him thinking of me as something separate from him.

Once I had begged to come back to the circus. I had sat and cried in the trailer office.

"Be serious, Charlotte" was all Hale would say to me. "The whole country knows your face now. Do you think you can go back to sweeping sawdust and selling Sno-Kones? They own you now, baby. You belong to the world. And you have to go with it the best you can." He was as kind as he'd ever been, and as inflexible.

The circus. With its glitter and deceptions, more real than where I was now. Its free-floating sadness my only anchor. The unnatural acts performed at the end of a cracking whip not so dissimilar from—and more honest than—the slavery of Hollywood. But I had been severed from it.

That had been my mistake. When the scout approached me just outside the big top, direct and persuasive behind expensive shades, I somehow hadn't realized I could simply say no. I'd let myself be abducted and now it was irreversible.

They had taken me from the circus, but nothing was going to take me from Jorgé. I was going to marry him, finally, in spirit as well as flesh. Just when he thought no one could understand what he was feeling, I was going to join him in that land outside the living. Just when he thought no one would want to share his water glass, let alone his bed, I was going to draw in his tears, his spit, his semen, and his sweat. He would understand; in some way he already did. "You don't move forward" was something he frequently said.

I didn't know what forward was and I didn't care. I only knew what made sense for me, and that for once in my life, I had to make it happen. Come hell—I would risk that—or high water, I would go where he was going.

Night was falling fast outside the window, filling the room as if it knew it was welcome. I pulled back the covers and motioned him under.

"Mother hen," he complained, but I could feel him relax when I crawled in after him and pressed myself to his side. And I could see him smiling, softly but definitely, just before I turned off the light.

The Houseboy

The Sergeant was standing at the head of the room when Troy Caretta's class filed in. He was in full uniform, army drab, with boots and a Smokey the Bear hat. Upon seeing him, the students rolled their eyes at each other, exchanged smirks.

It was April. They were seniors, agonizingly close to being done with high school forever. They were above this, whatever this was; they were above everything. And yet, tiresome as it was to see another clown at the head of a room who thought he had something to tell them, it was better than regular class.

It was a surprise assembly. Everyone had been brought here without explanation at the beginning of sixth period. All the fourth-year language classes were present. And restless.

The French teacher, Miss Marceau, made an effort to address the group. "Students. This is Sergeant Brannon. He is fluent in seven languages, an accomplishment which has served him well in his military career, among other places. We are very glad to have him with us this afternoon, and I'm sure you will benefit a great deal from his discussion."

Nobody paid the slightest attention. Everyone had already chalked the period up to a study hall. Troy had his calculus book open in front of him and was accepting a handful of M&M's from a wrestling teammate when the man stepped forward and spoke for the first time.

"I want your full attention and I want it quiet in here while I'm talking to you. The quieter and more attentive you are, the better off you'll be for the rest of the time I'm here. Be on your guard because I'm going to call on you, I'm going to have you participate in some exercises, I'm going to put you on the spot, and I'm going to embarrass you. It's nothing personal. Don't take it personally."

The room fell silent. Troy closed his notebook and without thinking pulled his hand away while the candy was still being poured. A few M&M's rattled to the floor in what seemed a loud and interminable cascade. Troy froze, cast his eyes downward, and waited for whatever devastation the man would bring down upon him.

Mercifully he ignored it. "I went into the army at age seventeen," the Sergeant began. "I let it determine the course of my life, and it was a good decision for me. I'm not a recruiter and I'm not here to push the military on anyone. That's a personal decision and it's yours.

"You've all got your whole lives in front of you right now and it's time for you to make some crucial decisions. You've been in school ever since you can remember and now you're almost out of it, you're the big fish in a little pond, and that's going to make you cocky. It's going to give you something I call the John Wayne Complex. But I've seen a bit of the world through the work I've chosen, and one thing I can tell you from my own experience, it's the John Waynes that crack first out there, so for the next forty minutes I want you to put that attitude aside on the faith that you just might learn something."

Slowly, painstakingly, trying not to make a sound, Troy fished a dirty sock out of his gym bag. The M&M's were a melted mess in his sweating palm, and he certainly wouldn't dare to eat them now. With a few surreptitious, vicious motions, he wiped the chocolate off his hand and replaced the sock.

"Now," the Sergeant said, "the first thing I want is a volunteer."

No one moved a muscle.

"I should tell you right now that I like to zero in on the most reluctant people in the room. Don't be afraid to volunteer. Be visible. Get involved. That's very important."

Nearly every hand went tentatively up.

"Now, as I understand it, you're all fourth-year language students. Aren't you? You." He singled out Matt Carlisle, a surly, gangly boy near the front row. "What's your name?"

"Me? Uh, Matt."

"Matt?"

"Matthew. Matthew Carlisle."

"Please stand when you're spoken to, Mr. Carlisle."

Matt rose instantly. He kept one hand on the desk behind him, as if for support.

"All right, Mr. Carlisle, what language are you studying?"

"Spanish," the boy answered.

"Spanish. And you've been doing so for four years now, is that correct?"

"Yes sir." Hearing the word "sir" come out of Matt's mouth was definitely a first, but somehow it seemed natural in this situation.

"Okay, Mr. Carlisle, what I'm going to do is give you a very simple sentence in English and you will translate it for me into Spanish. You must translate it in the order it is given to you. You may not stop and you may not say, 'I don't know.' When you've finished you may sit down. Are these instructions clear to you?"

"Yes sir," Matt repeated.

"All right, then. I think you'll agree that this doesn't involve difficult or unusual words. Here is the sentence I want you to translate." He spoke very slowly and clearly, giving each word equal emphasis. "The table is flat and brown."

Matt hesitated. "*La mesa . . .*" he began, and stopped, coloring slightly. Everyone waited. The Sergeant waited. Matt looked around a little desperately. Then, apparently remembering his instructions to sit down when he was finished, he sat.

"Okay, now that I've embarrassed Mr. Carlisle, is there anyone else in the room who would like to try the same sentence in his or her respective language?"

In the silence that followed, Troy could hear the snip of the workman's shears, trimming the hedges outside the window.

"Mr. Carlisle, clearly you are not alone, and it's to your credit that you were willing to stand up and take a chance. My point applies to everyone in this room, and for that matter to most of the young people in this country. Your education is something you take for granted and acquire almost against your will. You're here six hours a day, five days a week, surrounded by experts in a whole range of fields, all of them here for the sole purpose of imparting their knowledge to you for free. You think you're working for them. It never occurs to you that they're working for you. You have to be here anyway, so why not milk the situation for a fraction of what it's worth? That never occurs to you either. You learn to say what the weather is like, and you think that's enough. You're just not interested."

The Sergeant paused to let his point sink in. "It's an American disease, and spreading like a cancer. Apathy. Why learn about other cultures, other ways of thinking and doing things? You're Americans, and your way is the best way. You've got your MTV and that's all the entertainment you need. Well, I've got an interesting story for you. When I was in Vietnam, I was one of the only American soldiers who took any interest in the local Vietnamese people. I was the only one in my regiment to try to draw the civilians out, to talk to them and get to know them. And it saved my life, because one of them came to me one day and told me about a bomb that had been planted in my jeep. I climbed up on a roof, sat there, and watched it explode."

The students shifted uneasily in their seats. Every pair of eyes in the room was fastened upon the Sergeant.

"Well," he said after a moment. "Let's move on." He nodded at a girl sitting near him. "Suppose I cook you two eggs. . . ."

Now that was something to imagine. Troy stopped listening and tried to imagine the Sergeant standing in front of a stove. Impossible that such a man would have to cook for himself. He couldn't picture it.

He was excited. The discussion was exciting him. He thought this was the most exciting thing that had happened in weeks, though he didn't know why the man would be here if he wasn't a recruiter. He liked the way the Sergeant looked, stern yet approachable, starched and pressed and immaculate from hat to boots. He'd been places, done things. He *understood* things. Look at the way he'd taken control of the class. When was the last time they'd accorded a visitor such respect?

Now the Sergeant was wrapping up the egg exercise, whatever it had been. "Are there any questions?" he asked.

Troy's hand shot up.

"Yes, go ahead."

"Would you ever really cook for a woman?"

It was a phase he was going through just then. A phase in which he had the idea that he could say anything he wanted, the more unseemly and challenging the better. Anything that would take someone aback, take them out of context, but even more important, set him apart, make him memorable. He knew this made him unpopular with many teachers, who considered him a troublemaker. A heckler. They didn't understand that it was a passion, a passion for a certain kind of intimacy created instantly and infallibly by inappropriate questions.

He couldn't have been more delighted by the Sergeant's reaction. The man actually stepped backward and broke into a flustered little grin. Several people laughed. After a brief interval in which the Sergeant was visibly trying to decide what to make of the question, he recovered himself smoothly.

"I would cook for anybody because I happen to be a damned good cook. And I can sew too," he added. "That's also come in handy on several occasions. But then, you've all seen Rambo giving himself stitches in the movies without so much as a whimper, so I don't need to go into that."

He filled the rest of the hour in this way, letting the students' responses guide the discussion, working their questions into his agenda, never missing more than half a beat and never at a loss for the moral of any story. It was a strange, rambling, seemingly off-the-cuff sermon, and it wasn't clear to Troy why he wasn't resenting it. But he wasn't, not at all. He was enthralled.

The Sergeant said he'd been an interrogator in the army, and that he'd never failed to get any information he wanted out of anybody he questioned. "And I'm not talking about splints under the fingernails. Nothing crude like that," he said. "I'm talking about knowing when a person's lying and when he's telling the truth. I can always tell the difference. And when someone's lying I can bring him around. Don't need to lay a hand on him. It's all in the mind."

"What if someone won't talk? I mean, not at all?" someone asked. "What if he just won't open his mouth?"

"Everyone talks," the Sergeant said. "That's never a problem. People love to talk about themselves—they never pass up the opportunity."

Troy could feel the familiar ache. It was lodging itself in his chest again. He tried to see himself in a soundproof holding cell, across the table from the Sergeant. Why was he there . . . ? Maybe he was a smuggler. Or even a spy. But definitely tough, even under the lights, or whatever it was they used on you. He could take a lot; he knew what endurance was about. . . .

The seventh-period bell snapped him out of the fantasy. From the hall came the usual commotion between classes; lockers slammed, mock scuffles erupted, sneakers pounded in the corridor. But the class was still under the Sergeant's spell; no one moved until he touched the brim of his hat and wished them luck.

Troy found himself in front of the man. "I—could—can I write you a letter?" He forced himself to make eye contact.

"Certainly," the Sergeant said, extracting a pen from his shirt pocket. "Though I won't be home for another ten days."

He wrote down an address in New York City.

"Thanks a lot," Troy said, not feeling that he had to explain. He folded the piece of paper carefully and turned to go.

That night Troy couldn't eat dinner. He couldn't do much of anything, in fact, let alone study. He sat at his desk with his calculus text open in front of him and stared out the window. He kept seeing the Sergeant standing at the head of the room with his arms folded across his chest.

He was glad when Arthur called. Arthur was a professor at the local university; he lived just down the block. He was also a fan of Troy's, coming to watch nearly every one of the boy's wrestling matches.

"I just bought a VCR," he announced, "and all the pretty boys in this godforsaken city are invited to come over and watch movies."

Arthur always knew when to call. Arthur knew what Troy was, though he pretended otherwise, claiming he'd resigned himself to the young wrestler's being straight some time ago. But they both knew that what he'd really resigned himself to was not pushing the issue. Not now. The professor treated him knowingly but gingerly, like a skittish horse he didn't want to break.

"All the pretty boys" referred mostly to a handful of student disciples, graduate and undergraduate, who hung on his opinions, read what he recommended, and wore their jeans at least one size too small. Troy liked Arthur, trusted him, and found himself glad to be included in these gatherings where he was same and not-same. He even liked the flirtation, as long as it never went past that point.

"Great," Troy said. "I'll be there in a while."

On the way to the older man's house he pondered the old puzzle of his longing. Troy wasn't afraid of what he was, he was only afraid that there was no place for it, and so far there had been no reason to announce it, advertise it, or act upon it. He wasn't in the closet and wasn't out of it. He wasn't a *faggot* but he didn't shun them; they aroused in him neither desire nor chagrin.

People speculated about him and he let them, uncaring. The one he did care about didn't give a rat's ass what he was, as long as he captured the trophies and broke the tape. The Coach was married, though, with three kids, and had never given any indication of being anything but straight. It didn't matter. It was enough to run for the man, to lift the cold circles of steel and execute endless push-ups beneath that impassive gaze. Oh, he had suffered for Coach Hanley, and all the ropes and hurdles and stadium stairs, every pounding mile, each lungful of dust was for him. It was enough to be with him every weekday afternoon, and to know he was the man's dearest hope. His personal project.

The other one he cared about made no sense, none at all. Troy whispered the name to himself dropping into sleep each night,

Jesse, tightened his jaw around it as he laced his shoes, *Trueblood*. His rival and archenemy, Gladstone's star wrestler, a lithe half-Sioux, unbelievably difficult to grasp and hold down. Those lean arms had twisted him and pinned him, brought tears to his eyes, shown him agony. And yet . . .

Troy's daydreams were shadowy, involving not consummation but a hard hand clapping the back of his neck in approval, grudging respect in a pair of dark almond eyes. These were the private yearnings he carried with him always: quiet, exquisite. He could impart them to no one. Not to his family or his friends, not to Arthur and his entourage, certainly to no one on the team. They blossomed unbidden when he was trudging to school alone, head down, through sleet or snow; when he was studying by himself in the basement beside the churning washing machine; in any one of the solitary, half-lit places he might occupy or pass through. Coach Hanley's hand holding a stopwatch; Trueblood locking against him limb to limb on the hard blue mats; and his own body pared down, chiseled out, muscles glinting under the sheen of hard-earned sweat.

Troy felt his own beauty keenly. No one had to tell him he was desirable. He was a hero among the student body, an asset to the school, a teen fantasy to Arthur's gang, and a sweet, sweet enigma to the girls. He worked hard to maintain his own miraculousness and he ached to give it all to someone as a gift. His body and his soul, on a silver plate: but only to a man. A Real Man.

In the meantime, he did what he could without sacrificing his leverage or his integrity. He performed like a prize horse, put out everything he had. He loved Coach Hanley and Jesse Trueblood with his diligence and his effort, his exhaustion and his pain, his silence and his aloneness. Up till now it had been enough.

The Sergeant's arrival had thrown everything off somehow. Nothing was the same. He was more sharply aware than ever that high school was almost over. He would no longer be around the Coach, not in the same capacity, and he would never again grapple with his only real opponent. He would have to find something else. . . .

Arthur greeted him at the door. Three men were already seated on the floor before the television, watching *The Wizard of Oz*. Troy could hear their falsetto from the foyer.

"Lions and tigers and bears—oh my!"

Troy joined in as he settled onto the sofa, their crescendo drowning out the television. It was then that he noticed a boy about his own age moving unobtrusively about the room, collecting beer cans and emptying ashtrays. Unlike anyone else in the room he was stripped to the waist, so that his carved little chest was on display for all of Arthur's company.

"Thank you, Scott," Arthur said in his direction. "And we'll need a beer for our newcomer."

Troy started to demur with his old excuse—being in training—then changed his mind.

The boy grinned good-humoredly and disappeared into the kitchen.

"That's my new houseboy," Arthur whispered. "I can't decide which acquisition I'm more excited about, him or the VCR."

"Your houseboy?" Troy repeated.

"He gets room, board, and tuition in exchange for housework, errands . . . and a little . . . heavy petting," Arthur explained.

"Heavy petting?" Troy echoed, then: "Tuition! You pay his tuition?"

A satisfied smile from Arthur. "See what kind of arrangement you—uh, straight boys—miss?"

Scott returned with Troy's beer. He also brought two bowls of popcorn. He placed one in front of the three men on the floor and the other on the end table beside Arthur. Then he went back to the kitchen.

"Well, boys," Arthur said. "Is everybody ready for the feature attraction?"

Someone inserted *Kiss of the Spider Woman*. William Hurt appeared on the screen.

"Where's the bathroom?" Troy whispered to one of the men, not because he didn't know, but to explain his leaving the room.

"Down the hall and to the left" was the answer.

Troy got up and followed the directions. Once inside, he locked the door and sat on the edge of the bathtub. He wasn't sure what he meant to do, but he wanted badly to talk to Scott alone. He waited a minute, then made his way silently down the hall. He got past the entrance to the living room without diverting anyone's attention from the TV. Then he slipped into the kitchen.

Scott was doing the dishes. Troy stood a moment just looking at him. The other boy seemed so innocent: sweet, impressionable, like a kid ready for anything his older brother might suggest.

"Scott?" Troy said tentatively, moving up beside him.

Scott turned, smiling. The peace in his face was something to see. "Hi," he said. "Can I get you anything?" He had a soft, southern drawl.

"Me?" Troy was caught off guard. "No, I'm all right, I just . . ." He trailed off, not knowing how to begin. He cast about for some opening remark and his gaze found the sink. "Looks like a lot of dishes," he heard himself say.

"Yeah," the other agreed, matter-of-factly and without regret.

Troy worked a dish towel free from the oven door and dried a just-rinsed plate.

"Do you like being a houseboy?" he asked idiotically.

"Sure," Scott said. "It's a good deal."

"How'd you find Arthur?"

"Answered an ad in the paper."

"Really?" Troy said. "Can I ask you something else?"

"You can ask me anything you want."

"Did you have an interview?"

Another bright question. No, Troy, Arthur hired him over the phone, sight unseen.

"Yep" was all the other boy said.

"Well, what was that like?"

Scott finally turned his blue gaze upon Troy full force. One corner of his mouth went up, with something like recognition.

"It was in his study," he said. "Arthur sat behind his desk while I stood. He didn't offer me a chair and I knew instinctively not to sit."

Troy held his breath, waiting.

"It was like standing at attention," Scott continued. "I kept my hands behind my back. He appreciated that, I could tell. He asked me what I could do and I told him . . . everything."

"Everything?"

"I said, Sir, I can cook, drive your car, mow your lawn, trim your hedges . . . and do anything else . . . you might require."

"You called him sir?"

"I call most older men 'sir.' It's the way I was raised."

"I bet he liked that."

"Oh, he did," Scott said.

They had finished the dishes.

"So now what?" Troy asked. "Are you going to go in and watch the movie?"

"Oh, I don't know about that," Scott answered. "Those are his friends, not mine."

"Well, can't they be your friends too? Most of them are closer to your age than to his. They're students like you."

"There's a difference," Scott said lightly. "Maybe not outside this house. But inside there is."

"Did Arthur tell you that?"

"Arthur didn't have to tell me. That's the point. That's what he likes about me."

They looked at each other for a long moment.

"I understand," Troy ventured.

"I know," Scott said.

Another pause.

"Well, I guess I should go back in," Troy said finally.

"I reckon so."

"It's been—good talking with you."

"Enjoy the movie," Scott said.

But when they stepped out of the kitchen and Scott turned toward the stairs, Arthur summoned him from the sofa.

"Come here, darling!" he called. His voice was full of tenderness.

They reentered the living room together. Troy took his seat on the sofa, and Scott went to Arthur, crossing behind the television. He seated himself on the floor, at Arthur's feet, his head resting against the older man's knee.

It was all so incredible. He pictured Arthur composing an ad for the newspaper, writing what he wanted, and Scott understanding all it said and left unsaid. A brief phone call leading to a meeting—the interview in the study—where most of the crucial information was imparted without words. Where nearly everything had relied on instinct and recognition and surrender to the inevitable.

Troy stared unseeingly at the screen for about ten minutes before whispering to Arthur.

"I'm going outside," he said.

"Outside? For what?" the older man whispered back, startled.

"I just need some air."

"Do you feel all right? I can drive you home."

"Oh yeah, I'm fine. Don't get up. I won't be gone long."

He found his backpack in the foyer. On his way out the door, he heard one of the men ask, "Doesn't he like the movie?"

Dear Sergeant Brannon,

I hope you'll remember me. You came to my school last week and spoke to the language students. I was very affected by what you talked about, but more than anything I was amazed that you got the attention of about seventy-five rowdy, know-it-all kids in less than a minute, and held it the entire time you were there.

I guess you have to know how to take that kind of control in order to be an effective interrogator. It must be something to have that kind of power. What is it like to interrogate someone? And how do you learn how to do it? Do you ever kind of get to know the person you're trying to crack, and does that ever make you regret your success? If these questions are too personal, or if you're not allowed to talk about it, I'll understand. I hope you don't mind me asking.

Now that you've seen Gladstone, Pennsylvania—which is where I've lived all my life—I'm sure you can understand the fact that I've often thought of going into the military just to get away from it. My real hope is getting a full scholarship to a good school—because my mother basically has no money for something like that—but I won't know what that situation is until the end of the month.

Well, anyway. I appreciate your willingness to correspond with me. I never knew my father—he died before I was born—but I know he was a military man also. I've always wanted to know more about him—he apparently led an adventurous life—but it makes my mother sad to talk about him so I don't like to ask. One thing I feel sure I inherited from him, and that's a desire that's so hard to describe: to know more, do more, work harder, go places. See the world. That's what you were really talking about, wasn't it? I haven't been able to stop thinking about it; I really wanted to thank you.

Sincerely,
Troy Caretta

Troy copied the letter over before mailing it and worried about it long after it was gone. Was it in any way presumptuous? The Sergeant hadn't really expressed a "willingness to correspond" with him, after all—he'd just said it was all right if Troy wrote to him. And what about the rest of it? Had he painted the picture fully enough, the one he wanted the Sergeant to see? That first letter had to be the foundation for all that followed. It would probably be the factor which determined whether the rest of his plan would work.

Two weeks later, the Sergeant's reply arrived in the mail.

Dear Troy,

Of course I remember you. I enjoyed the afternoon I spent at your school, and I always feel that if my message reaches only a handful of young people, my time will have been well spent.

You remind me of myself in one respect: you don't sit back and let life happen to you by accident, you go out and make it happen on purpose. And I think that's very commendable.

I have no problem with your asking me questions. In fact, it might be refreshing to be on the other side of the table. But you'll have to understand that this is something I'm not used to, and it may take some time to overcome my natural reticence when it comes to talking about myself.

Your desire to experience life fully and keep it an adventure is a positive one. A lot of people seem to have no idea that the world goes beyond their hometowns. That was one of the main points of my discussion, yes. I'm always glad to know when that message has found its mark.

I hope everything is going well for you. Good luck with the schools. Where have you applied, anyway?

Till next time,
Michael Brannon

Troy read the letter at least five times and then had to go for a run just to have something to do with himself. It had worked. It was working! The Sergeant obviously expected him to write again; he had ended with a question almost as if to insure it. And he was taking an interest in Troy's future.

Troy did little with his evening besides compose a reply, which he wanted above all to seem unhurried and casual.

Dear Sergeant Brannon,

I've applied to a few different schools, and two of them are in your city: New York University and Columbia College. Actually, New York City has been where I've wanted to live since I was a little kid. It just seems like the backdrop in every movie and where all the action is.

Of course, I know it's supposed to be a hard place to live. A friend of mine, Arthur, is from New York and he's always going on about how dirty and crowded and overpriced it is. He claims that unless you're really rich, the apartments aren't much more than modified closets. But then he admits that he's mostly suffering from a case of sour grapes, and that his heart never hurts so much as after he's looked at the entertainment section of the Sunday *New York Times*.

What do you think of the city? I was surprised you live there. It doesn't exactly seem like a place for military headquarters or anything.

Maybe by the time you write again, I'll have heard from all the schools. I hope so, anyway. Waiting is the worst.

Sincerely,
Troy Caretta

There was some truth in what he'd written. He *had* always wanted to live in New York City. Columbia had accepted him some weeks ago, but the Sergeant didn't need to know that. And he'd been there several times; he had an uncle on his dad's side in Battery Park. But the more he seemed like a starry-eyed kid from the sticks, the better off he'd be, he was sure.

The Sergeant's second letter came in just over a week.

Dear Troy,

You're right about New York being a surprising place for someone with a long-term military career to live. But you see, I'm not a regular soldier, I'm in a division of the army called Special Intelligence. Now and for an indeterminate length of time, which should be at least a year, I'm on a mission which involves some work at the United Nations. I can't say more about that right now.

New York has, as your friend pointed out, a lot of drawbacks. It *is* dirty, and violent, and one of the most apathetic places I've ever been, in certain respects. But there are also endless opportunities at your fingertips. And few other places, if any, have the cultural diversity that New York has.

The cost of living is extremely high, and no one where I'm from would believe what people pay for rent. But I've been lucky in that respect, since the army is covering the cost of my housing. They've set me up in a two-bedroom apartment. Here, that's practically living like royalty.

Ultimately the choice of a city is very personal. What works perfectly for one person is intolerable to someone else. Hopefully you'll get into most if not all of the schools you've applied to, and have a wide range to pick from. And remember, no matter what obstacles, financial or otherwise, appear to be in your path—where there's a will, there is a way. Let me know what happens.

Best of luck,
Michael Brannon

Troy couldn't believe how perfectly everything had fallen into place. His idea still wasn't guaranteed to work, not by a long shot, but the situation could not have been better constructed than it now was. The Sergeant had virtually set his own trap.

Everything depended now on this third letter. It had to be flawless. Simple and straightforward, almost businesslike, full of boy-scout integrity, and devoid of beggary. It was drafted nearly a dozen times during the next several days.

Dear Sergeant Brannon,

Well, I'm very happy to tell you that I've been accepted by Columbia, and with a partial scholarship. I'm sure that wrestling had a lot to do with it, but my grades are good too, and it makes me think that everything I did in high school has started to pay off.

The bad news is, with a partial scholarship, they'll pay for my tuition but not for room, board, expenses, and so on. And I can't afford to pay the kind of rent even the cheapest of places in New York would demand. You know, it's funny, I was kind of resigned to going to Penn State, but listening to you talk that day made me change my mind. I no longer feel I can waste any valuable opportunity that comes my way. And then in your last letter, you wrote that if the will is strong enough, things can be made to happen.

So I had this idea. You're the only person I know in New York, and you mentioned having a lot of room for one person. I wondered if there was any possibility of an arrangement where I could work for you in exchange for a small space to study and sleep. I could clean the apartment, type for you, cook, whatever. And working part-time I could even pay some rent. I'm very quiet and neat and I'd never get in your way.

I'm asking you because I know how much you value education, because I really want to go to this school, and I figure you would want it for me. Maybe you could just give it a trial period, try it out for one semester—if it didn't work out, I'd at least be in the city already and in a better position to set myself up elsewhere.

If you see another way for me, please let me know. And if you don't see another way, but for whatever reason you can't help me the way I'm proposing, I won't have any hard feelings. I hope you won't mind the fact that I've asked.

—Troy Caretta

There was a tiny room just off the front hall and the Sergeant let his applicant have that. It was exactly what Troy wanted—about six feet by ten, with a window opening onto the street, a desk, a chair, and an army cot.

"It's little but functional," the man remarked when showing the boy in.

"It's just fine . . . sir," Troy said sincerely, and waited for the Sergeant to laugh; to say, You can call me Mike. He didn't.

Troy hadn't brought much, just a duffel bag, a tape deck, and a minimal amount of bedding. He arranged his belongings neatly in the closet and made up the cot. Then he lay low until the Sergeant left: "I've got to be at the Ukrainian embassy for a few hours this afternoon. See you later."

Troy waited until he heard the elevator doors clang shut on the tenth-floor lobby before venturing out for a real look at the place. The apartment was uncluttered and austere, with high ceilings, dark wood floors, and a fireplace in the living room. Nothing on the walls. No pictures anywhere, no throw rugs or houseplants, with the exception of a single bonsai tree. Troy walked around as softly as a burglar, gingerly opening drawers, closets, kitchen cabinets. The Sergeant's room (the *master* bedroom) was nearly as plain as his own, and immaculate. The bed was tightly made, papers lay in orderly stacks on his desk, and metallic venetian blinds covered the windows. In the closet, military clothes were separated from civilian. As in the cartoons, several identical uniforms hung from evenly spaced hangers, and his boots (his *boots)* were lined in a neat row beneath. His bureau drawers were no less fastidious. The shirts and pants might have been fresh from a Chinese laundry: starched, pressed, each article fitting squarely over the one beneath it.

Troy also cased out the kitchen, taking inventory of what the Sergeant had: pots and pans, an electric wok, a toaster, a waffle iron. Troy sat down at the kitchen table and made a list of things he knew how to cook. It wasn't long, and was made up mostly of breakfast items: French toast, eggs, stuff like that. But he supposed he could learn to do everything else. Anyone who could read a recipe could cook, his mother always said.

The main question, the real question, was still unanswered. Troy had imagined that seeing the Sergeant's apartment would reveal at least some clues, but he saw now that he had been mistaken. Was he or wasn't he? Troy usually knew, but with this one he didn't. He only had a feeling. And there was nothing more to go on, not even in the man's living quarters. No photographs of women, no girlie magazines, as far as Troy could tell. No condoms, at least on the premises. For all the apartment revealed, the Sergeant might think of nothing but military matters around the clock.

Who are you? Troy asked the walls. What do you care about? he implored the ceiling. What do you need, why did you let me come here, are you glad to have me around? Did you ever have a boy before?

The Sergeant returned in high spirits. "I got a new assignment today," he told Troy. "A real hard-core subject, top of the line. Too tough a nut for anyone to crack so far. I like that."

"You like the challenge, you mean?" Troy asked.

"The challenge, yes. The opportunity to test out my skills. You know, when people think of war, all they can imagine are toy soldiers blasting away at each other from their trenches. But I go to war every day. And a decisive victory in one of those rooms can be worth more than a thousand bloody clashes out there on the field. Innumerable lives might be in the balance, depending on the information at stake."

The Sergeant had taken off his jacket and was hanging it up. Suddenly he turned to face the boy, thrusting an index finger in his direction. "Anything I say about the work I do—anything at all, no matter how insignificant it might seem—never gets repeated to anyone, not one word. Is that understood?"

"Perfectly. Sir." Troy spoke carefully, looking into the other man's eyes, his words measured and serious. He watched the Sergeant's jaw relax.

"Good. I want to think I can speak freely in my own apartment. Not that I'd ever reveal any real information, beyond first names; I wouldn't do that, if only for your sake. And you'd have no way to know anything about the issues I'm dealing with anyway. It's not in the news, it's all behind the scenes . . . but it's crucial, that I can promise you. So whatever superficial details I might choose to relate to you must never go any further."

"I understand that, sir. And you can count on my . . . discretion."

"Well, that's fine, then. Now this fellow today. His first name is Xavier. The boys like to call him X. He's going to give me one hell of a hard time, I can tell already. And I don't know if you can understand this, son, but I enjoy nothing more than that."

"I think I can understand, sir. It's kind of like that in sports, too. Having a tough opponent is what keeps you going."

"Yes. That's right. That's exactly right . . . say now, have you eaten yet? Do you eat pizza?"

"Sure."

"Why don't you call Ray's and get one sent up here. With anything but anchovies. I'm going to shower and then I'll be hungry."

The Sergeant disappeared into his bedroom. Troy wandered into the kitchen and found a Ray's take-out menu pinned to the refrigerator with a magnet. He ordered the pizza, his heart pounding with exhilaration at the exchange they had just had. The Sergeant had told him something important already. Something intimate. And he had not only understood, but he'd *known* it, known what the man was saying.

When the Sergeant emerged again, he was in semicivilian clothing—white undershirt and khaki pants. It was the first time Troy had seen him out of uniform. This, along with his damp, slicked-back hair, made him look younger. The Sergeant had bottles of dark beer in the refrigerator; he offered one to Troy. They ate their pizza out of the box and drank their beer from the bottles.

"So when do you register?" the Sergeant asked after they had eaten awhile in silence.

"That'll be tomorrow, sir. I was thinking of running early in the morning, though. Do you know where I could go?"

"Well, sure. Central Park is less than half a mile away. A lot of people run around the reservoir. How far did you want to go?"

"Oh . . ." Troy considered. "Maybe eight miles or so."

"Eight miles?" Was there a glimmer of admiration in his tone? "I thought wrestling was your sport."

"That's right, sir, but I go out for track also. It helps wrestling, actually. Keeps me in better shape. Clears my head."

"Well, I'm glad to hear it. There's not enough emphasis on physical fitness in this country. The new arrivals at boot camp never cease to amaze me. Over the years, I'd say it's only gotten worse. We get kids that can't run half a mile, do a single pull-up."

"No way," Troy said, detaching another slice of pizza from the pie. "That must be a drag."

"It's a national disgrace," the Sergeant continued. "I'd like to know what they're doing in their phys ed classes. I don't think kids are being pushed enough these days to find out what they're made of." He leaned back in his chair and clasped his hands behind his neck. "Now back when I was a kid, the most respected person in school, after the principal, was the coach. He was a hard man—and hard to please—but something just made you want to put out for him. Practically everyone went out for a sport. Even the real academic types played tennis or something."

Troy suddenly lost all desire to eat. He leaned back in his seat and looked at the man. It took all his control to speak casually.

"Is that right?"

Troy set his pizza carefully back onto the cardboard.

"That's how it was. And probably the only way to reverse the unfortunate situation on our hands today is to bring back that kind of system. Those values have to be instilled in early youth."

"I felt that way about my coach," the boy said, staring at the wooden grain of the table.

"Yeah? Was he a tough guy too?"

"I guess you could say that. He didn't give praise easily or lightly."

"But you busted your ass for him anyway."

"Yeah."

"Because a word from him was worth more than a song and dance from anyone else."

"Right."

"Well, consider yourself lucky. You had something of a mentor, someone who probably showed you what you had."

Oh, Coach Hanley. Who was the focus of that narrowed blue gaze now? A wave of homesickness washed over the boy.

There was a pause and then the Sergeant changed the subject. "I suppose now's as good a time as any to talk about the terms here. You offered to do some work for me in exchange for room and board. I could use some assistance in a few different areas. You said you could type?"

"Yes sir . . . I'm not as fast as some, but I've typed all my own papers for school and I'm pretty good."

"You can type for me. There's no end to the paperwork I'm required to turn in. Assessments, reports, all sorts of bureaucratic bullshit; and it's begun to weigh me down. But again. What you type for me you will never discuss with anyone. At any time, in any capacity."

"You can rely on that, sir."

"You won't understand a lot of what you're typing. That's all right. You don't need to understand it."

"That's fine, sir."

"All right then. Now. Cooking was something else you mentioned. You want to cook, that'd be great. One less thing for me to worry about at the end of the day. It'll save me money, in the end, because when I come in late, at eight, nine, in the evening, I'm more likely to call for a pizza or something, like tonight, than to play chef. I wouldn't expect you to do it every night, of course. And I don't mind cooking myself. I'm thinking you could do it a couple nights a week."

"Sure," Troy said.

"Nothing set in stone," the Sergeant continued. "Just pick up the slack for me. And I don't care what you cook. Fix any damn thing you want. As long as it's edible."

"Well, hopefully I'll be able to manage that," Troy said.

"Shouldn't be a problem. I eat anything. Something I learned to do spending so much time overseas. We're talking raw fish—and I don't mean the clean, pretty sushi variety—seaweed, all kinds of insects, snails and eels, goat, monkey, dog. When it's a matter of survival, the taste buds get real adaptable."

The Sergeant shot a glance at the boy. He was hanging on every word, open admiration written plainly on his face. With such a captive audience, the man grew expansive.

"The only true hardship was the days I didn't eat at all. And there were plenty of those."

"In Vietnam?"

"Vietnam, Korea, and son, a lot of other places. Not every military mission reaches the media, remember. A lot of important maneuvers take place under wraps. Secrecy is often crucial for the security of an operation. Our country is involved with everything that happens on this globe. And that's as it should be. The United States is a world leader, and that kind of position carries a certain responsibility."

"I guess you've kind of put serving the country above everything else," Troy ventured carefully.

"No true patriot does anything less. I'd lay my life down at any minute."

"What about family? Have you—" Troy broke off, uncertain of how to continue. The Sergeant waited, tilted back in his chair, fists jammed in his pants pockets.

"Did you ever want a family? A wife?"

"If I wanted one I'd have one." The man's voice was flat. The answer revealed nothing.

Troy couldn't think of anything to say.

"I never saw a necessity for any of that," the Sergeant continued after an uncomfortable pause. "I enjoy the company of women, but I can have that anytime I want it. Never saw a reason to tie myself down, and I deal with kids all the time at boot camp anyway. They're kids to me. I don't need more at the end of the day, that's for damn sure." He grinned suddenly. "Unless they're cooking my dinner and typing my reports."

The next morning Troy's alarm went off at 5:00 A.M. He recognized the sound with pure dread, although he wasn't sure where he was. He reached out and found the metal on the frame of the cot. And then he remembered.

It was still dark out and the air in the room was chill. He fought the urge to burrow back into the warmth of sleep, and struggled into a sitting position. His running shoes were waiting where he'd set them out the night before. He meant to run his eight miles before breakfast.

Lacing his sneakers, the familiar sense of virtue stirred within—the feeling that had taken him through a thousand workouts. He was someone special, unusual, disciplined and resolute. And this fact would etch itself upon every inch of his body, for all the world to see. For the man to see.

The apartment was silent. The Sergeant apparently hadn't risen yet; Troy noted this with something like triumph. He stood at the kitchen sink and drank a glass of water, then left the apartment jauntily, just as if the man was watching him go, not still asleep behind his closed door.

Even at five-thirty in the morning, there were signs of life all around, so different from his hometown. Stray taxis cruised the wide streets, winos peered at him from open doorways, ragged cats slunk in and out of alleys. When he reached the reservoir, Troy saw that there were at least a dozen runners already circling the water.

It was an earthen track. He could feel how easy it was on the feet the minute he started. Nonetheless, the first few steps were a special kind of agony. His head was still drowsy, heavy on his neck. And his body was stiff and awkward and afraid of the long haul ahead.

Half a mile into it, he found momentum and knew going the distance would not be a problem. He rounded the curve onto the eastern side of the track, crunching through withered leaves. Long-tailed rats moved unhurriedly out of his way. Troy glided along smoothly now, waiting for the glow he knew would come after a few miles.

It hit him just as the sun slid onto the water. At one with nature, he thought, smirking inwardly, and: five down, three to go. Happiness fluttered beneath his ribs. His whole body fell into a sweet, working, sweat-bathed rhythm and he found it, that soaring high, the awareness of his body as the most miraculous of machines: limbs pumping in tandem, pressing forward, shining and tireless.

When he got back to the apartment the Sergeant was awake. Troy could hear the sound of water running in the kitchen and he went down the hall to make an appearance. The man was sitting at the table barricaded behind the *New York Times* and the air was fragrant with coffee.

"Morning, sir," Troy announced himself as he headed for the fridge.

The Sergeant lowered his paper. "Morning," he answered, sounding surprised. "I didn't know you were up."

"Yeah," Troy said casually. "Remember, I told you I wanted to run?"

"Yes, that's right, that's right. Eight miles?"

"Yeah, about that. Maybe a little more."

"Well, good for you, son."

Son. How he loved that word. He peered into the fridge to hide the hot pleasure he knew was staining his face. The man had white bread and eggs.

"Hey, have you eaten yet?" Troy asked. "If I make some French toast, do you want any?"

"Well, now, that sounds good. I usually don't have a decent breakfast."

This was something Troy knew he could do. He'd learned from his mother to mix vanilla extract, and plenty of sugar, into the egg for extra flavor. He stood at the skillet while the bread browned and observed the scene as if from outside it: the boy in from his morning workout, serving the man before he'd even had a shower.

As he slid the first several slices onto a plate and set it down before the Sergeant, the man sighed with satisfaction and picked up his fork.

"I could get used to this," he said.

By the evening of the second day, Troy had memorized the Sergeant's features, down to the smallest detail. The man stood just about six feet tall, with a medium build: not bulky, but well-defined. Iron tinged his light brown crew cut and mustache; his eyes were gray-green, with faint lines radiating from the corners.

His hands were beautiful—pale-veined, square-tipped—the nails kept clean and pared down to almost nothing. He wore a digital watch set to army time, thin steel-rimmed glasses for reading, and he smoked a pipe after dinner. His clothes were always sharply pressed and immaculate.

In the man's presence, Troy had a heightened awareness of his own physique and its contrasts. He himself stood only about five-foot-eight, but his body was solid, deeply cut, and golden-bronze. His own eyes and hair were the color of honey and he wore softly tattered broken-in things: thermal underwear, T-shirts, sweats.

The boy could see immediately how they would complement one another, take up opposing roles: where the Sergeant was forceful, Troy would be mild; where the man was didactic, he would be a disciple. The image of his own persona became clearer every day: he would be quiet, hardworking, diligent, grateful. He would do the housework so unobtrusively as to call no attention to it. The kitchen table would clear itself; dishes would vanish from the sink. No matter what hour the Sergeant arrived home, his dinner would still be warm.

Troy would spend hours at the dining room table, bent over the heavy textbooks in a halo of lamplight. Every few months the flawless grades would come, to be placed wordlessly on the Sergeant's desk in the afternoon, justifying his investment. All this on top of his dedicated regimen: the running, the lifting, the jumping of rope as his muscles swelled ever tighter and more voluptuous under his taut and gleaming skin. Until it went without saying that he was the son the man hadn't even known he'd wanted.

"X is one smart son of a bitch," the Sergeant reported in the middle of the second week. "He's been playing the boys in our department like a record. We've had him on hidden camera during each of the questioning sessions, and when we review the tapes in succession, it becomes clear that he has a whole array of personalities. Which he can put on and discard at whim. Like a chameleon."

"Depending on who he's dealing with?" Troy asked.

"Depending on who's dealing with *him*," the Sergeant corrected. "He's slippery—trickier than anyone gave him credit for at first. Even trapped and cornered in enemy hands, he's got a working strategy—divide and conquer. He's given each of us very different, even conflicting, impressions of who he is, and as a result, no one's in agreement about what approach to take with him."

"So I guess that's something you guys are going to have to resolve first," Troy said.

"Right. And the obvious solution to that situation is to eliminate it. Let one person interact with him exclusively and consistently. He'll exhaust his repertoire much sooner, and the one dealing with him will have the prerogative of taking whatever course of action he thinks is best. It's better that way. More efficient. Wavering back and forth, debating with a committee—that's not the way to win a battle."

"Which is why the president gets full and executive control of the military in a war," Troy suggested, recalling last year's American history material.

"Exactly. Good, son. You know something about the way this country works; that's more than I can say for a lot of your peers." Nothing caused quite the same flush of pleasure to spread over his body as the Sergeant's approval.

"The rules of the game are always changing," the man continued. "Sometimes it's not always a team sport. This has revealed itself as being one of those times. So it's going to be one-on-one from now on with him."

"Is it you who'll have him?" Troy asked, but he could already sense the answer.

The Sergeant's smile was barely detectable, but there was a sudden, unmistakable light in his eyes. "That's right, son. The man is mine."

September was golden. The days took on a rhythm of their own: running, school, housework, and then evenings with the Sergeant. For several hours nightly, Troy studied ancient Greek literature, urban sociology, Spanish, and advanced calculus with equal and undivided concentration. Sometimes the Sergeant did his paperwork in his own room, but more often he was nearby, reading the newspaper with a serious, almost pained expression. Crumpling its edges in his white-knuckled grasp as though it were something to be tamed. At odd times, Troy would catch a glimpse of the scene they created, as if peering through someone else's living room window. Boy and man. Man and boy. And then, later: man, boy, and cat.

Near the end of the month, Troy spied an emaciated gray kitten shivering in an alleyway, and carried her home in his woolen hat. While she ate her fill of raw hamburger and milk, he tried to think of how to convince the Sergeant that keeping her would be a good thing. He had a feeling the man wouldn't like the idea.

The Sergeant was late coming home that night, but by the time his key could be heard in the lock, the kitten was where she needed to be: asleep on the hearth. Troy was sitting next to her on the floor, pretending to read Plato's *Republic*. The man strode in, unbuttoning his military overcoat as he walked. When he saw her, he stopped short.

"Where did *that* come from?" he snapped.

"Sir . . . ? Oh, the kitten? I rescued her from a bunch of juvenile delinquents this afternoon. There was a mob of second- or third-grade boys on that stone bridge in Riverside Park. They wanted to drop her over the side. To see if she'd land on her feet."

The man snorted. "Well, what are you going to do with her now?"

Troy tried to sound offhand. "I thought I'd ask around at school, see if anyone wants her before I take her to the pound. Isn't she cute?"

"How do you know she isn't carrying all kinds of vermin?"

"She seems pretty clean to me," the boy said.

"Bringing her here wasn't a good idea."

"I'm sorry, sir. I didn't think it would be a problem."

"Well, see about getting rid of it as soon as possible," the man said, then added, with a faint, relenting smile, "One stray is enough for me."

"Yes, sir. In the meantime, maybe she'll catch some of those mice."

The Sergeant had been starting to leave the room, but at the boy's last words, he turned around. "What?"

For a moment, Troy thought he'd gone too far. The man was never, never going to fall for it. But with nothing to do except plunge on, he said, "The mice in the kitchen. That live under the refrigerator. Don't you ever hear them?"

"What? I've never heard anything. There are no mice here."

"Oh, there are, sir. I've even seen 'em a couple of times. When I've studied late in the kitchen some nights. That's when they come out. And if anything's carrying vermin, it's going to be them."

"I've never seen any trace of mice in the six months I've been here. Your eyes are playing tricks on you."

"But do you ever stay up really late? In the kitchen?"

"Well, I usually turn in early, as you know. But I'm sure if there were a mouse problem, I'd be aware of it."

The next morning, Troy went to the deli down the street, where he'd noticed baited snap-traps in the back corner. The owner told him, with some dismay, that he couldn't imagine what a well-intentioned young man would want with a dead rodent. After some time, however, Troy persuaded him to give up the catch of the day.

That night he positioned his stiff and slightly bloodied mouse about six inches away from the fridge. When the Sergeant came home, he was in his own room as if immersed in schoolwork. The kitten was with him, curled up on the cot. First the man went to his own room. Troy could hear the scrape of hangers as he hung up his coat, and then his footsteps as he crossed the dining room to the kitchen.

"Well, I'll be damned," the boy heard him say.

"X," announced the Sergeant, home from work early in October, "is without a doubt the most demanding challenge I've had in my career to date."

"What's happening with that, sir?" Troy asked.

"Oh, I'm getting my information. But slowly. Slowly. It's like pulling teeth." The man passed his hand wearily over his eyes. "I've got a mean headache. And an even meaner crick in my neck."

"Did you wake up with it?" Troy wanted to know.

The Sergeant seated himself at the table, his movements uncharacteristically tired. "I may have, I don't remember. But even if I did, the hours I put in today across the table from that stubborn bastard didn't help any."

"Where is it?"

The Sergeant looked up blankly.

"The pain. Is it in the tendons?" Troy stood up and moved behind the man's chair. "My coach showed me something. . . ." And for the first time, Troy put his hand against the man's warm skin. "This might hurt a little right now but it'll kill the real pain for good. It's all in the pressure points." He pressed his fingertips deep into the nape of the man's neck, kneading slowly. He'd done this for Coach Hanley all the time—all the athletes had. They'd done it for each other too. But it had been so long since he'd touched a man's flesh that his own was tingling, little tremors running from his fingertips up his arms and down his trunk. He felt his erection straining against the denim of his jeans and was grateful for the long flannel shirt which fell to mid-thigh, shielding the evidence.

The man sighed low in his throat and leaned back against the pressure. "Your coach trained you well."

Had anybody ever said anything to him which had meant as much as this? Joy washed over him in sharp waves. He worked on, mesmerized by the sight of his own square hands on the nape of the Sergeant's neck. From his vantage point he shot a searching glance at the man's groin, but a copy of the *Washington Post* lay folded—strategically?—over his lap.

"My coach knew everything," Troy said, talking to cover his nervousness, his thrill. "He could tell you what to do about any physical problem, put dislocated bones back in place. . . . Whenever anyone got injured at school, they'd page him over the intercom."

"A little lower, son. A little lower . . ."

"Lower" could only mean the shoulders. Troy's hands moved to the top of the man's spine and across his back. The Sergeant leaned into it with a barely audible but definite growl of pleasure. Troy could feel the tension in the man's muscles and how it was ebbing, slowly, under his grip.

It hadn't been the boy's night to cook. He'd only assembled a large salad, which was all he would eat for the next several nights—there was the need to make middleweight division. This meant days of drinking only water and skim milk, snacking on celery sticks, gnawing cabbage cores. Still, he wished now that he had thrown together something else for the Sergeant, who had come home with a paper bag from McDonald's.

When Troy wasn't cooking, the man didn't eat right.

The boy felt a pang of regret. If he were that *other* type of . . . well, then he might soften the edges of the man's life. Fill the kitchen with color and texture, like Arthur had with his own. He thought for a moment of that cozy room, with its strings of garlic and hot red peppers, bright enameled tea tins filled with fragrant leaves, colored bottles that lined the window above the sink and caught the sunlight. He recalled the professor's dinner parties and his mouthwatering, elegant dishes. He tried to think of their names but could only recall details: translucent half-moons of celery floating in clear consommé, radishes cut into elaborate roses.

But then, if the Sergeant had wanted such things, he would have provided for them. He'd said he didn't want a wife. Troy had never even heard him mention a woman. Women did not seem to be part of the man's world.

Troy was sure about this now. He knew from listening hour after hour that the Sergeant was riveted upon men. Men who slipped in and out of the woodwork like spies, men who cradled fire in their arms night and day, men who wore bullet necklaces and dirt smeared on their faces. Cagey men who changed under the spotlight into cornered animals; men who knew they'd met their match. Men in his power. His power.

He also knew the Sergeant's closet was complex, wrought as much out of patriotism as fear and denial. The man was so religious in his devotion to the military that he probably couldn't afford to look at himself. Not even out of the corner of his eye.

And just as Arthur used to honor Troy's silence, the boy was honoring the Sergeant's. There was no other choice, really. There was a delicate balance, a harmony, between them, based as much on this silence as on recognition.

Sometimes during the day, when he was alone in the apartment, Troy stood in the middle of the floor and tried to fathom his life. Here he was doing it all, and someone was watching. He was living with a man. A military man, a drill sergeant, a broker of boys, a breaker of men. And he himself was a manservant, houseboy, wonder kid and confidant. It was a fantasy and it was a reality, unfathomable and undeniable.

He would not compromise it.

Autumn wore on. The Sergeant became more excited as the interrogation continued; every night he reported what X had said, what X had done. X revealed another piece of the puzzle inadvertently. X seemed to be launching an unspoken hunger strike. X was growing gaunt; circles were appearing under his sharp black eyes.

The days grew shorter; evening fell faster. It was no longer pitch-black in the mornings when Troy rose to run. Midterms were coming and wrestling was going well. Life was sweeter than it had ever seemed before.

That's what Troy had to hold on to, afterward. The fact that it had been perfect, or nearly so: a little capsule in time, set apart and self-contained. A situation he had conceived and then conjured into existence. How many people could say they'd ever done the same?

Scott and Arthur could. But they had the incredible advantage of having nothing to hide, from themselves or anyone else. For all Troy knew, they might be together still, with no disastrous ending to their story.

The ending with the Sergeant was disastrous all around. And Troy would mark the beginning of the end, like a dark omen of all that would follow, with the end of X.

It was late October. The leaves in Riverside Park were fiery, drifting. It was a little before five, and Troy was heading home after a gruelling wrestling practice. He felt deliciously tired, each limb singing with what he thought of as "the good burn."

He could sense something wrong the minute he entered the apartment. From the front hall he could see the Sergeant's military coat, draped over the back of an armchair, which was strange. Troy had never known him not to hang it up. He wondered if the man could be home already. It was too early.

Walking down the front hall, he registered another irregularity: the air was heavy with alcohol. And upon entering the dining room he saw the Sergeant at the table, a half-empty bottle of vodka in front of him. He was staring glassily into space.

Troy felt a stab of shock and fear. What was going on? He waited for the Sergeant to look up, to speak, but the man didn't acknowledge his presence. It took the boy several seconds to find his voice.

"Sir? You're home. . . ."

"Yeah," the Sergeant said, after a pause. "I'm home." He sounded unnatural, confused.

"It's early," Troy said uncertainly. "Did something happen?"

"Oh, something happened," the man said, and laughed, a quick bark without humor.

Troy set his gym bag down and stood awkwardly in the middle of the room, not knowing what to do. The Sergeant lifted the bottle and took such a long drink that it might have been water. In the silence that followed, Troy took the seat opposite him at the table.

The Sergeant set the vodka down and spoke again. "Cracked him," he muttered.

"What?"

"Cracked him open," he said, and began to croon. "Cracked him open, cracked him open, cracked him open just now . . . just now I—cracked him open—cracked him open just now . . ."

Troy went cold all over. "Is it X?" he asked. "You cracked X, finally? Is that it?"

"Cracked him open. He sang. Just this morning. Sang like a canary." The man picked up the bottle and took another lengthy swallow.

"Well . . . ," Troy said, bewildered. "That's great . . . isn't it? You got your information. After all this time. He was your toughest challenge ever, and you came out on top. Like always . . . right?"

"Like always," the man agreed, and laughed again. It was an awful sound. "Just like always . . ."

"Sir, what's the matter?" Troy asked, hearing the plea in his own voice. "Was it a bad scene, this morning? Too heavy?"

The Sergeant finally raised his head. When he spoke again, his voice was soft and wondering. "He killed himself," he said. "Hung himself. In his own cell. The cell was only four feet high."

Troy stared at the man.

"I don't know why it surprised me," the Sergeant continued between gulps of vodka. "That's the kind of man he was. And I should have known it."

"You couldn't have known," Troy said. He searched frantically for something reasonable to say. "Besides, you were just doing your job. Fighting your war. You said it was war. And in war, people die."

"I should have known," the Sergeant went on, as if the boy hadn't spoken. "I knew him, knew what he was. Knew he couldn't live with himself after betraying his side." His hands were trembling.

"You told me innumerable lives could be in the balance, depending on the information at stake," Troy said in desperation, recalling the man's words. How he had taken those words to heart! He had paid such close attention for so long that quoting them was effortless. "Wasn't it all for the greater good?"

"I knew him," the man repeated, ignoring Troy entirely. "I knew him! I—I loved him. . . ."

In the stillness that followed, Troy thought he could hear his own heart, pounding in his ears. Across the gulf between them, the boy watched the Sergeant's gray eyes fill with water and, seemingly in slow motion, spill silently over. And then the man pitched forward onto the table, passed out cold, hitting his head hard against the wooden grain.

That had been on a Monday. The next day, incredibly, it was as if nothing had happened.

"Guess I really tied one on last night" was all the Sergeant said in the morning. He didn't look at the boy as he spoke, but busied himself at the toaster. Apparently he was going to work as usual. "My head is killing me. Well, what can I say—you can kind of get to feeling for a guy, even when he's on the other side. Had to admire the son of a bitch."

That was all he said about it, all that was ever said. He went to work in the morning and came home that evening. He read the paper. He smoked his pipe. Conversation was somewhat stilted at breakfast, but was by nightfall as smooth as it had ever been. And their safe words closed over the dangerous ones of the day before, like water over a sinking stone.

On Friday of the same week, it all came to an end. Troy never learned how the Sergeant found out the truth about him. It could have been anything, he supposed. A telltale piece of mail, a phone call from the school's financial department—the possibilities were endless. And the Sergeant, presented with any fragment of startling information, could then have made additional phone calls, conducted his own investigation. He never bothered to tell Troy, and the boy supposed it didn't matter.

Early Friday evening, for the second time that week, Troy came home to find the Sergeant there ahead of him. Again at the dining room table, this time without the vodka. The boy, on his way to the kitchen for a glass of Gatorade, was startled to see him sitting there.

"Sir. Hey, I almost didn't see you."

"Sit down," the man said.

"What?"

"There's something you and I have to talk about."

There was a still, incredulous pause. "Sir?"

"What part didn't you understand?" the man asked.

"I . . . I was going to take a shower. I was just at practice."

"That can wait."

Troy's heart began to pound with dread. "Can I ask what this is about?"

"Do what I told you to do."

Troy approached the chair across from the man and grasped the back of it. "Please tell me what's going on."

"I told you to sit down."

Troy stared at him in disbelief, then wordlessly pulled the chair out from under the table and sat. The Sergeant looked at him steadily and in silence for several moments, until he shrank back and crossed his arms over his chest, steeling himself against trembling.

Finally the Sergeant spoke. "I think you know what this is about by now. And it will be to your advantage to admit it."

Troy found that his mouth was almost too dry for speaking. "I—I really don't know . . . but I wish you'd tell me. . . ."

"Of course you know. It's written all over your face. And you're shaking like a leaf." There was a pause. Then: "What I don't understand . . . is *why* you lied." Another pause. "Lied so much, about everything, for so long." The man tilted his head to the side, as if in deep thought. "It boggles my mind to think about it. Why in the world would you *want* to make all those things up?" He leaned forward suddenly. "Tell me this—is there anything of importance you've told me in the last eight weeks that *hasn't* been a lie?"

Troy could feel how futile it would be to resist. "How did you find out?" Could the Sergeant hear his terror?

"I'm asking the questions now. It's funny that I haven't before this. Because of course, the real question, the *correct* question, is how the hell *didn't* I find out for so goddamned long? I'm supposed to be the goddamned CIA agent. It's hard to believe, isn't it? It's like a joke. A joke on me. But the thing is, I let all that down with you. I trusted you."

Troy was finding it hard to breathe. His whole setup was crumbling. "How—how much do you know?"

"Didn't I just say it was me doing the asking here?" The Sergeant flared. "I don't even want you to open your mouth again except to answer the questions I have for you. That's about all I can stand at this point. So. Let's start. And if you lie to me now—and believe me, I'll be able to tell, because the chump is gone and you're dealing with the professional you've been lucky enough never to meet—I'm going to put you out of here tonight."

He paused to let his words sink in. "Now. Your father is not dead, is he?"

All right. He'd do what was being required of him. What else was there to do? "No, sir."

"Your parents are still together, for that matter."

"Yes, sir."

"And your family has plenty of money."

Troy nodded.

"Answer when I talk to you," the man said.

"Yes, sir."

"You're not even on scholarship. You don't qualify for a financial scholarship. Your tuition has already been paid in full."

"That's right, sir."

"And yet, you told me just after I met you that your father had died before you were born, that your mother had very little money, that you'd gotten into Columbia but couldn't go because you couldn't afford to pay rent in New York City. All this so I would take you in."

"That's all true, sir."

"And it worked. Partly, no doubt, due to my own brand of naïve idealism. Always trying to help save the youth of America. You proposed this whole arrangement. You would live here with me, in my tiny spare room. You would clean, cook, run errands, do typing for me in exchange for room and board. You would maintain a 3.8 grade-point average. I believed you, and I agreed to it. I wanted to make a real difference in at least one kid's life."

"You *have* made a difference in my life, sir," Troy said. Talking was an effort.

"What life is that, Caretta? I don't know a damn thing about it. It's all been a fabrication."

"But . . ." the boy began. His head was spinning. "The arrangement . . . you've found it a good one, haven't you? Sir?"

The Sergeant recovered his coldness. His voice resumed its hard tone. "There you go, asking questions again. But I'm not done with mine yet. Suppose you tell me what your family is really like."

Troy was quiet for a moment, considering. "My father owns a lot of Pennsylvania real estate. And he invests very successfully in the stock market. My mother's a society queen. She plays a lot of bridge and he plays a lot of golf. They mostly spend weekends at the yacht club. They don't have a very good idea of what I'm doing. I've told them I'm squatting in Alphabet City and don't have a phone. I told them it's political. They write it off as cheap college-liberal bullshit. They don't really care, as long as they can tell their friends that their son is at an Ivy League school."

"They don't know anything about me?" the Sergeant asked.

"They've never heard your name, sir."

"So you've been lying on both sides."

"Yes, sir."

The man shook his head. "Doesn't it get exhausting? Frightening? Tricky?"

Was he granting the boy something—some kind of reluctant admiration? As he had with X?

"All those things, sir."

"Well, that leaves me where I started. I want to know why you've done this."

Troy braced himself to ask that which he feared most. "Do you hate me for it?"

"I'm asking the questions," the Sergeant said. "I'm not going to tell you that again. And you haven't answered my last one."

"It's . . . hard to explain," Troy said softly.

"You've got all night. And if it comes to that, all morning too. Because you're not getting up until I'm satisfied that I know why I was deceived."

Well, here it was. The man was asking. Was this what he had fantasized about? Being forced to confess what had always been unsayable?

"All right," Troy said. "I'll try. Maybe you could help me. Do you think you could? After all, as you've said, you're the professional."

"I'm an interrogator, not a shrink," the Sergeant said.

Of course. He would not let himself be implicated. Of course not.

"Well, all right," the boy repeated. "I'll tell you what I know." He supposed he had nothing left to lose. "As long as I can remember, I've been different from everyone else. I never fit in, not even in my own family."

"Different in what way?"

This would be the tricky part. Troy decided to play it safe for a while. "Well, for one thing, I was just never interested in what they were all about. I didn't respect them. They never seemed to do any real work. And my sister and I never had to work for anything either. Whatever we wanted, they just handed to us."

"You have a sister?"

"Yes, sir, I do. I know I've never mentioned her. I guess she was one less person to have to lie about."

"I don't know why I'm even surprised," the man said. "But go on."

"I hated the way things came so easily. I never liked things that were easy. I was always happiest with the strictest teachers at school. I liked the ones all the other kids hated, the ones that were the most demanding and the hardest to please."

"Go on," the man repeated.

"Well, and then there was the Coach. He had a city-wide reputation for being the slave driver he was. He was why I started wrestling."

Troy stopped for a moment. This was getting harder. But the man was waiting him out, staring him down, nothing but command in his face.

"I guess—," the boy continued. "I guess I had a crush on him. I wanted to suffer for him, knock myself out, make him proud at any cost."

Still the Sergeant said nothing.

"And then you showed up at school. I remember that day so clearly. When we saw you in our classroom, we thought it was a joke. Some moron from the army there to recruit. But you surprised us. Surprised me. It was the most exciting lecture I'd ever heard. I wanted so much to keep knowing you. So afterward, I asked if I could write you a letter."

"I can follow you that far, but I still don't understand all the lies," the man said.

"It was just a fantasy. My fantasy," the boy admitted. "All those circumstances. And since you didn't know me, and didn't live near me, I could be whoever I wanted to be for you. And I wanted to be saved by you, the way you thought you were saving me."

"But I didn't save you."

"In a way you did. I could keep performing as I had before. School, sports . . ." He hesitated, then: "Discipline."

"I'm hardly responsible for that. I don't make you do anything."

"You're there," Troy said. He was finally starting to relax. In a way, it felt good to come clean. "You're watching me do it."

So far the Sergeant had been unexpectedly calm. He hadn't balked at the word "crush." It was as if a weight had been lifted off the boy. He continued, suddenly without fear. "And I have to tell you something else. I've loved this. I've loved every minute of it. I wanted to serve you, and I've loved serving you. I've been happy knowing I've done it well. You might think that sounds sexual. Maybe it is sexual. But I knew there wasn't going to be any sex."

He paused briefly. "I guess I expected that sooner or later

you'd find out—and I was hoping you'd understand. I didn't want you to feel betrayed; I hoped you'd realize that I had to do it, to get to you. You see, I thought you'd get as much out of this as I did. I knew in some way you were like me. . . ."

Troy searched the man's face for something to help him through the rest of what he had to say. It was unreadable, unyielding. He pushed on anyway. "When you spoke at my school, you said that you could always tell if a person was lying. I've been lying to you for months and you didn't know. I think you probably chose not to know. I think you wanted me here as much as I wanted to be here."

The Sergeant remained silent.

"It's about power, isn't it?" the boy continued. "Power is what makes you tick. You like to control things and call the shots. And that's all right. Because other people want the opposite. It can be a good arrangement, as long as it's understood."

What he was saying was taking on a momentum of its own. He was articulating thoughts he hadn't put into words before, even to himself. But here they were, and they felt strong and right. He stopped trying to gauge what the Sergeant was thinking and gave himself over to his truth.

"I know two men from my hometown. They have a setup a lot like this one. But they both understand what it's all about, and they went into it with their eyes open. Arthur's the boss and Scott does what he's told. They're happy.

"You don't have any way to get what you really want," Troy continued. "You're into men, into all things male. Combat and struggle and dominance. You loved X. You said you did the other night. But you have no place in your life for that kind of love, and no space for that kind of—of, I don't know, that kind of drama. So you have to do it for real. You had to destroy him."

There was a long silence before the Sergeant spoke.

"That was very eloquent," he finally said. "Very compelling. Are there any other speculations you would like to make here? Anything else that you'd like to say?"

Only what finally had to be spoken.

"I love you," said the boy. "And I'm sorry."

He saw a muscle jump in the man's jaw.

"That's all," he added.

"Good," said the man. "And that *will* be all, because I wouldn't dignify any of it with a response. I'll only say that you need some serious professional help, and I'm not going to be the one to provide it."

He stood up. "I've got to return to the UN this evening for about an hour. You can start packing. And you'd better not waste any time. When I come home, I want to find you gone without a trace."

It was nine o'clock in the evening and Troy was in a Chelsea bar. A bar with boarded-up windows. *Rawhide.* Men in leather were all around.

He tried out the word *shock*. Was he in shock? The life he had so lovingly contrived, the dream, was in ruins. He had been kicked out like a dog. The Sergeant had kept the cat but kicked the boy out like a dog.

"You look like you're a long way from home, little buddy." Troy looked up. The speaker was at least six-foot-three, with a long, tawny mane and golden eyes. He was clad all in black: shining motorcycle jacket, leather chaps which revealed one tantalizing patch of blue denim, and heavy, broken-in boots. He was also holding a helmet.

Troy studied the stranger, adrenaline flooding his body. Could he do it? Receive the messages, send his own, in an arena where it was not only permissible, but the point? Was it really as easy, as possible, as this?

"Never been closer," he said to the man.

The other grinned, showing teeth. He wasn't quite handsome. But very leonine. And . . . sexy . . . he was . . . oh God, he was sexy.

"I'm Brian," the other said. "Brian the lion."

"And I'm Troy. The boy."

"Hey, Troy. Boy. Let's go for a ride."

Therapy

"I want you to tell me where it hurts."

These soft words were spoken to me by Dr. Isaac Landau somewhere in the course of our first session. It was the turning point of the consultation, the moment I knew I was in the hands of a pro. It was when I knew I would want to keep seeing him. And it was when I started crying as if I'd never stop.

I can remember just a single moment like that in my own career: my interview with Spot, the only client I've ever reserved for my own personal use. I called him Spot because dark birthmarks were splotched all over his body. He had never been to a dominatrix before and his epiphany came with my first question:

"How long have you known you were a slave?"

He looked at me in wonder and tears came into his eyes. No one had ever recognized him before, and I waited while he wept with gratitude and disbelief.

I'd heard that Isaac was extraordinary, special. This came from my friend Ione, who should know. She must have tried forty shrinks and he was the only one she ever liked. She couldn't have more than a consultation with him, though, because she worked at the same small firm as his wife.

It was exciting to make that first call to his office. To finally admit that something was really wrong. I called on a Monday, a slow day for me.

"Hi, my name is Vanessa; I got your name from Ione Matthiesen. I've never had any form of therapy before, but I would like a consultation with someone very soon. I've recently become quite unhappy at work."

I didn't mention what kind of work it was. I left my number and the times I could most easily be reached. It happened that he was out of town, so when the phone rang several days later, I had nearly forgotten about him.

"Hello?"

"Hello. This is Dr. Landau, returning your call." His voice held just the faintest trace of Israel.

"Oh. Yes. Hi."

"I'm sorry it has taken me a few days to call, but I just returned to New York this afternoon. Do you have a few minutes to briefly discuss some things?"

I had another hour before my next session. "Yes, that's fine."

"You mentioned, in your message, being unhappy at work. Could you say just a little bit about this, to give me an idea of what you mean?"

"Yes, all right." But I hesitated, unsure of how to put it. "I—well, actually I work out of my own home. I'm a dominatrix. Do you know what that is?"

"I believe I have some idea," he said. "But it would be best for you to tell me in your own words what it is."

"Well, generally speaking," I said, "I am paid, usually by men, to dominate and discipline them."

"I see." A pause, during which I thought I could hear him writing. "And how long has this been your line of work?"

"I guess it's been a little over three years now."

"And when did it take, shall we say, a turn for the worse?"

"It's hard to pinpoint exactly. I'd say somewhere in the last few months."

"Has anything changed about the job itself? Or only your feelings?"

"It's me. Everything is just the way it's always been."

Another pause, a rustling of papers. Then: "I imagine you set your own hours?"

"That's correct."

"Would it be a problem to come to my office tomorrow evening at seven?"

I glanced at my schedule. "So far, so good."

"There's a one-time consultation fee of one hundred and thirty dollars. Is this within your means?"

"Yes it is." I felt smug for a minute about making more an hour than a doctor.

"Good. Then I look forward to meeting you tomorrow."

When I make an appointment with a first-timer, it's very common for them not to show up. I wondered if it were the same for shrinks, because until the last minute, I didn't know whether I would really go. Even as I stood outside his office, beside the doorbell marked with his name, I considered just turning around and going home. There would be many times I wished I had.

After I'd waited a few minutes in his waiting room, he appeared in the doorway of his office. There was nothing physically compelling about him at all. He was thin and Lincoln-solemn, with a receding hairline, dark mustache, and beard.

Good, I thought. Clearly, everything I'd heard about tortured transference would not apply to me. He couldn't have been further from my preferences; the men I'm attracted to are imposing, and I have a specific aversion to facial hair.

He ushered me inside and indicated my seat. His was directly across from it, maybe three feet away. I sat down and waited expectantly but he said nothing, just looked at me. He looked at me like a Red Cross doctor might look at a starving woman. His gaze was direct and unwavering, full of pained empathy.

"Hello," I said. The word itself was a challenge; I was already annoyed.

His head tilted ever so slightly to one side. And his silent inquiry seemed to intensify a notch.

"Look, I don't know how this is supposed to work," I said. "Can you help me out here?"

"I'd like you to talk for a little while," he said quietly.

"Just talk? About what?"

"Whatever you think is important." He spoke so softly I could barely hear. "And why you're here."

I took a breath. "All right. I told you on the phone that I'm a dominatrix. This seems to be bringing me a lot of misery lately. I don't like doing it anymore, but it would be almost unthinkable to quit. I've invested too much, too many people need me, the money's too good, and *I'm* too good. It's spoiled me. I couldn't stand a regular job."

"But what brings you here today?" he wanted to know.

"I just told you. What I just said."

"But why now?" he persisted. "Instead of last week, instead of next week?"

"I don't know. What does it matter? Here I am."

He resumed his sorrowful gaze. It irked me. What was so fucking tragic?

I tried to go on, looking past him and through the window behind his back. "It's started to spill over. Into my real life. I'm becoming a full-time bitch."

Silence.

"I've started to believe my own PR. You know? That I'm a goddess, someone entitled to worship, and that I should have my own way all the time. It's hard to just snap out of it after so many hours."

Silence. Sorrow.

"Every encounter seems to become a battle of wills." And then, as if to illustrate my point: "Would you say something already? I mean, what are you waiting for?"

"I'm waiting to learn why you're here," he said.

"I *told* you already. I've been telling you this whole time! What the fuck do you want from me?"

"I want you to tell me," he said, and his voice seemed to go even softer still, "where it hurts."

It caught me completely by surprise. My mouth opened but for the first time, no words came. My eyes filled instead and spilled over as I stared at him in amazement. I thought then that I knew how a tree must feel when a siphon is tapped gently, unexpectedly into its side. Past the layers of bark and wood to a deeper place, where something it didn't know it had begins to flow.

My tears ended a few minutes later, as abruptly as they had begun. But things had shifted. I had been humbled. And I wasn't sure I could forgive him.

"Are there any questions you would like to ask me?"

It was an offer I would not hear again. I didn't know much about the therapeutic process, but that much I could guess, so I took it.

"Oh yes," I answered. "Many inappropriate questions."

"In here," he told me, "there is no such thing as an inappropriate question. I may not always answer your questions. But you should never hesitate to ask anything."

"Fine," I said. "Do you ever get aroused by your patients?"

"That's a general question," he remarked. "Perhaps what you really want to know is whether or not I am aroused by you."

"Well, yes," I said. "That too. I'd like to know whether you get aroused in general, as well as if you are aroused by me."

He was silent a moment. Then: "That does sometimes happen," he said. "In your case . . . I would prefer not to answer the question."

Good, I thought. He's good. That was a perfect response. If he'd said he wasn't aroused by me, I would be upset. But if he had said he was, that would bother me too.

"All right, then. What if," I said, "I came in here wearing this transparent dress I have? What would you do?"

"What would this mean to you? Why would you be wearing it?"

"Just to fuck with you," I said. "To see what you'd do."

"I think it would depend on whether or not I could do therapy in that context," he answered slowly. "If I were too distracted by it, unable to get beyond it, I would call off the session."

I felt a rush of hope. At least he wasn't easily taken aback, wouldn't shy away from confrontation.

As if he could hear my thoughts, he said, "Let's go back to something you brought up earlier. About every encounter becoming a battle of wills. Tell me about that."

"When I meet someone for the first time," I said, looking at him pointedly, "I find it hard to relax until I've established a certain control."

"And who do you think will be in control here?"

"Well, obviously, if I can intimidate you and control you, you won't be any good for me. On the other hand, since I've said this, I can envision you going overboard to prove you're on top. And if you do, I'll be too irritated to want to even deal with you. I guess if you're exceptionally good—though maybe it's too much to hope for—you'll be able to walk that line."

I heard myself. I was no different from any of my clients. I was asking him to be the boss, on my terms. And in the slyest, most manipulative of ways. Setting it up as a challenge: "If you're really good . . ."

He didn't rise to the bait. Instead he said, "Tell me about the line you walk." He would do this over and over. Turn my statements around, make them about me, with no transition.

My line. It was thin as the edge of a knife and I had to keep it honed and glinting all the time. Could he ever understand what a delicate balance I had to strike every time? Could I ever explain it?

"I have to give my clients what they want without appearing to care what it is," I said. "I've got to . . . *accommodate* as I dominate. I need to inflict exactly as much pain as each man can take—no more and no less. And I have to instill terror and dread, yet make the net equation yield ecstasy."

"That sounds like a lot of work," he said. "And if you're going to work that hard, one would hope it would be at something that's personally rewarding."

"Well. I guess that's my problem."

"Tell me, do you think you'll be able to work well in here with me?" he asked.

"I think . . . that I'm going to piss you off. Get under your skin. Make you wish you'd never taken me on."

He studied me for a moment before speaking. "My main concern about that," he said, "is that you seem to be anticipating an adversarial relationship with me, whereas this process relies greatly upon our alliance. If you feel you could achieve this condition more easily with someone else, I can give you several excellent referrals."

He would give me up? That easily?

"No," I said. "I want you."

Spot was waiting outside my building when I got home, just as I'd told him to be. I wordlessly brushed past him and unlocked the door. He followed me up the stairs to my apartment. I turned my back so he could ease the jacket off my shoulders and hang it up. Then he stripped down to a leather thong and put his folded clothing out of my sight. Only after he had done this did I speak to him.

"Cigarettes. Coffee."

He took my pack of Marlboro Lights from the mantel above the fireplace, put a cigarette between my lips, and held the light while I drew. Then he went into the kitchen.

I loved watching him move in near nakedness around my apartment. He was lean, well muscled, and I secretly thought his birthmarks were beautiful. He looked jungle-spotted, wild: an exotic animal I had tamed.

Spot was the only client I'd ever found who could take what I gave out. Who truly wanted to serve me and had the endurance to do it. I wore myself out on him, beat him till I couldn't lift my arm anymore. I raised welts. Drew blood. Left bruises that lingered for weeks. He was my prize, and because of this, I no longer charged him. He was my slave, my only real slave.

Tonight I was feeling tender. When he came in with my cup of coffee, I almost thanked him.

"Do you want your own?" I asked him. It was an unusual gesture for me.

"Oh no, I'm fine, thank you, Mistress," he said in surprise.

"Come here, then," I said. "My feet need some attention."

Massaging my feet was Spot's special fetish. He knelt beside the divan where I was sitting and happily took my shoes off. A moment later, his strong, warm hands were enclosing my tired left foot. He always started with the left foot. They all had their particular ways, and I knew them the way I imagine a lion tamer knows his cats. In any case, he was making me feel good. I leaned back and began to give myself over to it.

After a few minutes, I realized—maybe from the way he kept glancing up at me—that he wanted to ask me something. It was my rule that he could not speak until spoken to. This made for many long and peaceful hours. There were times when he came over, carried out every instruction on a written list, and left without a word exchanged between us. If ever he felt the slightest resentment, he never betrayed it. He was a good boy.

"Go ahead," I said to him.

"Mistress?"

"Go ahead and ask me about whatever's on your mind."

"Forgive me, Mistress. It's none of my business."

"Of course it isn't. But I just told you to ask me. Don't make me repeat an order."

I enjoyed his brief panic as he tried to decide which was potentially more dangerous, an audacious question or an attempt to evade a command. Some mistresses create these situations deliberately, to have an excuse to punish a slave regardless of what he does. This was something I never did. I punished Spot only when I was genuinely angry.

"I was wondering where you went this afternoon," he said, lowering his eyes. Trying not to cringe.

"If I tell you it's all right to ask me something, then it's really all right," I told him. "It doesn't mean I'm going to answer you."

"Yes, Mistress."

"I would, however, like to know why you were wondering."

"Mistress, it's because you seem . . ." He trailed off.

"Tell me," I said.

"You seem more relaxed, or happier, or something."

It occurred to me that he knew me as well as I knew him. Maybe even better.

"Well, Spot, for some reason I can't begin to fathom, I'm going to tell you where I was." I paused and studied his face. It was flushed with pleasure, though he didn't dare to raise his eyes.

"I was seeing a shrink to find out why I keep you around," I said. He laughed softly, then turned his attention to my right foot. I could see he thought I was joking.

In Isaac's waiting room, I watched a gray-faced, middle-aged man emerge from his office. This was the patient who was immediately preceding me. Last week it had been a little old lady.

He must look forward to seeing me. I have to be more interesting than these people.

"Tell me," Isaac was saying a few minutes later, "what you get out of domination."

"Up to five hundred dollars an hour," I answered.

"What else?"

"Expensive gifts. Clothing, jewelry, champagne. Roses. The men who can afford me are very wealthy. Some of them take me shopping for what they want me to wear."

"Yes, and what else?"

"A spotless apartment. Anything I want done. Essentially I have a chauffeur, masseur, cook, maid, and errand boy at my beck and call. Any or all of them. Around the clock."

I thought I could feel him hating me. How could you not hate someone who had just recited such a list?

"Anything else?" is all he said.

"Well. I'm good at it. Really good. These guys can't believe their luck when they find me."

"Tell me about that," he said.

"You have to understand," I told him, "that what brings these men to me is a need, a need almost no one understands. When you need something that badly, you'll overpay, and gladly, for any semblance of it that you can get. No one expects it to be great. They stopped expecting that long ago. The S&M scene is pathetic for the most part."

"And you?"

"I'm by far the best thing most of them have ever found. I'm young and I'm beautiful. My body is beautiful. My face is pretty and not too hard.

"Beyond that," I continued, "I have a deep understanding of their desires and how to meet them. I'm perceptive about the subtleties—intuitive, and discerning. I don't snarl, I don't yell. I never overact. They're incredulous when they meet me. Overcome by their luck. Do you know how it feels to be that good at what you do?"

I was sure he did.

"Is there anything else?" he asked.

"Well, the power. That's an incredible feeling. I feel desirable and untouchable. Like royalty—like someone men would kill and die for."

"And the work itself? What are your feelings about that?"

I considered this for a moment. "My feeling is, most people want to think that S&M has nothing to do with them. That it's over *there,* in that freaky leather bar. But S&M is everywhere I look; those dynamics are in all of us, and they pervade everything we do.

"Sometimes, I think that the practice of S&M is the healthiest, most honest thing in the world. That the people who do it recognize the truth about themselves and aren't afraid of it. They create a safe, consensual space to work it out and don't let it wreak havoc in their real lives.

"Other times, I think I can't do another session, can't stand one more grown man sniveling and begging and sucking on my toes. I want to kill them, or kill myself."

Okay, Doctor. What do you make of that?

"You seem very deeply conflicted," Isaac said.

Oh God. Add him to the list of people to kill.

"Is that the best you can do?" I asked. "I've never met anyone with such a passion for the obvious."

The smile didn't reach his mouth, but his eyes gave him away. "What is it you imagine I'm going to do for you?" he asked.

"You're the enlightened one, you tell me. What am I paying you for?"

"You're the one paying," he pointed out. "What do you think you're paying for?"

Maybe I should cut my losses. Just walk now.

"I can tell you what I hope you're here for," he said after an interminable silence. "I hope you want me to help you understand your conflicts. So that you can better make the decisions that will bring you the best chance for fulfillment."

I stifled a yawn. "Did you really need med school for this?" I asked him. "I could do this. It would be a lot easier than what I'm doing now. Just to sit there and utter shrink platitudes from some very short list of acceptable shrink phrases."

He wasn't smiling anymore. Not even his eyes. Well, he couldn't say I hadn't warned him.

"You're thinking I'm as much of a bitch as I told you I would be," I guessed.

"I'm thinking," he said, "that you left something out when you explained why you're drawn to your profession."

"Is that right? And what could that be?"

"Your rage," he answered.

Rage. It leapt within me as if answering to its name, a wild clawing thing that had taken me through a hundred domination scenes—and how I wished this were one of them. I wished I had a whip to crack, wished he were tied down and at my mercy. I channeled all the fury in my body at him, hated him with all my strength, and he looked straight back at me with nothing in his face. Therapists must wait for such moments, to prove they will not break under anger like the camel's back, nor turn to stone as before Medusa's gaze. It was an entirely new sensation, directing all my wrath at a man who neither cowered nor cringed, who wasn't afraid, who would do nothing to appease me.

Poor Spot. I almost pitied him. Someone was going to have to pay for this.

Later that afternoon I was in top form. I had demonic energy for my session with Peter, whose fetish was stiletto heels. He had given me the pair I was wearing, the black leather pumps that made me five inches taller. And I was in exactly the mood to give him what he wanted, to fuck his mouth with them as he knelt before me, naked, with his hands tied behind his back.

I put my foot against his face, the toes pressed to the bridge of his nose, and slid all five inches of the spike heel into his mouth. In and out, in and out, hard and fast and mean. He closed his eyes, sucking in a trance of ecstasy, and looking into his rapt face I saw security for the rest of my days. Nothing in the world could keep him from this. He would travel any distance, pay any price, to be force-fed the heel of a cruel woman's shoe.

Before the session, he'd presented me with an outfit he'd had tailor-made to my measurements. A cherry-red vinyl dress that was beautiful against my skin and clung to every curve. I wondered how I could find a pretext for wearing it the next time I saw Isaac. I wanted to make that bastard break a sweat.

"Am I supposed to call you Dr. Landau?" I asked during my next session. I was in jeans and a flannel shirt. I had been unable to concoct any earthly explanation of why I would be wearing the vinyl dress and besides, he had already told me what he would do if I looked too provocative.

"Why don't we talk about what that means to you?"

"Answer me first."

There was enough tension in the air before he spoke to let me know he did not like being given orders.

"You can call me whatever you want," he said evenly.

"Good. Because I don't think of myself as your patient."

"Oh?"

"No. I'm your client. Okay? I consider you a peer. After all, I'm a therapist of sorts myself."

In the silence that followed this declaration, my eyes found his shoes. They were unassuming black shoes, the leather slightly worn. Scuffed around the toes. They needed a spit-shine.

If I tried hard, I could remember the taste of boot polish.

"What are you thinking?" Isaac asked.

If you only knew.

I tried to recall what we had been talking about.

"I'm thinking you're irritated by what I just said," I answered. "That I would call myself a therapist. Compare myself to you."

"I'm wondering if you find it hard to imagine the idea of being a therapist and a patient at the same time," he said. "For instance, would it surprise you to learn that I myself am a patient? A patient of another psychiatrist?"

It shouldn't have. I'm the one who always says that true mastery requires an apprenticeship of slavery. But it did, it really startled me. It was hard to imagine, him in the other chair.

"No, I'm not surprised," I told him. "That's, like, practically a cliché by now. That shrinks are the most fucked-up people of all." And glancing at my watch, I added, "Looks like the hour's just about gone."

I watched the time. I was always the one to announce when it was up. He might have had the power to keep me coming back. But I wasn't going to let him dismiss me.

He probably sighed with relief each time the door closed behind my back.

The bitch is gone for another week.

In Jacob's fantasy, I was a queen. In my dungeon was a very ornate metal chair I used as a throne. Spot assisted me with this scene, dragging the shackled and terrified prisoner before me where I sat in my velvet gown. A tiara left over from New Year's Eve in my hair. Struggling to stay awake.

Jacob crawled to me slowly. "Your Majesty . . ."

I planted my foot in the center of his chest and sent him sprawling with a kick. "Were you granted permission to approach the throne?"

We would repeat this bit a few more times, varying it just slightly, before Jacob achieved his end result. Which was poignantly simple. What he wanted was to kneel between my legs, surrounding my calves with his arms, and rest his head against my inner thigh. He would hold this pose of supplication as long as I would let him. Occasionally he would cry. And sometimes, I would rest my hand on his head and stroke his fine light hair.

My sessions with my own clients began to affect my sessions with Isaac. My mind would start to wander as we talked. The following day, in his office, I pictured myself kneeling before his chair. Embracing his trousered legs and resting my head just above his knee.

"I've started looking at my clients more clinically," I told him. "Trying to imagine what went wrong."

He smiled. His whole face changed when he smiled. The stern angles melted and he became beautiful.

"And what conclusions have you come to?" he asked.

He had begun to take notes during our sessions. I watched him write on his yellow legal tablet. He had beautiful hands too.

"Oh, they're all so different. It would be impossible to generalize."

His shirtsleeves were rolled to just above the elbow. And his arms. I'd always thought of them as thin, but now I saw that no, they weren't thin exactly, they were sinewy.

"And what about with you? Did something go wrong for you?"

And something inside me flared up again, without warning.

"What do you think, Doctor? Do you think I'd be a professional sadist if nothing had gone wrong? Why do you play so fucking dumb all the time?"

I bet he'd love to wash my mouth out with soap . . .

"What do you think went wrong?"

"I think it's your job to figure that out."

. . . put me over his knee . . .

"It's not a job I can do alone," he said. "In fact, you're going to be the only one who will really have any answers."

. . . and sometimes I wish he would.

"You're lying," I said to Philip.

"No, ma'am," he whimpered.

"Do you think I can't tell? You're only making it worse for yourself."

We were at the table. He was stripped down to his underwear and handcuffed to a chair. I turned the desk lamp so that it shone directly into his eyes. I'd turned the heat way up, which would leave the apartment sweltering for hours after he left. Philip liked to sweat.

The lengths I would go to. Even now, when I was so burnt out. But then again, he was one of my highest-paying clients. And this was his standard scene: interrogation, torture, confession.

"I gave you very specific instructions a week ago," I said, "about what you weren't allowed to do." I paused to get up and walk over to his chair. He was trembling, sweating bullets. "But you couldn't resist, could you? You jerked yourself off against my orders—and if I'm not mistaken, just by looking at you, not only once or twice, but every single day. Maybe even twice a day. Didn't you? Answer me!"

"No, ma'am!" he pleaded.

I slapped him across the face as hard as I could, followed immediately by a backhand blow. It was an immensely satisfying moment. He cried out. Looking down, I saw the erection straining against his waistband.

"Do you really think you can get away with lying to me? I *know* what you do. I know all about you! But the worst offense you committed this week, Philip," I continued, "was thinking of me while you did it. Do you know how sick it makes me, knowing that I'm on your filthy mind while you indulge in this sordid habit?"

Always, the hardest part of this was keeping a straight face.

"I'm sorry." His voice cracked. "I won't do it again, I promise."

"That's what you say every week, you pathetic fucking scumbag. What do I have to do to you?"

"I can't help it," he sobbed.

"Yes, Philip, you do seem beyond help. But that doesn't mean I can't keep trying to beat it into you."

I uncuffed him from the chair and, pulling him up by the hair, bent him over the table. He begged for mercy as I selected a paddle, came up behind him, and jerked his underwear down. It always went like this. I would start out hitting him lightly, then increase the force of the blows until I was blistering him pretty well. I would beat him until he came, then resume the verbal abuse.

"You fucking maggot, did I give you permission to come? To shoot your repulsive wad all over my table?" And seizing the back of his neck, I'd force him to lick the surface clean. "That's right, you bastard, lick it up. Yeah, you better get it all. . . . If I find so much as a drop left . . . How many girls have you forced to swallow your scum? Next time you're tempted to believe it's God's gift to the female species, I want you to remember this."

Isaac's interrogation was gentler. He asked me about everything. My mother, my father, my sisters and brothers. Teachers and counselors, caretakers, lovers. And I told him everything. Almost.

It reminded me of being six years old, in the office of our family pediatrician, who tested my reflexes by tapping all around my knee with his rubber mallet. To see from where the involuntary kick would come.

But there was nothing involuntary about my responses with Isaac. I revealed what I wanted to reveal. I especially liked giving him the details of my clients. Unburdening myself of everyone else's secrets. I entertained him with my domination stories, served them up for his amusement.

He would only let this go so far. "Those are *their* fantasies," he said. "I want to hear your fantasies."

I was less forthcoming with these.

"For instance, what are your fantasies about me?" he asked. Did he think he was going to get them that easily?

I had many.

I fantasized that I was his favorite patient. That he scheduled me for seven on Saturday evenings because that hour marked the end of his analytic week and he was saving the best for last. That he then *ran* home, all fired up, and fucked his wife on the kitchen table while their rice burned on the stove. I didn't mind him fucking his wife as long as I had something to do with it.

I fantasized that he could see me as I dominated my clientele. He watched from the wings as I held them in thrall. He had more privileges than even Spot; he was there for every scene. I looked over at him and winked.

I fantasized about lying on the couch. He had explained that it wasn't for me; it was for psychoanalysis, not psychotherapy. I argued that it should be for any psycho who wanted it and he laughed but did not invite me to lay my body down. The truth was,

I was tired. I wanted to surrender to its gray safety, rest my head. Close my eyes.

Oh, Isaac. Take me in your arms. Cradle me against your chest. Croon to me until I fall asleep. I fantasized that one day he would reach for me, hold me like his own baby, and never put me down.

But he had no way to force these fantasies from me. He wasn't going to put me under the lights, turn up the heat, take off his belt, and work me over. So I didn't relate many of them. Instead, I gave him facts.

"You'll be glad to know I've decided not to take on any new clients," I told him. "I've withdrawn my ads from the underground directories. From now on, I'm only seeing the clientele I already have."

"*I'll* be glad?" Isaac asked.

"Well. I imagined it would please you."

He tilted his head and regarded me. "*Must* you please me?" he asked gently.

The question rattled me. The presumption of it. Half a dozen sarcastic answers sprang to my lips, but for once I checked them, and thought before I spoke.

"Yes," I said finally.

My answer pleased him. In spite of himself, his face lit up.

I was as good as my word. I pared down my clientele, seeing only about fifteen different men with whom I had established a considerable history.

Alan was one of these men, and in fact, I saw no reason to ever give him up. His craving was for sensory deprivation and he was by far my easiest client. He was the head of a multimillion-dollar corporation, and the three-hour lunches he took on Fridays were questioned by no one. All I had to do was supervise his transformation from corporate executive into latex-swathed mummy and secure him to my padded restraint table. There he lay for a full ninety minutes, in an interlude without time or space, in silent, sightless suspension. His entire head was covered along with his body. The only opening was a thin black tube inserted between his lips, through which he could take in air.

As the overseer of this strange ritual, my only responsibility was to make sure he was breathing. Next to Spot, Alan was my favorite submissive. He was sweet and polite, appreciative, had a certain dignity.

"What's it about, Alan?" I asked him. I was always curious, about all of them. "Is it just wanting to check out once in a while?"

"No, no," he said. "It's deeper than that. It's the deepest thing you can imagine. Beneath the ocean floor, the other side of a black hole. I could never convey it to you in words."

Once, as I was wrapping him up, I heard him sigh something under his breath. Eyes, ears, and nose had already disappeared, and I leaned down to catch the words escaping what was left of his mouth.

"Erase me," he whispered.

After several months of questions and answers, intimate disclosures, warmth and flirtation, Isaac suddenly pulled back. I came in one evening and he didn't speak to me.

"Hi," I offered.

He nodded briefly, held his peace.

"How are you?" I tried again.

"Good."

He was waiting for me to talk, as he had in the first session. But as on that day, it was hard for me to just start by myself. I said something about that morning's client, mentioned that my landlord was raising the rent. I rattled on for about five minutes before my voice became unbearable.

I thought maybe he was angry, though he didn't seem to be. He was looking at me as attentively as ever. But he offered nothing of himself. No assistance.

"Why are you so quiet?" I asked.

"Do I seem quiet?"

"You're not talking to me."

"What am I doing, then?"

"Come on. I mean, you're talking when you absolutely have to. But it's not the same as it usually is."

"That's true," he said. "And I'll tell you why. I think that the interactive therapy you prefer takes the focus off you and shifts a good deal of it onto me. And I think it's important at this point to intensify our focus on you."

Could he be serious? And did he mean to keep it this way for all time?

"But I hate it," I protested.

"I know it's not as comfortable for you. But I think it will ultimately be more useful."

I couldn't believe it. Couldn't bear it. "Well, why have you just arrived at this decision now?"

"Because now you can take it," he said.

It reminded me of the catchphrase used by so many dominants: "limits respected and expanded." To me it was a diabolical phrase, pure doublespeak: I'll respect the fact that your threshold only approaches A, while taking you on to B, C, and D.

But he held his position. It was a permanent measure. It was like a shade being pulled down over a window, and everything exciting about the sessions evaporated. The electricity was gone, the texture flattened. Only my monologues filled the stillness.

I had been punished with silence before. But that didn't make it easier. My throat started to hurt when I arrived in his office, and it continued to ache for hours after I'd gone home. I began to resent traveling all the way there from my neighborhood, only to return without feeling that I had ever truly arrived. If he didn't fully respond to me, I found it hard to believe that I was even really there.

Listen, I wanted to tell him. You're wrong—I *can't* take this. Only the fiercest pride kept me from saying it. I held my own silence.

I saw Peter in Taylor's Bakery. It was my day off, and I was exhausted. I was in thermals and a pair of those black slippers you can get in Chinatown for two dollars. My hair was tied in a knot, loose ends straggling out. No makeup. No nothing. He looked over at me and his jaw dropped.

Oh no, I thought. I was used to not acknowledging clients outside. Most of them kept me a well-guarded secret. But Peter wasn't with anyone.

"You—," he sputtered.

I waited.

"I—I didn't even recognize you!"

Well, this isn't my most glamorous hour.

"And you—I thought you were taller!"

Five-inch heels tend to create that impression, you asshole.

"My God," he concluded, in a kind of daze. "I guess—I guess I didn't think you were real."

I could feel his agony. He was more than disappointed; he was crushed. So I gave him what I knew he wanted more than anything. I gave his fantasy back to him.

"Have we met?" I asked. I gazed up at him, looking sweet and bewildered, and spoke in a warm tone he had never heard.

He gaped at me. "Aren't you—?"

"I don't believe I know you. I'm sure I've never seen you before. Perhaps you have me confused with someone else?"

He took it. It didn't matter that it was preposterous. He needed it and he took it, and his relief was palpable.

"I'm so sorry, miss. The resemblance is remarkable. But now I realize I was mistaken."

This encounter inspired an experiment. Before my next session with Isaac, I sat on the steps of the brownstone across the street from his office. Waiting for him.

I had never seen him on the street. Never seen him anywhere but across a three-foot space in his office. *His* office, his turf, which he presided over like the only adult at a children's party. Where a game of musical chairs never ended.

But there he was, at the end of the block. I saw him out of the corner of my eye, and knew it was him without having to turn my head. He was walking quickly, bundled into an old coat. He looked small inside it, like an old gray mouse. It was touching and terrible at the same time. What was incredible was his innocence, the idea that I could sit there at my vantage point and watch, like God, as he moved innocently down the street.

I felt that. And yet, at the very same time, I thought: He must know I'm sitting here. He's pretending not to know. In another second, he'll look over and drill me with his all-seeing gaze.

I toyed with both premises until the moment he unlocked the door and let himself in without glancing my way. And then I knew he'd been clueless. He wasn't omniscient. He wasn't larger than life. And he would never help me pretend it hadn't been him.

A few days later, during one of my sessions, a client named Cyril pressed his naked erection against my leg. And for the first time in my career, I snapped. In my scenes, my rule was no contact with genitalia. Absolutely no skin contact. If I jerked someone off, which was very occasional, he wore a condom and paid a hundred dollars extra. At this violation, I leapt away from him and let out a scream.

Spot appeared instantly at the door of the dungeon. "Mistress! What is it?"

"I want him out!" I shrieked.

Spot needed no information. He immediately advanced on Cyril, who backed away, shouting, "What the fuck!" I did not understand the extremity of my own reaction, but there it was. I was trembling with rage.

Spot wrapped one powerful arm around the naked man's windpipe. He didn't know what Cyril had done. He didn't need to know. He understood that I had been badly upset.

"Let me hurt him, Mistress," he begged.

I was tempted. I wavered. I stood there actually considering it, not thinking clearly.

"Look, I'm sorry!" Cyril panted. "I didn't mean anything!"

"Mistress, please let me hurt him."

I knew I couldn't allow that. But I could punish him. *Really* punish him; my way, not his. "Put him on the wheel," I told Spot.

Spot dragged him to the floor-to-ceiling torture wheel that he himself had built for me. It's a very specific torture, spinning on that wheel. The people who don't love it usually can't tolerate it.

"What—what the hell are you doing?" Cyril protested. "Is this supposed to be part of the scene? I never asked for this!"

"Shut the fuck up," Spot said. He slapped my client onto the center of the wheel, secured each of his limbs to the restraints, and set it to spinning with all his strength. Cyril began to howl.

I couldn't think with that noise. I had to leave the room. Spot followed and stood at a respectful distance while I tried to regain my composure. He kept his head down, chafing, clearly distressed. But he was too well trained to ask any questions.

What was I doing? This was insane. I breathed deeply and made myself count to ten. Cyril wasn't going to bring this into court, but that didn't mean it was all right. It was nonconsensual; it was wrong.

"Spot, take him down and just get him out of here," I said. Which, come to think of it, was probably the worst thing I could do to him.

I had barely gone over these events with Isaac when he said, "Okay. I'd like to talk about that some more next week."

"Next week? What do you mean?"

"I mean, I'm afraid your hour's up."

It was impossible. My eyes shot to the clock. It read 7:30, and I had arrived at 7:00. What was he saying? I felt disoriented suddenly, dizzy and sick. He was telling me to go.

"I'll see you next Saturday," he said.

Even in my confusion, I knew I was going to cry. I bent to gather my belongings, kept my head down while it clogged with tears. I let my hair hang in front of my face, hiding it.

Still bent over awkwardly, I pulled on my coat.

"Vanessa."

I couldn't look up, couldn't answer.

"Vanessa, would you really sacrifice a full fifteen minutes of your rightful time—the time you pay for—rather than protest to me?"

It was almost a minute before his words made sense. Another before I could speak. "You bastard."

"I don't blame you for being angry," he said. "That was a low-down trick on my part."

I stood up. Tears ran down my face.

"Vanessa, please don't go."

"What?" I choked out. "What did you just say?"

I needed to hear it again. Needed him to beg, or come as close to it as he ever would. And he gave it to me. It was the least he could do. "I said please don't go."

I dropped back into my seat and covered my face with my hands.

"You're what we in the profession call well defended," he told me. "I felt I had to try some guerrilla tactics."

He could've left me dangling upside down.

"I had to make sure," he said.

"Make sure of what?"

"That one of your most important issues is dismissal."

I heard myself whimper.

"Vanessa, who else dismissed you?"

How much time was left? Ten minutes? He was going to open this wound and then I'd be turned out onto the street, bleeding mortally. Again.

"We have time," he said. Another lie. There wasn't enough time to tell him, not even to start to tell him. I wouldn't know how to start.

"Who was it, Vanessa?"

His name? No, I couldn't say his name, couldn't even *think* his name. . . .

"What happened?"

He dismissed me from his service with no explanation. My own master. Mine.

"Tell me about it, Vanessa."

And I didn't contest it. I considered it a point of honor not to contest even that final command. My last service to him was to go away without a word. But I broke the way mercury breaks. Into a thousand shining self-contained pieces, irreconcilable and dangerous.

And I said: Never again. And I crossed the road. Just to get to the other side. Like in the joke.

"You're going to have to tell me," said Dr. Landau.

And if I didn't finally know better, I would've thought that was an order.

Missing the Boat

"I want to play a game." These were my words, sly and reckless. It was a rainy night and I wanted something to happen.

"What kind of game?" Samantha—everyone called her Sam—asked. She and Sean were looking at me with interest.

"A sex game that will fuck up our friendship," I said, and laughed.

Maybe I was feeling this way because Sam had stayed too long. She was visiting New York and had been with me for over a week, so that I hadn't slept with Sean in all that time. But of course that wasn't all of it; there was more to it than just that.

Sam was the big brother I never had. I was eight and she was nine when I moved to her town, and she already owned the block. Back then she was a lean little tomboy—everyone thought she was a boy on sight—taller than me then, tougher, headstrong and bossy. She alternated between bullying and protecting me, and I was in love with her.

She'd become a strange woman. Adolescence had stripped her of authority; puberty had distorted her image. No one would mistake her for a boy now. She's heavy, full-breasted, though she still keeps her honey-colored hair cut short. She's quieter now, with the quiet of a trapped animal: careful, watchful, as if waiting for an escape to present itself. Still, I always have the feeling that the nine-year-old Sam is inside her somewhere. And so I'm still a little afraid of her, and accord her the same skittish respect.

On the other hand, I had only known Sean for about six months. I met him when I joined his karate class early in the fall. This visit gave Sam the chance to meet him, though I had told her all about him long before. To my surprise, they hit it off immediately, and better than I ever would have guessed. She even went down to his office one day while I was in school—I was taking classes part-time at NYU—and met him for lunch. I knew they had to be talking about me at least part of the time, and I wondered what she was telling him.

I had decided to take karate because I wanted to meet a martial arts master. And I was amazed to find, at the head of the first class I looked into, an almost exact replica of what I'd dreamed up. Sean might have been a Marine or a Navy SEAL: just under six feet tall, hard and compact, with light brown hair buzzed to within an inch and cold blue eyes. His face habitually wore a grim expression: white-lipped, tight-lipped, severe.

He proved to be a good teacher, methodical and thorough. And he had the kind of presence I always imagined a karate instructor should have: commanding, closemouthed, with an air of keeping plenty of contemptuous judgments to himself. The members of his class treated him with something like reverence. Within minutes I decided to put my money down, and signed up for six months.

I loved the dojo, which was actually a dancers' studio for most of the week. Even for an outsider, to cross that threshold was to step into another atmosphere, hushed and strange. The acoustics were like those of a temple: voices echoed, the air was charged with diligence. A hollow stillness enveloped the sound of bare feet on the wooden floor.

Sean ran a tight ship. His rules were simple and inflexible. Shoes had to be removed before entering the room, even if one was only visiting. Students who arrived early helped to mop the floor.

Those who dared to come in late were to kneel at the back of the room until Sean acknowledged them formally, which he did with a nod in their direction and a single clap of his hands. The latecomers were then to bow, touching their foreheads briefly to the floor, before getting up to begin their stretches.

Sean didn't make up these rules. They're the standard rituals of Shotokan etiquette, which he himself obeyed, along with his fellow black belts, in his own master's classroom. Still, it was a thrill to see him enforce them, and I could never decide whether it was better to be early or late. I loved mopping the floor barefoot and in silence: head down, humble, a ship hand swabbing the deck. I loved wringing out the gray water, and leaving wide, shining arcs on the amber wood. But coming late might have been more exciting still. To slip to the back of the room and go to my knees. To lower my eyes, assuming a chastened, almost fearful, expression. To hold perfectly still, waiting for pardon. The longer Sean took to release me—the longer I knelt—the better. And then the signal clap like the crack of a short whip in the quiet, to which I would bend forward and put my forehead (and secretly my lips) against the floorboards.

Sometimes I thought he took longer to acknowledge me than he did anyone else. Watching him from beneath lowered eyelids, I thought he looked at me many times before clapping. Was it possible that he liked having me there, and in that position? The idea aroused me nearly to the point of pain.

For two months I lived for the Tuesday and Thursday evening classes where I flustered, stumbled, and temporarily lost the ability to tell left from right. It was an infatuation that literally kept me awake at night, staring into the dark, touching myself with a practiced hand and calling his image to my aid. I felt he was someone with whom there could never really be an equal relationship. I dreamed I could serve him; that he might allow this, even look for it. I never expected him to fall in love with me.

I remember the feeling of those nights, before he was mine. Emerging from the subway, across the street from the second-story classroom. It was dark and chilly outside, but the light was always on in that window, and it seemed to emanate heat as well. Sometimes on my way in, with the other beginners, I'd overhear conversation about the impending class: rueful jokes, ironic despair, bruises being compared. I felt wholly outside these sentiments. I wasn't afraid of being hit or thrown. The blows absorbed by my body were part of a natural order; I took them as my due, as a weaker wolf will offer its throat to a stronger one in battle. To me, the dojo was the warmest, the safest haven; it held an inviolate hierarchy, with everything—everyone—in place. I couldn't wait to get there, and I was never ready to leave.

Sean asked me out on the last night of November. The karate class went out for pizza and beer on the last Thursday of each month; this was the second such outing since I'd joined. I was seated directly across from Sean and could barely eat. My skin tingled with longing and I found it hard to swallow.

Afterward everyone crowded out to the sidewalk and milled around for a few minutes before taking their leave. I made small talk with several people, watching Sean out of the corner of my eye. Soon only he and I were left.

I made myself look straight at him. "I have so much work to do tonight," I said. "I hate the thought of going home."

"Been putting it off, huh?" he said.

"That's right," I said. "And I'd like to keep putting it off."

There was a light snow. Now, I thought. Now. Please.

"Well, you want to go get a cup of coffee?" he asked.

"I'd love to," I said. He hadn't smiled; I didn't either.

We went to a little Spanish dive. He liked his coffee strong, preferably Colombian; I made a mental note of this. It came; he drank it black, and then relaxed in front of me for the first time.

He did nearly all the talking, which shattered the cold, silent image I'd been nurturing all those weeks. He was easygoing, humorous, even gregarious, holding forth on a number of topics, including New York real estate, corruption in publishing, and all things political—he read at least three different papers every day. I held my cup of coffee in both hands for warmth and looked into his eyes. He was a regular guy. I felt the porcelain cool beneath my fingertips.

Dinner the following Saturday found him much the same. He liked me. I could see that he really liked me. And it was no longer impossible to believe. We'd eaten near my apartment and afterward he walked me home. I didn't invite him up. I didn't kiss him good-bye.

By Tuesday night, I was overwhelmed with schoolwork. I decided to sacrifice karate to do it. I had tentative plans with Sean after class, but I was ready to let them go as well. I made this decision on the street outside the dojo. The class wouldn't be starting for another few minutes; I decided to stop in quickly and let him know.

Sean was unlocking the broom closet when I walked in. I went right up to him.

"Sean."

He turned. "What are you doing in here with shoes? Take them off."

"I'm not staying," I protested. "I just wanted to talk to you a second."

"I don't care," he said. "Go back out and take them off."

Face burning, I retreated to the hall. Outside the door, I considered just leaving, bolting for home. Why had Sean been so cold? Had I offended him? I peered through the window. He was handing out mops. Apparently, I was the last thing on his mind.

I removed my shoes. My body was trembling for some reason. Had we really gone for coffee? Had dinner? Or was it only my imagination? I crept back into the room and stood timidly nearby as he advised a student about a swollen knee. It took a few minutes for him to notice me again.

"Oh. Cecilia. What did you want?"

"I, um—," I said. "I came to tell you I can't attend class tonight. Both of my final exams are this week."

He looked at me without any expression. It was the most awkward moment I'd ever experienced in that room.

"Fine," he said at last, as if wondering what the point was.

"But if you still want to get together later," I added in a rush, "I'm sure I'll have time to take a break. You could come by my apartment. I'd really like it if you would."

* * *

I was to see that it would always be this way. He was one man in the classroom, another out of it, and this sustained my attraction. I was gratified to see there was a part of him I'd never be able to touch.

I was comfortable with him before long. I stopped cleaning the apartment for his visits and no longer changed the sheets each time. I let him see me in glasses and ratty old sweatshirts. In the beginning I liked to cook him time-consuming and exotic dinners; now I was more likely to make spaghetti. But in karate class, I still looked at him and couldn't believe he could belong to anyone, let alone me.

The other place in which I remained in awe of him was the bedroom—in the bedroom games that started right away. I pulled him into them, but he knew instinctively how to play. I could give him the briefest sketch of a fantasy, and he would pick it right up and run. We created roles and inhabited them for hours.

Once I called him at work. "Guess what I just did."

He sounded amused. "What did you just do?"

"I wrote a personal ad. Just for myself, just for fun. I wanted to see if I could do it—say who I am and what I want in around forty words. I mean, of course what I wrote is just a fantasy. But I had fun putting it down."

"Well, let's hear it," he said.

I looked down at my notebook and read it into the phone:

Housegirl position sought.
Vagabond wants to come home.
SWF, wandering Jewess, charming
waif, love slave will cook, clean, and
entertain master of the house for
room and board. I'll be your muse,
masseuse, and charlotte russe.
Take me in? Serious replies only.

"I like that," Sean said. "Listen, though, I have a meeting, have to run."

I hung up feeling vaguely let down.

Half an hour later, the phone rang.

"Hello?"

"I'm responding to your ad in the paper," said a male voice. There was no laughter in the tone, no irony. I knew it was Sean, but my heart started to pound.

"Yes, sir," I said.

"I'd like to interview you for the position you're seeking, tonight if possible."

"Tonight is fine."

"I'd like it to be on the late side. I have a lot going on right now."

"Anytime, sir. Your convenience."

"I'll see you at ten o'clock then. Be on time." And he gave me his address, as if I didn't know it.

I arrived at his apartment that night in a blouse and skirt from the Salvation Army. He answered the door in a sharply pressed white oxford shirt and dark trousers. Silver cuff links were fastened at his wrists.

"Come in," he said. I followed him into the dining room, where he indicated I should sit at the table. He sat at the head and I took the chair to his left.

"I'm Sean Cafferty," he said. "And you are?"

"Cecilia Fox, sir."

"How old are you, Cecilia?"

"I'm twenty-one."

"You're seeking a live-in position here with me."

"Yes, sir."

"Where are you living right now?"

"I'm at the Ninety-fourth Street youth hostel. But my money's running out."

"I see. And before that?"

"I was with the circus."

"The circus," he repeated. "And what were you doing there?"

"I groomed the cats, sir."

"The cats."

"There were two lions, five tigers, and an albino leopard," I told him.

"All right. And your reason for leaving?"

"Unwelcome advances by the ringmaster, sir."

I watched him fight back a smile.

"Well, I'll explain my situation to you. I'm a busy man. I don't have a lot of time for housework. I need someone to pick up the slack for me, someone who'll do what has to be done without being told and make herself scarce when I need some space."

"I can do that. Sir."

"For instance, right now," he said. "What do you think needs to be done around here?"

I looked around the apartment. "I think the dishes need to be done, the floor has to be swept, and that you could use a Sloe Screw Against the Wall."

There was a blank pause. Then: "That's a drink," I added.

"Why don't we consider this evening a trial period," he suggested. "And let's see what happens. You can start now."

I stood rather shakily. I was actually quite nervous as I went to the liquor cabinet and mixed this man a drink. I brought it to him in his armchair, where he'd started to read one of the several papers he'd brought home. Then I found a broom.

It was calming to sweep. I found a rhythm and peace in it. I liked this apartment; I could see how it would be nice to land here after being rootless, adrift in the dead of winter. I was careful, fastidious; I evacuated the dust from every corner, angled the broom under each piece of furniture. And finally as I stood wreathed in steam, arms plunged into suds at the kitchen sink, I felt him come up behind me.

"Don't let me interrupt you," he said, and put a hand against the nape of my neck. I continued rinsing dinner plates and cutlery while he ran a possessive hand up the inside of my thigh. By the time the sink was cleared and the drying rack stacked, my underwear had been eased down several inches and he was penetrating me slightly, easily, with his fingertips. I was wet.

"Don't turn around," he said quietly into my ear.

"No sir," I murmured.

"Hold on to the edge of the sink."

I clasped the rim with both hands and closed my eyes.

"Little runaway," he chuckled. "Fleeing the evil ringmaster." I felt his lips against the back of my neck. "Are my advances . . . unwelcome . . . to you?"

"No sir," I whimpered.

"No? Tell me. Are they welcome? More than welcome, even?"

"Yes, sir . . . please."

"Please what?"

"Please, sir."

"Please, sir, what?"

"Please! Sir."

Still holding my neck, he bent me farther over the sink and took me that way. I came before he did, came harder than I ever had before, and was hired on the spot. I slept that night across the foot of his bed.

We played out such scenes all the time. Sean understood the inevitable link for me between sex and submission, and was glad to oblige. He liked to hit, knew how hard to hit, and how many times. He knew how to secure a blindfold and tie a good knot. He understood what I wanted, which had little to do with pain and everything to do with mastery.

Our relationship was held together by sex. Usually when a relationship is described as mostly sexual, what's implied is "animal." Carnal. Not to be taken seriously. I have never understood this dismissal. Sex is, after all, a partnership—a recognition, communion—as legitimate as any other, and as essential.

The three of us—Sean, Sam, and I—were together nearly all week. Sam and I spent much of this time reminiscing out loud, as we liked to do whenever we got together, boring anyone else around us with a dozen years' worth of escapades. Sean, though, was attentive to every word, concentrated and serious, particularly when Sam had the floor. It was as if he were trying to glean something from her, something he needed.

"Cecy was such a *good* girl," Sam told him, with remembered distaste. "I *hated* her."

"Cecilia? A good girl?" Sean said. "I can't imagine it."

"Oh, please. Too good to be true," Sam said. "I was too rough for her. Too wild. Too filthy a mouth."

It was true. I had become friends with Sam more from a process of elimination than anything else. We both stood out in my new neighborhood, which was full of little rich girls, all of whom had their own phones and color TVs and canopy beds and designer jeans. I had never even heard of designer clothing, and the idea of having my own television or phone was as incomprehensible to me as having my own house.

Sam lived two doors down from me. She was as much of an outcast on our street as I was, because while all the other girls were playing with the new Barbie and Ken Condominium, Sam was up in a tree, or racing dirt bikes with the neighborhood boys. Her mother made her come over to meet me the day I moved in. I was in my room, sitting on the floor, playing with my new printing set and trying not to cry. I missed my old friends already and wanted to go back to Baltimore.

"This is Sam," my mother informed me. "She's going to take you to the park to meet some of the neighborhood kids." I was being delivered. My mother had never before spoken of another child "taking me" anywhere. It was always *she* who had taken *us* places. This left me with some slight and unidentifiable panic.

"What are you doing?" Sam asked me after my mother had left the room.

"Making a newspaper," I answered.

She looked at me, then at my reams of paper, the stamp pad of black ink, and the rubber letters spread out on the rug. "What kind of fucking baby-toy is that?"

I stared at her in distaste. "Are you allowed to cuss?"

"Cuss? What's 'cuss'?" she demanded.

"You know. Like the f-word," I answered, thinking that she wanted me to trip up and say it.

"The *f-word*?! The f-word! You mean *swear*?"

But maybe because she didn't have another girl on the block for a friend, or maybe because I didn't own a single doll, she continued, grudgingly, to come over for the rest of the summer.

I accepted her company and her rule the way I accepted Mondays and Fridays, with the sense that these things were inescapable but not entirely lacking in promise. She was rugged, fierce, perpetually grass-stained. Dark blonde hair tumbled over her eyes, one of which was blue, the other brown. She came over nearly every afternoon, usually around four, for lack of anything better to do while her friends were doing their paper routes. She showed me around, taught me shortcuts and good alleys for smoking and which stores were safest to steal candy from (not that I would ever have done these things, but I was learning not to say so). She always came to my house, I never went to hers. We made and consumed endless peanut butter and jelly sandwiches, washed them down with tall glasses of cold chocolate milk. I tagged along with her to the baseball diamond, where there were heated games. Sometimes she would let me on her team, though I was never an asset. She liked my little brother, who was a year and a half younger than me, and often insisted to my dismay that we take him places.

We had two favorite activities. One was making a tent in Joey's—my brother's—room: an elaborate enclosure making use of all the blankets in the house. To enter it from outside, you had to crack open the bedroom door and crawl in on your hands and knees. This was particularly satisfying on rainy days, since we couldn't go outside anyway, and a storm added to the feeling of sheltering ourselves against the ominous. Our other favorite activity was simply called Boat. It was a pretend game like House, only we were on a ship instead. This always took place in my attic. We had seen the television movie *Orphan Train* the night before this game was conceived, and we had adapted it, I'm not sure why, to take place on a boat. My brother and I were the orphans and Sam was the captain, transporting us across the ocean to foster homes. En route, however, she, who was actually a "he," would decide to adopt us. (In any pretend game we ever concocted, Sam played a male, and I a female.) The guest bed was her cabin. I got the sofa, and Joey got the walk-in closet. His role was always an innocent one; he was the good kid. I was the troublemaker to whom Sam had to lay down the law. When I stepped too far out of line, she would push me against the wall and take off her belt. Joey always pleaded for me but it was no use. She would crack the belt against the wall and I would pretend to cry. Occasionally, as if by accident, the leather would really meet the back of my legs, and whenever it did, I would fall silent, hold breathlessly still. This game left telltale black marks on the wall's white paint. Last time I was in that house, in December for the holidays, I went up to the attic to study and saw that they were still there.

"Your ass is mine. Boy." This was Sean's voice, affecting a southern accent and soft in my ear. Sam was out—finally!—visiting some distant aunt to whom she'd promised an afternoon. Sean and I were alone at long last and I was getting my fix.

"Now this is your first day in the joint," he continued. "Maybe that's been enough time for you to see how it is around here, and maybe not. But a pretty boy like you ain't gonna last long without protection. You know what I'm sayin' to you?"

"Yes," I whispered. "Sir."

"Well, you catch on nice and quick. You're gonna want to keep on callin' me sir."

"Yes sir."

"Cause I ain't gonna take no disrespect. You got that? Now I'm gonna spell out the situation here." A pause while he took a fistful of my hair. "I been here five years now. I am the boss here. As far as you're concerned I'm the boss everywhere. In the cell, out of the cell. You do what I tell you."

"All right. Sir."

"That means you make up both these bunks every day, do my laundry when you do yours, and anythin' you get from the outside—cigarettes, stamps, whatever—it all goes straight to me. And there'll be other ways you'll be takin' care of me besides. Do you understand what I'm tellin' you, boy?"

I was thrust onto my stomach, the men's boxer shorts I'd borrowed from Sean jerked down. No one had ever fucked my ass before him, but I was liking it more and more.

"Yes, I do, sir. I do understand."

"Good. 'Cause it been a long time—too long a time—since I laid eyes on a woman, and there ain't no point in thinkin' about how much longer it gonna be." His hand was on me now, smearing Vaseline. My breathing came quick and hard. "A man be somewhere for five, six, seven years, he gotta fuck somethin' or go out of his mind. Do you understand that, boy?"

"I understand, sir." My voice low. He penetrated slowly, cleaving me inch by careful inch. It almost didn't hurt anymore. I whimpered partly in pleasure, partly in fear, then pleasure took over and I cried out involuntarily with each thrust. At these moments it was so easy to lose myself, to listen to my own cries as if to some intriguing and foreign orchestra.

"Oh yeah?" Sean's tone went up in amused surprise. "Yeah? Is that right? Have I got myself a little faggot in here with me? Well, what do you know."

I was always fascinated with incarceration. I seized the opportunity to try it out in many childhood games. I loved being in "jail" in Capture the Flag—even though it just meant sitting under a tree, apart from the action. I even liked landing in jail in Monopoly, just enjoyed the fact of my little metal iron or shoe stuck in that box where a crudely drawn man clutched the bars.

Sam and I played a game where she was a motorcycle cop like in *CHiPs.* This involved the forbidden use of an abandoned and near-dead little moped she'd found in a back alley. As a captured criminal I was forced onto the back and had to endure a few uncertain spins around the block before ending up in her backyard. Beside her garage there was a tall wooden shed where her family stashed the trash until garbage night. A sliding bolt locked it from the outside.

Inside there were metal trash cans and a cool cement floor. If I stood tiptoe atop the aluminum lids, I could just see over the shed walls. Usually I was only imprisoned for about two minutes; there wasn't a whole lot for either of us to do while I was inside. One fall afternoon, though, I remember hearing the bolt slide into place and suddenly knowing the game was going to take a turn.

I stood for a moment pretending not to know. Everything within the shed was the same as always: solitary, silent, the interior slightly darker and chillier than the outside. I strained to see Sam between the slats of wood. She wore a strange expression, satisfied and glinting.

Time slowed as in a dream, each moment widening to contain a world. My skin prickled and all my senses were heightened. I could feel Sam through the wall as I hadn't been able to before in the open air. Sam was jealous because I could read twice as fast as her, and play the piano. She both loved and hated me for being a girly girl, for wearing dresses and having long hair and getting good report cards.

I clambered onto a trash can and peered over the shed wall. "Sam?"

She was disappearing into the garage. I waited. In a minute, she emerged with a basketball under her arm.

"Sam," I tried again.

"You have the right to remain silent," she said, without really looking at me.

"When are you going to let me out?"

"When I'm ready." She set the ball to spinning on her index finger, a trick she was very proud of. "Maybe never," she added.

The top of the shed wall was sharp, each wooden slat ending in a point. The structure was too thin to support any weight, and I was in no position to vault over, even if I dared. I lowered myself back down to the ground and resumed my position at the spyhole. Sam began practicing layups against the backboard in her driveway.

I was surrounded on all sides yet I could still see the sky. My cell was cement- and wood-colored, but the ceiling was open and blue. I was quiet, taking in these details, marking the rhythm of Sam's basketball from within my prison. Panic was still at bay.

I didn't question why I was here. It was inevitable—hadn't I known it was coming almost before it happened? I was smaller and weaker and more than occasionally insufferable. What was unclear was how I was to appease her. Did she want me to beg, or would stoicism please her more? I didn't know.

Sam turned suddenly, without warning, hurling the basketball in my direction. I recoiled an instant before it crashed against precisely the part of the wall I'd been looking through. The entire structure trembled from the impact. I got the message: she didn't want me watching her. I just wondered how she knew.

I took a new position against the part of the wall farthest away from her, sitting with my knees drawn up, and studied the pattern of nail heads in the wood. All kinds of constellations were possible, depending on how you connected the dots.

What do dogs think about, chained in the yards?

Long minutes went by. The basketball pounded the concrete and swished in the net. I curled into myself and tried to fathom my transgressions. Sam and I had each been given a pair of gray mice by a boy up the street; I'd been allowed to keep mine, but Sam hadn't. We'd begun Hebrew school together some months ago, and I was already way ahead. In kickball the evening before, our team had two outs, Sam was on third, and I kicked the ball straight to the pitcher.

I ascended the garbage can once again. "Sam?"

Silence. Scorn.

"Sam, what did I do?"

She spat in the dust.

"Say something," I begged her.

"Something," she said.

"Come on, Sam."

"Come on what?"

"I'll give you my Halloween candy," I said, thinking of how it irritated her that I'd saved it so long, eating a piece a day for weeks on end, my pink pillowcase still half-full.

She spat again, like the ballplayers on TV. "I don't want a thing you've got."

Just then a fleet of dirt bikes, bearing five or six of the neighborhood boys, skidded into the backyard.

"Hey, Sam!"

She turned; I ducked. I felt it was important not to be seen.

I heard Vance DiCapriati, the leader of the pack, summoning her. "We're chicken-racing Homestead down at the Birmingham

Bridge. You comin'?" Homestead was a bordering neighborhood and the Birmingham Bridge spanned a steep ravine which the most daring kids negotiated on bicycles. Sam had braved it many times. I would have loved to have gone along to watch, as I often did. It was with a fierce and possessive pride that I watched her descend amid clouds of dust into the canyon. I was usually the only onlooker who knew she was a girl.

I heard Sam get on her bike and leave with them.

It was late in the afternoon on a Thursday. I had homework I couldn't start, and there was a test the next day. Evening would be falling in another half hour; it would be dark. I wished I had my schoolbooks, wished in fact that I had any book. I wished I had a heavier coat. Already the temperature was dropping with the sun.

I sat, alone and shivering, and listened to the sounds of freedom around me. Shreds of conversation drifted over the fence; there was the rhythm of a hammer against some rooftop and trees rustled in the wind. I memorized every splintered board of my cell before the sky changed from blue to black. Not long afterward, a sweep of headlights afforded me a brief and hurtful moment of vision as Sam's parents pulled into the driveway. They were home from work.

Here was my chance to be sprung. All I had to do was hop onto a trash can and announce my presence. What kept me from doing this? I sat unmoving as the car doors slammed and my potential rescuers went inside without a clue. Leaving me alone with all the sounds of night: crickets and distant traffic and my own muted whimpering.

I was there for hours. I was to find out later that Sam had forgotten about me. She had come home, flushed with triumph over a victory at Chicken, and left her bike on the front porch. She had gone in to dinner and I'd never even come into her thoughts until the phone rang. It was my mother wondering where I was. Had Sam seen me at all that day?

Even then, it took Sam a minute to remember where I was, and the realization was a sickening jolt. But she never let on; she never even blinked. No, she said, after appearing to think about it. She hadn't seen me at all. And then she made herself finish not only dinner but, to avoid suspicion, even dessert.

After putting down a dish of chocolate chip ice cream, Sam took out the garbage without being told for the first time in her life.

"Are you gonna tell?" is what she asked. Then, quickly: "I know you're going to." Her voice an attempt at flippancy. But I could hear everything: fear and anguish and regret, and most agonizing of all, her inability to show these to me.

I ran home without speaking to her. But when I got there I told my mother that I'd been in the library and had lost track of the time.

I can see the ways in which I've never changed. The blurred and broken line running down my life as on a highway—where the most ordinary, even dreary moment drifts, shifts, into the sublime—has never changed. And I'm in the backseat of the car, curled against the door and staring out, a passenger borne through the night. There are headlights, red and white; there are raindrops on the windowpane. There is coziness and safety. I don't want to drive. I never wanted to. I am seat-belted, rocked by the motion, lulled, contained. In a trance.

I might as well be on a boat—out in the middle of nowhere, surrounded by ocean, floating, suspended, anchored to nothing.

Children can instinctively make those journeys together. Sam and I could, anyway; we lost sight of shore for days on end. We had it all: ropes and rigging, cabins and chambers, flags, a plank, an upper deck and one below. We had it all and we knew where everything was.

When you grow up, something hardens around that world. It shuts like a shell. You can be left within it or without it, but what was once semipermeable is now sealed off. Only the ones who mapped that original terrain can preserve some semblance of access.

To his credit, Sean recognized this, consciously or not. He paid as close attention as he could. He must have sensed he couldn't afford to do otherwise, if he wanted to get on board.

Over the years, my relationship with Sam became more equal. She no longer intimidated me as much, and I was more likely to challenge what she said and did. Occasionally the old dynamics would kick back in; like once when we were having a heated argument on her front lawn, and she told me to get out of her yard.

"Make me," I sassed.

And she picked me up and threw me over the hedges.

At other times she could be amazingly benevolent. She came on her bicycle some evenings to pick me up from swim practice, and rode me home on her handlebars. And she had a few words with some of the girls on the swim team. The ones who called me "the Scum from the South" and asked me couldn't I afford a hairbrush. She had something to say to them, or maybe she just looked at them in her special hard way, but whatever it was, she said they wouldn't be bothering me again, and sure enough they never did. I was hers to bully; no one else was to have that privilege, if she could help it.

Defender or overseer: there was no telling which she might be, or how long each mood would last. Sometimes she would disdain both. The summer that I was twelve and she thirteen, she suddenly stopped coming over in the afternoon. I was alarmed by her absence and would call her on the phone.

"What are you doing?" I'd ask.

"Nothing much," she would say.

"Do you want to come over?"

"No, not today."

"Why not?"

"I just don't want to."

"But why don't you?"

"I just don't. No reason."

We had this conversation, or slight variations on it, every afternoon for several days.

"Well, when *will* you want to?" I finally whined.

"I don't know when. I can't tell you."

"Are you upset with me?"

"No, I just don't feel like doing anything with you. Okay? When I want to, I'll let you know."

This state of affairs made me thoroughly miserable.

At the beginning of that August, I went to my grandmother's house in upstate New York, where I spent a week nearly every summer. Each night there I lay awake, unable to get used to the silence and planning a strategy for getting Sam back. I would do something to get her attention, out in the street in front of our houses if need be, something she'd have to notice and be unable to resist. I'd set up a car wash with my brother, rake in big bucks, and she would beg to get in on it. I would construct a Japanese box kite, build a tree house. Some ostentatious thing she'd be dying to help with. As it turned out, none of these projects were necessary. The very night I returned home, she appeared at my back door with Popsicles, asking if I wanted to see the new Clint Eastwood movie.

As I grew older, I became a dedicated student of the art of manipulation. I actually worked on this for its own sake; I thought it might be the most valuable skill one could cultivate in a lifetime. And most of the time, I was very successful. But not with Sam, never with Sam. She didn't seem resistant to my strategies as much as just immune. She called the shots and there was nothing that could touch her. When she made up her mind, there was no swaying her decisions; when she said no, she meant no.

This wasn't true of Sean. He was easy to control. As long as you left him with the idea that he was calling the shots. I'd present him with two self-serving choices, for instance, and let him think he was making the decision. If I wanted him to do something for me, I could usually, with slight pressures and hints, get him to think of it himself. I made the favors I asked for few and far between.

I saw early that he was afraid of my displeasure. This big man. The same one who ruled the dojo, the one who handed down orders all day as assistant manager of a major publishing company. He was anxious in my presence and tried to figure out what I might want before declaring himself in any way. "Do you feel like seeing a movie later, or not really?"

This was at once disappointing and convenient. Convenient because I did, after all, want my own way whenever I could get it. So I was careful, pulling the strings in silence, and averting my eyes so as not to watch him dance. It was a discreet collaboration; we were equally invested in his appearing to wear the pants.

He took me out frequently, and he cooked a lot more often than I did. He would iron my waitressing uniform if I was in a time crunch before work, and I soon came to rely on it. He would also come to the café to pick me up if my shift ended in the middle of the night, which was not unusual. This involved setting his alarm for two-thirty or three in the morning, even if it was a weeknight. By the time we got home, he'd have fully awakened and was likely to be aroused. I, on the other hand, would have just finished waiting on eight hours' worth of tables and my only lust would be for sleep. Sometimes I'd indulge him. "Go ahead," I said to him once, "as long as I don't have to move." I recognized that sexual gratification ought to be his due for coming to get me. More often, though, I let him go to bed frustrated, and he didn't push it. When fantasy was too exhausting to forge, I was the boss.

The long stretches where Sam withdrew from me, as she had that summer when we were twelve, recurred on a regular basis for the next several years. They bewildered and hurt me, but I learned to keep these feelings to myself, to put on a great show of indifference. I hardened myself against her, not wanting to give her the satisfaction of my pain. It got easier. We were changing.

Puberty was as infuriating to Sam as it was delightful to me. The metamorphosis I prayed for and wore padded bras to enhance brought Sam nothing but chagrin. She was no longer indistinguishable from the pack of boys she had run around with for so many years. At the same time, she seemed to have little in common with other girls. She scorned makeup and curling irons, cliques and gossip. I exulted and suffered through crush after crush; my romances were full of sexual initiation and high melodrama. Sam remained dateless and apparently indifferent through four years of high school. You couldn't say she was an outcast; you wouldn't describe her as a wallflower. She was simply a loner, standing more apart with every passing year.

She gained weight. Her clothes were always loose and ill-fitting, concealing her body: men's hiking boots with baggy jeans, oversized sweatshirts. She regarded my fashion experiments—the ongoing trials with lipstick and eyeliner, tight sweaters and short skirts, fishnet stockings and spike heels—with the gruff amusement and fleeting interest one might accord a mildly ridiculous spectator sport.

During our periods of closeness it could feel as if we were travelers reuniting by chance in a foreign country. The strange territory we'd ventured upon seemed to fade before our recognition. Small world, we might have said. It's been a long time; or: There's no place like home.

"What did you guys do for fun?" Sean asked at one point during the week.

I don't remember what we said; it was something vague about barhopping and the lame small-town night scene.

Less and less: that would have been the correct answer.

Sean and I were alone in the apartment only one other time during Sam's visit. She'd said she was going out for a walk by herself. Lone walks were something she took quite frequently at home. We didn't protest, and we lost no time.

I had just stepped out of the shower and was standing, wrapped in a towel, in the middle of the bedroom floor when Sean turned and stared at me for a moment, as if seeing me for the first time. Then: "Get dressed," he said, in that curt tone that means he's beginning something.

Hastily I dried off and drew on some underwear. Then I tried to think of what he'd want to see me in. First I chose a sheer pink negligee, then changed my mind and climbed into a black catsuit instead.

"Get in bed," Sean said coldly.

I went over and sat down cross-legged in the middle of the blue patchwork quilt.

"Kneel." It was almost a sigh. As usual, he was making me believe him. Whenever he talked to me in that abrupt, impersonal way, like a cop writing up his hundredth speeding ticket of the day, it was easy to forget we were playing a game. I knelt, trembling as much from apprehension as from the still-wet hair dripping down my back.

He stayed at the desk, pretending to be busy with something. He let me kneel there for about five minutes while he shuffled papers around, and then he came over.

"Back straight. Head up."

I complied, shivering. He sat down on the edge of the bed and regarded me, lifting my chin with two fingers and running his thumb over my mouth. With the other hand he popped the snaps which closed the catsuit between my legs. It sprang open. He put his hand there, as always, to feel the wetness, but something was wrong. There was another barrier where none should have been, a thin cotton sheath between his hand and my flesh. I'd forgotten to take off my underwear. It wasn't any sexy silk underwear either. It was a plain white pair, printed with pink flowers, that might have belonged to a six-year-old. Against the black lace of the catsuit, it was ludicrous. I felt heat rushing to my face.

"What is this?" Sean asked, ominously calm.

"It's my underwear."

"Why are you wearing underwear?"

"When I put it on I was going to wear something else," I said. "But then I decided to wear this and I forgot to take the underwear off."

"You forgot?"

"I'm sorry."

"You forgot. Can you tell me," Sean asked softly, "what you were thinking about—what it was you had on your mind—that took precedence over getting dressed for me?"

"I . . . I don't remember," I said.

"It must have been very important."

"No."

"Then how do you explain this?"

"I don't know."

Sean rose and disappeared into the bathroom without another word. He returned a moment later with a razor blade.

"Now tell me," he said in that same flat tone, "is this one of your better pairs of underwear?"

"No," I answered.

"Is there anything special about them? Any sentimental value here?"

"No, no . . ."

"That's almost too bad," Sean said, and with the razor blade he slashed a line through the white cotton. The material yielded easily, and a moment later was hanging in tatters around his invading hand.

I stared down at myself where his two fingers were disappearing inside me and felt inexplicably forlorn. I thought it almost would have been better if he had ruined a fancy pair of underwear—some article of lingerie which, by its lascivious nature, would have declared itself part of the game. To take such action against those pink and white flowers seemed a terrible and heedless cruelty: how could anyone want to slash and punish them? A stricken ache took over my body, pulsing outward from my heart, spreading through my chest to my arms and legs, and somewhere inside it was my orgasm, blooming like a dark rose. My eyes welled up and spilled over silently, but Sean was kissing my neck and didn't see this. For which I was grateful; I didn't feel capable of dealing with startled questions. I stared straight ahead, willing myself to breathe normally, and felt my tears drying, unnoticed and unexplained, in their tracks.

"I could never do those things," Sam told me over dinner that week in New York. I was skipping karate to hang out with her, but we were going to the class just before the end, to watch the last fifteen minutes. She wanted to see how Sean taught. "Why deliberately bring pain into a relationship like that?"

"The pain is beside the point. I mean, it's there, it's fine, but it's only a means to an end."

"What end is that?"

"If you don't understand I don't know if I can explain. And anyway, if we both like it, what could be wrong?"

Sam was silent for a moment, regarding me. "The whole idea is just so strange, that's all. That that's all you two ever do. Don't you ever just want to make love?"

I thought about it before answering. I thought hard for almost a minute and then answered honestly. And I had to tell her no . . . no. "No. I really don't."

We slipped into the dojo, where the karate class was almost over. Everyone darted furtive glances at us except for Sean. He was explaining the side thrust kick and was too intent on the class to pay us any mind. I felt the familiar thrill as we watched him demonstrating techniques, correcting students individually on their stances, counting in Japanese. At the very end, he led the higher belts through an advanced kata, which is what he does best. As always, I was awed by how gracefully he moved, how easy he made it look.

Sam leaned over and spoke into my ear. "I can't believe," she said, "that this is the same man I met downtown the other day for lunch."

"Yeah, I know," I said.

"Let's make a tent."

It was Sam's suggestion. We had been sitting in the apartment at a loss for what to do, having just tried to get into a movie which was sold out. It was raining outside, and still fairly early, nine o'clock on a Saturday night.

"Come on, like we used to when we were little kids." She was already standing up, gathering the satin blanket to her body.

I felt a strange premonitory thrill. "Well, okay, why not?"

We started to work together. Sean watched with amusement for a while, then his boy-scout instincts took over and he rather arrogantly took charge.

"No, put these two chairs back-to-back and secure the blanket between them, you see? Like this."

When we were done, the bed was canopied by my two quilts, the edges forming a heavy curtain which parted to permit entry. We crawled inside and lay down. I was between them. For a minute all three of us were quiet. It was raining harder now, pelting the windows. Every now and then a blue flash of lightning lit the interior of the tent, and then we would hear the thunder. Finally Sean spoke.

"This is what you two used to do all the time, isn't it?"

"Right," I said. "Didn't you do something like this yourself as a kid?"

"We made barricades with the cushions of the living room couch," Sean reflected. "And played a modified Cowboys and Indians."

"We made tents, and played Boat," I said. "It's amazing, the way we played. For hours on end, day after day. Sam, when did we stop? I mean, *how* did we stop? Did we wind down and play every other day for a while, then once or twice a week, or what? There had to be some final day when we played for the last time, and we didn't know it. Does that seem strange to you, or is it just me?"

"No, I've wondered about that too," she said.

"Don't look back," Sean said, his tone heavy and mocking at the same time. "You can never go home again. Your playing days are over."

"But we play, Sean," I said. "We play all the time. Pretend games. Don't we?"

He was silent for a moment, then spoke seriously, as he hadn't before. "That's not playing for its own sake. That's sex."

"Was it ever for its own sake? Aren't childhood games very sexual? Innocent, unrealized, or whatever . . . but essentially sexual."

"I think you're right," Sam said. "The way I always had to be the boy, and order you around. I loved doing it, too."

"Well, now you're making me jealous," Sean said lightly.

"And you're turning me on," I said. I wasn't completely joking, either.

"Oh yeah?" Sean growled, pretending territoriality.

"Yeah . . . it's true," I murmured. I looked straight up at the ceiling, rather than at either of them. "So let's play a game."

"What kind of game?" Both of them were looking at me with interest.

"A sex game that will fuck up our friendship," I said, and laughed. "Let's play Boat!"

"I'm the captain," Sean said immediately, and we were all startled into silence. "I mean," he qualified quickly, "if we're actually going to play, I get to be the boss. You can be my sidekick," he added generously to Sam. "The ship's first mate."

"Then who am I?" I asked.

"You're our prisoner, taken in battle from the enemy ship. You can consider yourself lucky to be our slave," Sean continued. "It is only our incredible mercy that kept you from being thrown to the sharks."

I laughed at this. He wrapped his hand in my hair. "You won't be laughing for long," he said softly into my ear, and I stopped. He brought his other hand up to my face, made a fist, and lightly passed the knuckles over my cheek. Immediately my breathing grew rapid and shallow.

"Well, look what we've got here, mate," he said to Sam.

"Fine specimen of a wench, Captain," she replied with a straight face.

"That she is," he agreed. "But an enemy wench just the same."

"You're right, Captain. As usual."

"Well. What do you think? Should we have a look at our property?"

"I think that would be in order, Captain," the first mate replied.

"Let's strip her, then. Get her hands." Sam grasped my wrists and secured them above my head, and then Sean pulled off my tank top. I was wearing my favorite bra, strapless white lace with a circle of tiny imitation pearls in the middle.

"That's pretty fancy stuff this wench has got on. Too bad she won't be needing it anymore," Sean said, springing the clasp. The bra fell away, baring my breasts in the bluish light. Sean passed the palm of his hand over them casually, as he would have stroked a cat, or a bolt of silk.

"Lovely," he said. "Mate, would you care to touch the wench?"

I looked at Sam. She seemed taken aback all of a sudden, as if my half-nakedness had woken her up to what was going on. She glanced at me, then quickly averted her eyes, and shook her head no. Sean was excited, though, that much I could see. He was in his element, showing her the ropes, running the game. I looked at him and then at her, waiting to see what was going to happen. I felt suspended between them, calm, floating, open. Reasonable, flexible. I could have gone either way. Why not, I could only think to myself, much stranger things go on every day. I felt curious, devious, glinting, mocking. I was pleased also at having Sam all flustered. She didn't have the slightest clue what to do.

I was looking at her and thinking these things when all of a sudden she looked straight back, with a new expression I couldn't read. As if she could hear all my gloating thoughts and knew something I didn't. At any rate, it wasn't friendly.

"Go ahead," Sean urged her. "Look at her. She thinks you won't do it."

Maybe both of them could read my mind. Whatever the case, Sean's words seemed to release her. She reached over and twisted my nipple. I protested this by glaring at her and trying to squirm away. "Don't touch me," I challenged.

There was a frightening silence. Then: "What the fuck did you just say to me?" she asked.

I didn't answer.

"Can I do anything I want with this wench, Captain?"

"Do what you want," he told her. "I wouldn't let her get away with that," he added.

Her hand came back to my nipple. "Repeat what you just said," she ordered. For the first time I began to feel afraid.

"I didn't say anything."

She slapped me hard across the face. I saw stars, little orange bursts behind my eyelids. Amazement left me mute.

"How dare you lie to me," she hissed. "How dare you! You know what you said, now say it again."

Not knowing what else to do, I repeated myself, speaking low. "I said don't touch me."

"Can you believe this, Captain?" Sam said, addressing Sean.

"She's a brazen little bitch. Let's strip her all the way down and see if a whipping changes her tune." Disbelief and excitement made me cold, and fear pricked my flesh. They pulled off my jeans. Sean went to my closet and took the riding crop from where it hung on the hook inside. He came back to the bed, jerked my underwear down around my thighs, and handed the crop to Sam.

It seemed as if everything I had ever said and done with the two of them had led inevitably to this moment. My refusing to follow Sam around anymore, catching up to her, surpassing her. Now I was the one who was good friends with the boys, though for different reasons. I had become the athletic one, the bold one, the manipulator, the bully. But here she was; she had found me. She was holding the whip. And I wanted it. I could not remember ever having wanted it so much before. Not with Sean, not with any man.

She beat me. Sean held my hands above my head and she wielded the crop, hitting me hard all the way down my back and legs. When I was striped from neck to ankle and crying with abandon, she stopped and regarded me with immense satisfaction.

"Now," she said, "there's a lot more where that came from, if you don't do whatever I tell you to do."

She made me kiss the whip. She made me kiss her feet. She made me go down on her, something I had never done to a woman. I could sense Sean watching from somewhere on the periphery of things; he seemed far away. I had a vague hope that he was impressed with what was either my inherent skill at this or considerable beginner's luck. Only after I had satisfied her this way three or four times did she deign to touch me in turn. It was all she had to do.

Through the open window came catcalls from the street. They could hear me eleven stories below.

"Write to me soon," I said to Sam on the way to the train. It was five o'clock in the morning, and the streets were bluish and still.

The morning after. I had expected, just before falling asleep, to be incredulous in the light of day, but I wasn't at all, and neither was she. We were calm, unsurprised, and unapologetic.

"I will," she said.

"Tell everyone at home I said hello."

"Tell Sean I said good-bye."

That was the closest we came to even mentioning it. By the next time we saw each other, it would just be another episode in a dozen years' worth of memories.

I stood with her on the subway platform until the downtown IRT screeched into sight. We hugged each other and the train took her away. Then I climbed up to the street, where day was breaking, and instead of turning east toward my apartment, I found myself walking down to Riverside Park. I wanted an hour or so to myself before going home, where Sean was still asleep in my bed.

Turned Out

Nelson was out of prison and waiting to believe it. It was a fine day and he was in it, walking under the bright and newly bewildering sun. He squinted in the glare and took halting steps. There was nowhere special for him to go.

He had talked for years, like everyone else, about what he would do the first day out—a dream that seemed then as impossibly distant as winning the lottery. Theirs were elaborate fantasies, involving champagne, limousines, penthouse suites, and pussy of every color. But Nelson, who had a sweet tooth and wasn't ready for the rest, went into a drugstore for a chocolate bar.

Even this was dangerous. The candy counter held so many of them, rows on rows, some wrapped in a way that made his heart hurt. The sight brought on a rush of nostalgia, like the memory of some boyhood Halloween. There were new ones he'd never seen and old ones he had all but forgotten: fluffy Milky Ways and Three Musketeers, bright Mr. Goodbars and glinting Peppermint Patties. And good old Hershey's; that would never change. That was all the Axe had ever eaten, plain without almonds. Nelson hadn't even tasted another brand since falling in with the Axe, and how that had irked him all those years. The choices at the canteen would have been slim enough without the Axe insisting on the same damn thing week after week.

He stood and looked for a long time, which he could see was making the cashier nervous. Finally he decided on a plain Hershey's; what the hell, chocolate was chocolate.

It was autumn. Last week, this would have meant a pumpkin-flavored processed square on his dinner tray, along with a scoop of cranberry Jell-O. Freedom translated the season into chill air, bare trees, and fire in the sky as evening fell at five o'clock. Each inhalation brought something new: pipe smoke, ripe leaves, the promise of snow. Too much, it was all too much. Nelson wandered into a little fenced-in area—one of those tiny islands the city called a park—and sat down on a bench. He didn't want to cry.

So much time had passed. Nelson could recall whole afternoons squandered in porn theaters when he was a teen. He remembered the feeling of emerging in twilight, the day irretrievable. It was that same feeling all over again. Nelson was now thirty-four but felt fifty. He had done twelve years, eleven and a half with the Axe.

The Axe was never getting out. He was working on the second of three consecutive life sentences with no possibility of parole. He had killed many times, in prison and out, but he was undeniably the reason Nelson was alive. He had taken everything else from the younger man, maybe, but he had secured his life in no uncertain terms: no one was going to fuck with the Axe's boy. Nelson almost wished the Axe were here with him now, because he could not imagine what he was going to do out here all alone.

He thought he knew what any other ex-con would do in this situation. And that would be to go find a whore, if there was no woman waiting. But the very idea made him scared and cold. Could he trust himself to get it up, get on top? Arrange her body as he wished and take possession? That was what a man had to do. For so long, his only sexual responsibility had been to make himself available. To assume a position: facedown on the bunk, or bent over it. There were occasional variations: interludes of tenderness in the dark, where he lay between the rock thighs of the mighty Axe, sucking blindly like a baby animal. For the Axe had cared for him, a little, after a while. At least as much as someone like the Axe could care for anyone.

There was no point in thinking about it. Here was the world returned to him. It was like a painting come to life and almost too bright to look at. Even the pigeons around his feet were shining, iridescent at the neck. He watched as one aggressive bird, puffed up with purpose, chased its chosen one in erratic circles and finally overtook her. They coupled in the dust, the female held fast by the other's beak. She seemed to be purring, an ambiguous sound that could have been either pleasure or pain. And now he felt them, the tears on his face; and there was nothing to do but let them come.

The YMCA was faintly comforting. It was spare to the point of austerity: there was a bunk bed, a crude dresser, and a black-and-white television. Almost like a cell.

He remembered having heard the phrase *sensory overload*. That may have been what had come over him on the street. He wished he had someone to talk to about this. Maybe even someone like the Axe, with whom any of his own feelings would swiftly become irrelevant. Satisfying the Axe left no room for anything else.

Nelson sat on the lower bunk and struggled for the fragments of a plan. A plan for the evening, and the next day, and the day after that. He had some money—not much, but enough to live on for a couple of weeks. But no home, no family, and no real friends on the outside. His relationships had melted away with more than a decade of incarceration.

Getting work was his first concern. He'd learned to do a few things in the pen other than license plates; he could weld, for one thing, and had worked as a lift station operator for the main prison maintenance department. But there was a suspicion eating at his heart—unbearable, unspeakable—that his deep and real skills had been honed against the Axe.

It had been slavery. And it had been rape. But these factors were inescapable for someone like Nelson, who had gone in at twenty-two with a slight build, a smooth chin, and long-lashed blue eyes. And it was as inevitable that someone like the Axe—a giant who towered over prisoners and guards alike at six-foot-six, 240 pounds, all of it hard muscle; a man who warmed up at the bench with a dozen easy reps of his own body weight; a killer nicknamed for his weapon of choice—it was as natural that such a man could choose his own slave in any joint. It was better to service one man than to be open game, or the joint property of a gang. It was good to be off-limits to other predators, to receive as much respect as was possible for a "bitch." The other men averted their eyes in the showers and in the yard, not wanting to be caught surveying the Axe's property.

It was something to be the chosen one of such a man. And the Axe had trained him. It went beyond the physical, though that realm was not unimportant. Nelson could do things, incredible things, with his mouth and his hands without even thinking about it anymore, while his mind wandered like a stream, eddying and snagging, and strange bits of debris floated up, unbidden. Strains from kindergarten songs, for instance: *There was an old lady who swallowed a goat. . . . She opened her throat . . . to swallow the goat. . . .*

But it went beyond the physical. It was about intuition, anticipation. Nelson could read the Axe like a drawing on a cave wall, knew what he wanted before he spoke, could finish most of the man's sentences for him. He knew how the Axe took his coffee, how he wanted his laundry folded, how much pruno would make him mellow and how much would make him mean. He could work the hard knots out of that broad back and neck, dissolve a tension headache in minutes, ease wooden slivers from the skin without pain.

Most important, he could feel the Axe's emotions, knew his rage, his frustration, and even his fear. Oh yes, even the Axe had fear, more than anyone would have believed who wasn't lying beside him in the middle of the night. They didn't talk about this fear, not in words, but his sheets were soaked with it, sometimes, and his body racked and stiff. Here lay Nelson's most pressing, though unspoken, call: more important than any domestic chore or sexual obligation, it was his place to absorb the great man's fear, bring him solace. And he knew it was this ability, along with his intuitive delicacy and tact, that had made the Axe unwilling to replace him while he was there.

Who would the man take in his place? Amazing, the pang of agony this speculation brought with it. Wasn't it all behind him? He'd led the unnatural life of a caged animal, and he had done certain things to survive. But that was the past and he would never have to do them again.

Nelson left his room and within an hour found himself at a midtown strip joint. It seemed to hold no risk; all he had to do was sit and look. He settled into a shadowy corner and found himself watching a slim girl on the near stage. She was wide-eyed and tangle-haired, festooned in pink feathers, achingly young. She saw Nelson and smiled directly into his eyes. He was flustered and dropped his gaze.

Within minutes she was beside him. "Hi, baby," she said. Baby. This girl, who looked barely nineteen, was calling him "baby."

"I'm Jeannie," she said. "What's your name?"

He almost said Nellie. It was what he had been called on the inside, a name meant to reinforce his female status. He caught himself in time, but his real name stuck in his throat. What right did she have to know who he was?

"John," he said.

"Johnny and Jeannie. Goes together, right? Is this your first time here, honey? I haven't seen you before."

"First time," he confirmed.

"Well, welcome to the Catwalk," she said. "Glad you decided to check it out." She slid an arm around him and with her other hand found his left nipple, rubbing it lightly. Nelson stiffened.

"What's the matter, sweetheart, you shy?"

"Yeah," he said.

She smiled again, a teasing grin. "That's all right. I'll be gentle with you."

The idea that this place—dimly lit, smoky, and full of half-naked girls—was supposed to be some den of corruption, and that this child thought she was seducing him, would have been laughable if he could laugh.

"So what do you do?" she was asking.

Vague panic. How to answer that one? "I'm between things right now," he said after a moment.

"Times are hard," she said sympathetically, and finally he had to smile.

"So," she said, leaning closer, "do you want a lap dance?"

"A lap dance," he repeated. "What's that?"

"Oh, baby, where have you been? A lap dance. What does it sound like? Come on. I'll make you feel real good. Okay?"

When he didn't protest, she stood facing him and straddled his thighs. Her smooth cheek caressed his own as she started to gyrate, grinding into him. He held his breath, willing himself erect. Nothing.

She was singing along with whatever was playing, her fingertips grazing the back of his neck. He breathed in the scent of her skin, perfume mingled with light sweat. Her lips brushed his ear and she moaned into it softly. She was a sweet little thing. She was trying hard.

Nothing. He felt nothing, except for faint wonder that someone was trying to take care of *his* desire, was concerned about getting *him* off. And some small regret for her wasted effort.

On the street again, on his way back to the YMCA, Nelson saw it in the storefront window of Rooke's Collectibles and Sports Memorabilia, a sight which sent a sharp pain of recognition through his temples. There before him, through the glass, was the same photograph which had graced whatever wall he and the Axe had been allotted for—what? Ten years at least. It showed Muhammad Ali winning the Heavyweight Championship of the World. The boxer's bruised face was suffused with his victory—smiling and open, radiant with something like deliverance. He was wearing a robe of purple and gold and holding a trophy above his head.

Ali was, as far as Nelson knew (and he supposed no one could know better), the Axe's only real hero. He understood that the Axe identified with him and took a vicarious pride in his triumph. That worn photograph went with them from cell to cell long after the boxing world had gone on to Larry Holmes and Mike Tyson.

It took a moment for Nelson to register the rest of the display and to realize that this photograph was only a reference for it. Hanging just behind the photo was the immense gold and purple robe. Ali's boxing robe, the colors of royalty, faded with the years, but still in one piece.

Nelson went weak with longing. An irresistible picture came instantly into full bloom: a picture of himself giving this robe to the Axe. If anyone was the rightful owner of that robe, it had to be the Axe, ruler of the roost, prince of the prison, king of the motherfucking jungle. He was the only one Nelson could think of who could actually wear it around and not be ridiculous. It would fit him.

Nelson entered the store. An older man was behind the counter, looking at a catalogue and smoking a cigar. Nelson had to clear his throat twice before the other looked up.

"The robe in the window," Nelson said. He sounded hoarse in his own ears and cleared his throat again. "Uh, how much would that be?"

"Seventeen," the man said briefly.

"Seventeen," Nelson repeated, uncomprehending. "Seventeen . . . dollars?" He spoke without thinking, mortified as soon as the words were out.

"Seventeen thousand."

"Oh."

For a moment he imagined explaining to the man that he had to have the robe, that he knew someone who needed it, who *deserved* it. Then it came to him that he wasn't thinking straight, and abruptly he went back out into the street. The night air was cold and his jacket thin but he found that he was sweating.

What the fuck was wrong with him? Pipe-dreaming about a robe for the Axe? Fuck the Axe! The Axe had twisted him and warped him and taken his manhood away. Maybe even made it so a woman didn't do it for him anymore. He was finally out from under the yoke, and what was he fantasizing about? Getting the son of a bitch a present. It was fucking sick.

Nelson picked up a bottle of Crazy Horse on his way back, and when he reached his room, he knew it had been a good move. The space which had looked small in the afternoon now seemed immense—far too much for one person to fill. He knew he never would have been able to sleep without the liquor to blur the edges of his day, warming him through, taking him out.

* * *

In the morning, knowing a maid would be stripping its sheets for the wash, Nelson nonetheless made the bed. When he'd finished, it looked better than he'd found it the day before, the hospital corners sharp and the blankets drawn taut enough to bounce a quarter on. He found himself wondering if the Axe would actually have to make up his own bunk during the interim before he found himself another "wife." He wanted to be amused at the thought, but instead it was strangely appalling. There were some people who weren't meant to make beds. Well, probably he wouldn't have to, not even for a day. There would be someone else to take over that task.

Wouldn't there?

'Course there would. For the Axe?

But already?

You think he's conducting fucking interviews? How much time does it have to take?

To replace *me*?

What's the matter? Did you want to get married to the bull-elephant? Want to stay locked up in prison? What have you turned into, some kind of faggot?

But who could do what I did, the way I did it?

Get a fucking *grip*.

He had to get a job as soon as he could. Or the voices in his head could make him crazy. He got a newspaper on the way to the corner diner and studied the want ads over a couple of greasy eggs. One thing he knew for sure: he wanted a man's job. Something hard, rugged, backbreaking even. At least till he had nothing left to prove.

He borrowed a pen from the waitress and began circling whatever seemed acceptable. Construction. Roadwork. Auto mechanics, furniture moving, loading and unloading boxes in a shipyard. All work that would build muscle, blot out thought, and guarantee a good night's sleep. When he'd marked out enough for a full day's search, he finished his eggs, folded the paper, and went out to pound the pavement.

By the end of the third day of his job hunt—after standing in different lines for hours with other unemployed men, filling out dozens of bewildering forms, and writing down so many lies about his past that he knew he would never be able to keep track of them all—Nelson felt as if an invisible, ever-tightening hand were choking off his very life. There were three or four workers competing for each opening wherever he went, and he knew no one was going to pick him. He had little experience to speak of, no resumé, no references. He did not belong to any union. The application forms revealed still more that he didn't have: things like insurance, emergency contacts, a home address or even a phone number. In the unlikely event that someone would give him a chance, where were they supposed to call?

This was bad. He was just beginning to see how bad it was. It could be weeks before he landed something, and what was he going to do until then? He couldn't go on paying forty dollars a night to stay at the Y, and he knew there was nothing cheaper in the city.

These past few evenings, after each day's frustrated scramble, Nelson had found himself in front of Rooke's, staring at Ali's robe. He'd gone in again, once, but the owner had glared at him with recognition and suspicion. Like he somehow knew Nelson had just gotten out of prison.

The robe made him feel better, anyway. It held sweat and power, vindication of the underdog. It contained the dream of having risen above. It was a reminder of how close he'd become with the Axe, a man who made a point of keeping everyone at a respectful distance. Nelson still couldn't look at it without wanting to get it for him.

He stood in front of the window for a while and then went to a nearby delicatessen for his dinner. While trying to decide what kind of sandwich he wanted, he noticed two children at the front of the line, a brother and sister. The boy was older; he looked about seven. His sister was maybe five, with long light brown hair. She stood close to the boy, one mittened hand holding his. They wanted pickles out of the jar on the counter.

"Well, you're lucky," the cashier said as he picked up a pair of tongs. "We've got exactly two left." He fished them from the brine and placed them on sheets of waxed paper. They were dramatically different in size.

"I get the big one!" the boy asserted.

"I get the little one!" his sister said in the same bright tone. The counterman chuckled as he wrapped up their purchase.

Nelson was breathless. The little girl hadn't even realized. That she'd claimed the lesser share. Or maybe she had realized, but didn't care. Her brother was big; she was little. Her eyes were so untroubled, so . . . He tried to swallow and couldn't.

It was his turn to order. He asked for a turkey sandwich, shoved his money at the man, and nearly ran out to the sidewalk, but the children were nowhere in sight. He craned in every direction: gone. For a moment Nelson was overwhelmed with a sense of loss, though he couldn't have said why. What would he have done anyway? He couldn't very well follow them home.

He wandered back to Rooke's. There it was, hanging like a ghost. What would it feel like to slip it on?

Just to Nelson's left, the store's glass door swung open and the owner appeared with a broom. He began sweeping the pavement in front of the store with short, almost angry strokes. Nelson backed up a few feet without averting his gaze from the window. It was a moment before he realized the man was addressing him.

"Sir, is there something you want?"

A warning bell went off in his head, his instincts honed over the years to even the subtlest hostility. He waited a moment before answering.

"Somethin' I want? I reckon that'd be a long list. You gonna do somethin' about it?" With surprise, he realized he was imitating the Axe's drawl, as if summoning the other man's persona would help him in a confrontation.

The owner's knuckles whitened around the broom. "You've been loitering outside my store for the past several days. If you're intending some legitimate business, all well and good. If not, I'll ask you to please remove yourself from the premises."

Nelson was incredulous. The nerve of this son of a bitch! His eyes narrowed into murderous slits and his voice went low. Hushed and dangerous. "Am I botherin' anyone?" he asked.

"You're bothering me."

Nelson felt his hands twitching. He took a step toward the other man, who immediately backed up. He felt a rush of adrenaline, certainty that he was the stronger here, and a cold rage that had been building all week. But when he spoke his voice was a shade softer than before. The Axe had always gotten quieter and more menacing the angrier he'd become.

"Didn't know there was a law about standin' on a sidewalk."

"There are plenty of laws about loitering and you don't look like you're up to anything good. If I continue to see you hanging around, I'll call the police." With these last words, the man was already scurrying back inside the store, and Nelson heard double bolts slide into their locks.

His body was trembling with fury. Everything was bathed in a red haze. He moved off almost blindly, not knowing where he would go. He wished with all his might that the Axe were beside him, or within him. *He* would have known what to do, and done it by now. If the Axe had suffered such an insult, the owner of the store would be lying right this minute in a pool of his own blood, maybe even hacked into a hundred bloody bits.

Oh, Axe. Too proud and fierce for this world. They had to lock you away from it. You took whatever you wanted and they couldn't stand it no they wouldn't have it and they took it all away from you. They took everything away and then they even took me away. I understood you Axe better than anyone else ever did but never the way I understand you now. Oh Axe I understand you now I can even feel you now and how I wish I could show you

What he needed was a weapon. He was naked out here, defenseless. Nelson knew he would never be able to get a gun, not here in the city where you needed a license. But he could get a blade. There was an army-navy store not far away, a place no questions would be asked.

You wouldn't believe this robe Axe it's the real thing it was on the shoulders of Muhammad Ali right at the moment of victory I'll bet it's got traces of blood on it

The army-navy was everything the memorabilia shop was not. The guys behind the counter nodded at him pleasantly when he came in. No one appeared nervous when Nelson began examining hunting knives and switchblades. On the contrary, they kept up a running commentary on the special features of each one as he picked them up.

He had it narrowed down to a butterfly and a bowie when he saw the axe, and then it was like a joke and he had to laugh out loud. It was a beautiful thing, about four feet long, heavy in his hand. He gripped it lovingly where the sleek wooden body met gleaming metal and a delicious shiver ran the length of his arm.

"That's fire-department issue," one of the counter guys said. "A pick-headed axe," and Nelson could see he was as prepared to detail its virtues as he had been with the knives. But there was nothing to decide.

"I'll take it," he said.

Yeah Axe I can definitely see the attraction here feels good in your hands real good gonna go pay a visit to that tightassed maggotfaced pansy with his seventeen thousand dollar robe fuck with me now bitch let's see if you want to fuck with me now

The axe cost more than two nights' lodging at the Y, but what did that matter now? What the fuck kind of life was this anyway, scrounging for a bed, scraping for a job, counting and recounting his money, figuring and anxious all the time? And that was the least of it.

You did it to me Axe you did a real fucking number on me and I thought I hated you for it but I don't no I don't I can't anymore

He didn't belong on the outside anymore. He was a specter from an earthly hell, haunting the fringes of the happening world. Everything that had made him valuable inside had turned like wine to water on the street. Water in the deepest well of shame.

What am I supposed to do Axe you tell me I don't recognize myself anymore don't know what I am

With no real plan he was heading back to Rooke's. With an axe in his hand he didn't need a plan. That withered scumbag had threatened to call the police. Well, let him call, it might be the last thing he ever did. The police suddenly held no threat for Nelson. Why should they? He had faced up to bigger and better than a bunch of pigs.

After you Axe what could ever frighten me again I'm gonna get you that robe you're gonna flip out I know you're the one who should have it Axe it should never belong to anyone else

At Rooke's again. There it was. Hanging there and waiting for him. Behind the wide expanse of expensive plate glass—

Ah look at that fuckin' pussy he sees me Yes sir it's me did you think I was that easy to scare away?

—begging for an axe—

Break your window and I'll break your head open too

—sweet sound of shattering glass, a symphony, alarm going off already, the wall splintering and falling and him coming through it, bursting through it, barely aware of stray shards of glass cutting him, and uncaring—

Coming through the wall invincible unstoppable

—sirens in the distance, ah the robe in his hands, it was everything he had imagined and more, velvety, lovely, gave him a rush just like a woman did once—

Worth it all Axe worth more it's for you

—sirens wailing closer, flashing red and blue lights around him and—

And all right Axe you miserable fucker you bully you bastard I'm coming back

The Illustrating Man

I was coming back from interviewing a voodoo practitioner when I saw him. I was on 147th and Lenox Avenue and he was being hustled down a tenement stoop between two cops. There was so much commotion that I couldn't even see what was going on at first. There were at least five police cars parked out front, with more zeroing in from every direction in that way they have, like football players diving onto an already-accomplished tackle.

Sensing a story, I stopped to find out what was happening. I never expected to know the man. But I did know him, knew and placed his face instantly, though he wouldn't have known me. Though it had been more than twenty years and we were in another city, another state.

They put him in the back of their black and white car, then stood around talking importantly into their radios. I approached the nearest cop.

"Excuse me," I said, a little unsteadily. "The man being arrested? Is that Darwin?"

"That's right."

"Darwin Godfrey?"

"Yes ma'am." Then, apologetically: "Friend of yours?"

I wasn't sure how to answer that one, so I let it go.

"What's he being arrested for?" I asked, hearing myself snap into my aggressive press persona. But I think I knew the answer, knew before the cop confirmed it that it would have to be homicide.

When I moved from a rural part of Maryland to Pittsburgh the summer before fourth grade, there was a lot I didn't understand. For instance, that I was supposed to be afraid of black people. The first day of school, a girl with tight cornrows went up to every white girl on the blacktop, followed by a snorting entourage, and recited a poem.

I'm black
And you're white,
So baby you better
Get out of my sight.

At which point, the singled-out would hastily oblige.

When she approached me, I blinked at her in amazement.

"Girl, are you out of your cotton-pickin' mind?" That was the way people talked where I came from.

"Ooohh!!!" howled her cohorts, startlingly in unison.

"You gettin' smart with me, girl?" she said in disbelief.

"I'm already smart," I sassed.

"Oohh!!"

"You gonna take that sass, Renee?"

She looked me over critically, then her face relaxed.

"Awww, you ain't nothin' but a baby iguana," she concluded.

"Well, you ain't nothin' but a *mother* iguana." I tried to imitate her queenly air.

"Oohh!"

The crowd sounded more appreciative with every outburst. I was beginning to enjoy myself. But her face was suddenly full of genuine rage.

"I'm gonna get you, girl," she said. "Just wait. You feel safe now 'cause you know I'd get suspended if I jumped your ass on your way home later on. But the last day of school I'm gonna be layin' for you. And I'm gonna kick your little white butt inside out."

The last day of school! I could barely keep the scorn from my face. This was only the first day of school. The last was an unfathomable amount of time away. As I turned to go I saw the rest of the white girls standing a respectful distance away. Their faces were a mixture of awe and pity.

After that day, I had a reputation. I was approached by many other girls over the next several months. My tongue got sharper and I got cockier. The list of people who were going to kick my butt on the last day of school grew longer, rivaled only by the number of people who couldn't wait to see it happen.

Eventually the last day did arrive. On that June afternoon, I began to feel uneasy at recess. Everywhere I turned, I met eyes wild with anticipation. There was a party in the afternoon. I stood around with all the other kids in the class, holding my cup of punch and trying to act natural, as if all I could think about was the summer which would begin with the three o'clock bell. And trying not to think about what else might begin with that bell.

When it finally rang, I went to the locker room to get my gym suit, then to the art room for the crummy little ashtray I had made for Father's Day, two items I had "forgotten" to retrieve earlier in the day. Then I fussed at my locker, cleaning it out as meticulously as if I were preparing for a West Point inspection. Finally I ventured outside. The yard was deserted.

Strangely, I didn't feel any relief. I *knew*, the way the haunted ones know, the way you always know. Sure enough, about two blocks later, I heard a whoop from down the street. "There she is!"

I didn't turn. Didn't try to run. I am not and have never been a fast runner. I considered running a declaration of guilt, an invitation to be chased, and implicit permission to my pursuers to do as they saw fit when ("if" was not in question here) they caught me. I heard galloping footsteps behind me and I could tell there were at least a dozen in the herd. I squared my shoulders and stared straight ahead as they closed in around me. A fist drove into my back and knocked me down in the dirt.

I scrambled to my feet. Hands found my hair and pulled it; others were jerking at the collar of my shirt, popping the buttons. But these were lazy preliminaries; no one was attempting any real damage yet; the afternoon was young and they had waited too long to be hasty.

And the afternoon was Renee's, that much was clear. Most of the girls were already clearing aside to let her go.

"Get smart with me now," she said to me, her eyes snapping fire. "Get smart with me now, girl."

I was silent. My heart pounded in my throat.

"Come on and call me an iguana now."

I stared at the ground and waited for the first blow.

"I'm gonna make you cry, girl." She said this almost clinically, by way of information. And tears were, in fact, coming; I could feel them, hot at the back of my head.

But as I stared at the cracks in the sidewalk, I could feel the air around me change. There was a sudden, subtle hush, such that I dared at that moment to raise my head. Darwin was approaching from across the street. And then he was there, among us.

I had never spoken to Darwin, nor he to me, but of course I knew who he was. He was in the eighth grade but already inhabited the solid, clean-muscled body of a man. He had a dark, brooding face, full purplish lips, shadows cut beneath his eyes. He ruled the school. His authority was as absolute and uncontested as it was careful and lacking in pettiness. As he crossed the street, all action was suspended, as if we were puppets dangling from indecisive hands.

"What's happening."

"Girl's ready to get her butt kicked." Her tone was bold, but even I recognized it as a request.

"Renee, you 'bout twice her size."

"She grown enough to be gettin' in my face all year."

"What she do to you?"

"She be gettin' smart with me since way back September."

"It's right, Darwin. She got too much of a mouth on her," someone else put in. There was a scattered chorus of agreement. I didn't move a muscle or make a sound but I stared at Darwin with a sudden, desperate hope. His eyes came to rest on me, meeting my wild plea with the most impassive gaze I have ever encountered. He asked one question.

"How old is you?"

I scrunched as far down into myself as I could. "Nine," I said in a tiny voice. It was a pathetic little syllable.

He turned his head a fraction of an inch. "Renee, how old is *you*?"

"Eleven," she said proudly, and it did sound grand.

"Let her go," he said, as simply and unemphatically as "Pass the salt."

And that was it. I was saved. There was no protest from Renee, no murmur of disappointment from the crowd. Darwin did not so much as glance at me again, either to acknowledge his heroism or to warn me about watching my mouth in the future. I got the feeling, in fact, that I was incidental to all that had just transpired, to him. He had not been performing a rescue; he had just been making a decision. He was already disappearing down the street. And my tormentors had melted away, as if into thin air. I was alone.

"Does anyone know that man?" I fired the question into the sea of faces around me.

"Everyone know him," someone mumbled.

"What does he do?" I wondered out loud. What had that boy become?

"He do tattoos," said a light-skinned boy from deep under the brim of his hat. Right away I noticed a lurid green and red serpent undulating around his upper arm.

"Tattoos? Did he do that one?" I asked, nodding at the serpent.

"Naw."

"Well—where's his . . . uh, tattoo parlor?"

"He do it in his basement."

I turned my full attention on the boy. "Where does he advertise?"

"He don't."

"How do people find out about him?"

"They just know."

"Word of mouth?"

"Yeah."

"Do you, by any chance, have any tattoos that were done by him?"

"You with the press or somepin, lady?" he cracked.

"Matter of fact, I am," I answered, whipping out my badge without missing a beat. "But this is all off the record. So do you?"

"Naw," he said, grinning slightly. "He only do people who don't got none already."

"Really." I was intrigued past the point of no return. "How do you know all this?"

"He live in my building."

"And your name is—? Off the record."

"They call me Moe."

"Can I take you to lunch, Mr. Moe?"

Darwin was not only well-known throughout the neighborhood, but an icon in the tattoo world. His cult status in the underground was due as much to the startling nature of his designs as to the unusual prerequisites for their engraving.

First, as Moe had related on the street, the applicant—supplicant—had to be a virgin, so to speak. Darwin's mark had to be the first on any body he worked with. Second, the fee across the board, regardless of the size or intricacy of the tattoo, was a thousand dollars. This had to be paid up front and in full. Third, the client had to agree to accept, sight unseen, the design Darwin conceived for him (his work was never duplicated) and to have it etched anywhere on the body that Darwin chose. Discussion beforehand, negotiation during, or refund afterward was unthinkable—out of the question. The high price wasn't so much for the tattoo's application, but for the time it would take Darwin to think about the design.

I was so interested in all these details that for a full forty-five minutes I forgot about the arrest itself. I sat across from Moe in Copeland's, far too excited to eat, asking a steady stream of questions while he put away a plate of ribs and collard greens. Then, abruptly, I remembered the scene that had stopped me short on the street.

"So," I said, my lowered tone shifting the gears of the conversation. "Who did he kill?"

"Landlord."

"His landlord?"

"And mine," Moe said. He smiled.

"Did Darwin owe him a lot of money?"

"Didn't owe him a red cent. 'Bout the only one who didn't."

"Then why did he kill him?"

"Why don't you ask Darwin 'bout that?"

"If they let me talk to him I most certainly will. In the meantime I was hoping you could tell me what he would say."

"I could."

"Well, what would he say, then? Off the rec—"

"Darwin would say he needed killing."

It sounded so right I fell silent in amazement. It *was* exactly what Darwin would say. Our waitress approached and Moe ordered a piece of sweet potato pie while I mentally rephrased the question.

"Why did your landlord need killing?" I asked when she had gone.

Moe spun out the reasons why over several pieces of pie while I sat stirring my now-cold tea around in its cup.

The landlord—Mr. Ray, as Moe called him—was a bastard in all the usual ways, turning off the water and electricity, and the heat in winter, in his effort to collect from lagging tenants. He did not bomb the roaches and did nothing either about the rats or the crack addicts haunting the stairwells every night. But Darwin's reasons, Moe knew "for a fact," had to do with Tabitha Salazar.

Tabitha was a little girl of seven years who lived with her mother on the second floor. She had been born without arms—congenital something-or-other, Moe didn't remember exactly what. Her mother, Carmen, had quit her job of dispensing tokens in the subway several months before, confiding to Moe at the time that she was afraid she was losing her mind. She felt like the deep-sea diver she'd once seen in a Caracas aquarium, encased all her daylight hours in a Plexiglas cage and submerged in murky, shark-infested waters.

She was looking for another job and meanwhile she owed the landlord for three months. Last week, he had entered their apartment while they slept, and he had *taken Tabitha's arms.* He had confiscated the child's prosthetic limbs and wouldn't give them back until he had the rent.

"She didn't want to go to the pigs," Moe related, scraping the last of the orange filling from his plate. "She scared of them, and anyway she a illegal alien. She didn't want to go to the papers, 'cause that would mean puttin' the child in the middle of, you know, a mess with the press. She went to Darwin, I think, to borrow some money."

"And Darwin was incensed by her story," I suggested.

"He what?"

"He got mad."

"Naw," Moe said. "Darwin don't get mad. He just decided Mr. Ray needed killin'."

"So how did he do it?" I asked.

"Waited for him to come home from Bingo that night," Moe said. "Waited just inside the front door and snapped his neck like a chicken."

They didn't let me see him at first. His appointed lawyer had decided that media distortion would destroy Darwin's chance for a fair trial. So I ran the following ad in the *Village Voice*:

> Do you have a tattoo by DARWIN? Sympathetic journalist wants to talk to you. Share your special experience! Call (212) 802-7527.

I realized that "sympathetic" was ambiguous, referring either to Darwin or themselves. That was fine. They could decide what it meant.

That night I heard from Sadie.

"Well, they call me Sadie. They call me that now," she said. "But that's Darwin's doing too. My real name is Sara."

We made an appointment for the next afternoon, at her apartment. I offered to meet her at a bar or café in her neighborhood but she preferred it this way.

"Just come on over, and I'll make some tea," she said.

Sadie had a careless beauty, like a full-blown flower in its last glory. She was over forty and didn't attempt to disguise the silver streaking her long black hair. Her eyes were what caught you, a vulnerable aquamarine lighter than her skin. She'd been a high-class call girl before getting married.

"It was my girlfriend Charlene who got me interested in Darwin," she told me over a pot of chamomile. "She loves tattoos. She has five or six, some of the best I've seen. Like she's got a zipper on her left leg—starting at her thigh and unzipping down to her ankle. And this brilliant Japanese fighting fish, swimming out from between her breasts."

I murmured in appreciation.

"She was in the same business as me," Sadie went on. "The men loved it. The zipper and the fish. Men are like little kids; they like surprises.

"Anyway, she wanted another tattoo from Darwin, and of course he wouldn't do it. He won't touch anyone who's already been done. She offered him all kinds of money but he wouldn't budge. . . . Oh, it drove her *crazy.* Well, listening to her rant and rave about it all the time put the idea into my head."

Sadie smiled, drained her teacup, then rose to put the kettle back on. She moved languidly, a woman whose sensual indolence had been her bread and butter. She wore a robe of some shimmery stuff that hung in calculated tatters and brushed her braceleted ankles as she walked.

"I guess I originally did it to get to Char," she admitted. "I was always a little jealous of her. She was always in demand and she always had the best clientele—the sugar daddies and foreign royalty just had a way of falling into her lap. I think I liked the idea that I could have something she couldn't.

"So I went to see him, and I ended up staying all night. He was doing some electrical fix-it job in the basement ceiling. He worked and I talked. He had me hold a flashlight for him sometimes."

"What did you talk about?" I asked.

"Oh, everything. He had some pot; we smoked it together. Then he got his tools and we went downstairs. He climbed up a ladder until his head disappeared above the ceiling panels, and he started messing with the wires and stuff up there. After a while, I heard him say something. He said: 'Sara. Tell me.' Just like that."

She glanced at me, gauging something I couldn't guess at. Then, apparently satisfied, she said, "So I started to tell him."

At the time that Sadie—then Sara—had gone to Darwin, her career was in its decline. She was getting old for the trade. AIDS, paranoia, go-go clubs, and phone sex were edging all of them out anyway. There were three men in the picture, competing for her hand, and she felt cheated that after twenty-some years of flinging her ass around with the best of them, this is what it had all come down to. There was the manager of a rap group she refused to name. ("Please understand.") He had three floors of an apartment building, including the penthouse, directly across the street from the Metropolitan Museum of Art. There was the Senator, also necessarily anonymous, married with children, who wanted to set her up in a Georgetown brownstone. And there was Ty Hawkins. He was a joke. A math teacher in an east side public high school. Could barely afford her, and spent more than half of each paycheck on his monthly visits. Once he was there, though, he took his time. He rubbed her body down with oil before he made love to her, she facedown on the bed while he warmed the muscles in her calves, pressed the tender flesh behind her knees, and polished the delicate wings of her back. After he worked his way up the length of her, he would lift her heavy curtain of black hair—as reverent as if unveiling the lost ark—and kiss the back of her neck.

Sara stood by Darwin's ladder, handing him tools like a surgeon's assistant. In the shower of dust and ceiling debris raining down around her, she told Darwin that she had decided on the Senator. She couldn't see his face but she felt his total absorption in her monologue.

"I've never felt listened to with such intensity, not in all my life," she related now, looking past me to the opposite wall. "It was almost frightening. And you know what? I bet he wasn't fixing a damn thing in that ceiling. I think he was just taking his eyes out of my line of vision. Like maybe he thought the force of his undivided attention would spook me."

He told her to come back in a week if she still wanted the tattoo. She'd gone home and called Charlene. The other woman's outrage clinched her decision. She returned the following Sunday with a thousand-dollar bill tucked inside her bra.

Darwin reminded her that once he began the tattoo, he would have to complete it. With this in mind he asked her if she would like to be bound. It was, I was to find, a standard offer, and it struck her as a kindness. He had her lie facedown on something like an examining table, except it had metal posts at either end. He fastened her wrists to one of these, her ankles to the other, and got out the needles.

She felt as calm as if she'd been drugged, though she had ingested nothing since her arrival. She felt no fear, either of pain or disfigurement; such was her inexplicable confidence in the man readying his inks. She waited a long time, prone upon the table, lashed to the posts, while he put everything in order. She was almost asleep when he began to work.

And now, in the waning light from the kitchen window, Sadie pushed back from the table and came around to my chair. She knelt on the floor before me, facing the other way, and lifted her hair. On the back of her neck were seven sleek letters, intricately woven with hawthorn and thistles, etched in silvery slate and gleaming against her skin. HAWKINS.

Hawkins had discovered the tattoo during his visit, entirely of his own accord, and as if in obedience to an oracle, they had married. And now she was in love. With her husband. And very happy.

Two days later, Taylor called. I was on the phone already, talking long-distance with my brother, when he clicked in.

"Hello?" I said, aware that I sounded impatient.

"Ma'am?"

"Yes?"

"My name is Taylor. I'm answering your ad in the paper."

"Taylor? Would you mind calling back in about ten minutes? I'm on another line."

Very apologetically: "Ma'am, I'm sorry, I'm only allowed one phone call a week." He had a soft southern drawl. It sounded like

Charleston, or close. In my preoccupation with his accent, it took a moment for his words to sink in.

"You're only allowed one call a week? Are you in prison?"

"No ma'am. I'm a slave."

"What was that?"

"A slave."

I told my brother I'd call him back.

Taylor explained to me that he was the property of another man. It was a voluntary but inviolate arrangement. He kept his master's house and yard, chauffeured his car, served his guests, and warmed his bed. He had two visitor's days out of each year and was prepared to use one of them on me.

"That's very nice of you," I said, somewhat lamely.

"So what day would be best for you, ma'am?" I realized he'd been calling me "ma'am" throughout our exchange.

"Mmmmm . . . anytime after Wednesday," I said. "And you can call me Anne."

"Thank you, ma'am, but I couldn't do that," he said. "I'm not allowed to use first names to address any adult."

"Oh," I said. "I see. Okay. Well, how about Thursday, then?"

"Thursday is fine," he said. And gave me directions to his master's home on Long Island.

This time I saw the tattoo right away, because Taylor answered the door and he was stripped to the waist. A crimson horseshoe was scorched over his heart. Its edges were blurry, so that it resembled a burn. It flamed angry and raw against his smooth, chiseled chest. Something about it seemed vaguely familiar.

The rest of him was quite ordinary. He was younger than I'd expected—no older than twenty—about five-foot-ten, with a blond crew cut and hazel eyes. He wore jeans but no shoes.

"Please, come in, ma'am," he said, holding open the door for me. It was late in the afternoon, and the heat was sweltering. "Sit anywhere you're comfortable. Can I fix you a drink?"

I gratefully accepted a mimosa, using the minutes he took mixing it to survey "the master's house." The living room, where we were, was immaculate, and included a mahogany sideboard and full bar. The master himself was nowhere in sight.

Taylor handed me my drink. "He'll be home in a few minutes," he said, addressing my unspoken question. I was delighted with this news. I couldn't wait to see what he'd look like.

"He knows I'm here, right?" I asked.

"Yes ma'am," the boy answered. "Of course. Nothing happens around here without his knowledge. Or consent."

"How old are you?" I asked bluntly. I realized his subservience was affecting me. It didn't seem important to be polite.

"Nineteen, ma'am." He visibly relaxed as my manner changed.

"Are you in school?"

"No ma'am. That's over. At least for now. What do I need school for?"

Outside a military jeep pulled into the driveway. Swiftly Taylor knelt on the floor, hands behind his back.

"What are you doing?" I asked in alarm.

"I would never receive my master standing on my feet like a free man," he answered without turning his head. His gaze was riveted on the door.

"What should *I* do?"

"You're fine," he said. "Just stay where you are."

The door banged open. A powerful black frame filled the doorway. He stood well over six feet, muscles rippling through a drill sergeant's uniform. He was the kind of man who drives every thought from the mind except for, *Oh.* Oh my. I squashed an impulse to kneel on the carpet beside Taylor.

He stood for a moment in the doorway and then laughed. His was a deep, ringing, good-natured laugh. "You're the reporter, aren't you?" he said. He came over and extended his hand as if nothing were unusual about this scene. "Kevin's the name. Kevin Goodwin. Glad to meet you. So you're here to talk to my boy?"

"Anne Walker. Yes, that's right."

He crossed the room and seated himself in an armchair. Immediately Taylor was at his feet. Hands still behind his back, he leaned down to kiss each of the man's combat boots. Then he straightened to unlace them.

"He gave you a drink, that's good. Got to beat this heat somehow. Now you've come to hear about that tattoo, isn't that right? Well, good. It's a story worth telling. Have you talked to the brother yet?"

I realized he meant Darwin. "They haven't let me see him."

"You think you can help him?"

I bit my lip. "Me? No. I can't imagine how. I'm not a lawyer, I'm just a journalist. All I can do is tell a story—a fraction of a story."

"Well," he said, getting to his feet, authority as natural to him as breathing, "tell it then. Tell it right." He nodded pleasantly at me as he took his leave.

"Uh . . . yes, sir," I said to his departing back.

I turned back to Taylor. He was staring after the other man with glazed, love-struck eyes.

"Well," I said. "He's really something." The understatement hung in the air.

Slowly the boy brought his gaze around to me.

"But back to the tattoo," I prodded. "Taylor. Tell me."

So he told me.

It had begun with a fraternity initiation at NYU. Taylor had hated two groups of human beings with equal passion: blacks and gays. He wanted badly to join an underground white supremacist frat on campus, a group known for cross-burning and fag-bashing, major harassment.

"Have you ever witnessed a fraternity initiation? Usually it's a game of humiliation. That's all it is. Paddling, military bullshit, just games. But the schools have cracked down on hazing in recent years, and this particular frat had to cover its ass more than any of the others, being all but illegal.

"Most of these guys have tattoos. Some of them are skinheads—they've got 'em on their skulls, their faces. They read tattoo magazines; they all know who Darwin is.

"I'd just won a football pool, a little over a grand. And one of the guys—he was wasted off his ass—said, 'Hey! For his initiation, let's make him get tattooed by the Nigger.' That's what they called Darwin: the Nigger.

"Surprisingly, the others were into the idea. He's an icon in the tattoo world; most likely it was a vicarious thrill for them, seeing what he'd do. Plus they wanted to make me blow my winnings without actual extortion. 'If he fucks you up too bad, we'll go back and lynch him!' they said. It was probably the most interesting thing they'd ever come up with, I have to give it to them there."

Taylor paused. He'd broken a light sweat in the remembering.

"But I was shaking in my shoes. The idea was terrifying to me. I *hated* black men; I didn't want to go near one. Of course, it's obvious to me now that I was terrified of my own attraction to them. It was a deep and shameful secret I kept even from myself."

At this point, he noticed I'd drained my glass.

"Let me get you another drink," he offered.

"I'm fine, really," I said, but he insisted, and realizing he might need a break from the story, I let him go. What I really wanted was a cigarette. Badly. But I had none with me, as I considered it unprofessional to smoke during an interview.

Taylor returned with another mimosa, reseated himself on the floor, and continued his story.

Just taking the train into Harlem had freaked out the college boy from Magnolia, USA. *They* were everywhere, grouped on street corners, lurking in doorways. Clad in leather, in fur, in hooded sweat jackets and mirrored shades. Ominous, *knowing*. By the time Taylor reached Darwin's door, he was soaked in sweat, shivering, and faintly nauseous.

Darwin came to the door with a hammer in his hand. He was in the middle of doing a favor for an elderly tenant on the first floor, he said. Her kitchen floor was rotting. He was putting another one down for her. Did Taylor know how to drive nails?

Sure, Taylor answered, although he had no idea. He hadn't touched a nail since building a tree fort with some neighborhood kids at age ten. Darwin handed him the hammer.

Taylor followed him down the hall and into the woman's apartment. Apparently she was out for the afternoon.

There was a shallow pit in the kitchen where linoleum and corroded wood had been ripped out; three precisely measured boards waited to be fitted in place. Roaches skittered in all directions at their approach. A plaster Virgin Mary presided over the leaking sink.

They worked in silence for a while. Taylor concentrated as hard as he could on hitting the dead center of the nails so as not to embarrass himself. After about twenty minutes, Darwin asked why the boy wanted a tattoo.

"I told him it was a fraternity initiation," Taylor said. "It seemed impossible to lie to him. He asked which frat, like he was just making conversation. I actually told him. Didn't think it would mean a thing to him, any more than it would if I cussed him out in Greek. When his face didn't change, I figured I was right."

Taylor drew a deep breath. "I don't know about that anymore. I've thought about it every day since, and I still don't know what to think. We talked a little bit more, but he must have sensed I wasn't about to spill my guts to him like everyone else. My circumstances were different than other people's, anyway. Usually first-time visitors haven't made up their minds yet; they're feeling out the situation and they come back later. In my case, there was no decision. I was on a mission and I had the money.

"Besides," Taylor said after a pause, "I was having a lot of trouble with conversation anyway. I flustered and stuttered. Could barely meet his eyes."

Discussion tapered off as the two nailed the last board into place. Taylor felt a brief thrill as they stood together to walk across their handiwork.

"He took me down into the basement," he continued. "I gave him the money and he told me that, to ensure that he'd be able to finish what he started, he liked to immobilize his clients. I was afraid to let him do it, but more afraid not to. It had become some kind of insinuating challenge, though I didn't know what I was being goaded by anymore—whether it was him, or the fraternity, or just the whole idea of being put to a test. Anyway, I let him tie me to a chair. And then I wished I hadn't. Because as he was wrapping that cord around my wrists . . . to my indescribable horror, I . . . got turned on."

As he related this part of the story, Taylor flushed deeply. I found it amazing that he could play the part of a drill sergeant's sex slave with such ease, and yet be so shaken by the memory of what had brought him there.

"I know I have never been as mortified as I was in those moments. I didn't know if he could tell, but that was almost beside the point. *I* knew. For the first time in my life, this fact—which I'd never been able to look at, not even out of the corner of my eye—suddenly came into focus. It was dazzling in its clarity—dazzling and terrible. I couldn't accept it.

"I was wearing a white button-down shirt, nothing underneath it. Darwin told me he was putting the tattoo over my heart, and he unfastened every button on my shirt. His touch was completely impersonal; I felt like a kid being undressed for bed. But when he put his hands on me—when he touched the place on my chest where it was going to go—I broke out in the same cold sweat that had come over me on the street. If I hadn't been tied down, I would have bolted for sure.

"He went to work. It hurt. I was almost grateful for physical pain; it was a diversion from this unspeakable revelation. I didn't care what design he had come up with, because I was planning to jump off a bridge as soon as I was out of there. That was the extent of my shame.

"But after about thirty minutes, as he worked on me, this shame—by far the most overpowering emotion I'd ever experienced—began to yield to something even stronger. And that was ecstasy. I was alone with this man. Under his hands. I could breathe in the scent of his skin. I was, at that moment, his only concern. And I thought to myself, I could live if only for this. *This.*

"I don't know how long it took for him to finish. I lost all sense of time. Probably it was close to two hours. We didn't exchange a single word that whole time, and I actually imagined that he was oblivious to what I was feeling. When he was done he rose to sterilize his equipment, and for the first time I looked down.

"I recognized it immediately. It's the symbol that Omega Psi Phi, the black fraternity, brands into the chest of each of their brothers. It looks like a brand—doesn't it?" He glanced up at me. Then, without waiting for a reply, he added, "One that will never heal."

We studied it together for a moment. Then Taylor broke the silence. "I was overcome. It was like a miracle, a message. I saw what my life could be. I could never go home again, of course, and never go back to the university. It didn't matter. None of that mattered at all."

"Did Darwin understand the implications of the tattoo for you?" I asked.

Taylor looked at me as if at a very slow child. "Of course he understood. What do you think we're talking about here?"

I was clutching my pen so hard that my fingernails had left little half-moons in my palm, yet I hadn't written a word so far. "So what did you do then? After he'd untied you?"

"I was so grateful," Taylor said. "I wanted to kiss his feet. He wouldn't let me. 'I'm not the one' is what he said."

After this, I renewed my efforts to see Darwin. I called every press associate and pulled every string. I left half a dozen messages on his lawyer's machine, explaining that my motives at this point were more personal than professional, promising not to release anything I wrote until he gave me the green light. I offered to put this in writing. I said Darwin was a friend of mine from grade school. I said everything I could think of. And I was told by everyone involved that I would have to wait.

At the end of that week, Niles called.

"You the one with the tattoo ad?" he demanded gruffly.

I confirmed that I was.

"Well—this might sound a little strange," he began.

Somehow I wasn't surprised to hear this.

"It isn't me that got the tattoo. It was my friend Pete. But he's dead. Would it be awright for me to tell the story for him?"

I was startled into momentary speechlessness.

"See," he went on in a rush, "I think I was meant to tell it. Because me seein' your ad was like fate. I'm with Barnum and Bailey, right? And we just pulled into New York the week you ran your phone number in the paper. And I never read that paper nohow. I was on the train and it was there on the seat. Open right to that page. It jumped out at me, see? Now, I ain't a religious man, but this struck me as some kind of sign."

I recovered myself. "Of course you can tell your friend's story, Mr.—?"

"Niles. Just Niles," he said. "You can come down here to the circus anytime in the next two weeks. After that we go to Virginia. You can watch the show, too, if you want," he added. "I'm the sword swallower."

I hadn't been to the circus since I was a child. It was heavy with glitter and nostalgia, tawdry and seductive. Niles met me at the tent opening and escorted me to a ringside seat. The next time I saw him, his neck was arched back under the weight of seven gleaming sabers. He was a sinewy man, close to fifty, a widow's peak cutting into his iron-gray hair. I waited for him after the show, in my seat, as directed.

He emerged in street clothes a few minutes after the tent had emptied.

"Come on," he said.

"Pete was an electrician," he told me on the way to his trailer. "And an alcoholic. He worked the spotlights when he was sober enough. Not the most reliable guy in the world. He probably woulda been fired if he hadn't been here for so damn long. He been here since way back before I even joined up. Musta been close to twenty years. He had . . ." And here he stopped and groped for the word.

"Seniority?" I suggested.

"That's it. So if he was hungover once in a while and didn't show up for his call . . . well, the boss would just kinda let it go. The last coupla years we had Jason anyway, a kid who could fill in for 'im. I think that bothered Pete, no matter how many times it had saved his sorry ass. Didn't really matter if he didn't show, 'cause here was this young'un who was probably better at it anyway. Pete wanted to feel . . ." And he stopped again.

"Indispensable," I supplied.

"You got it. He wanted to be important. He stayed with the circus 'cause most people think it's somethin' special. Know what I'm sayin'? Glammer, that's what he wanted."

We had come to the door of his trailer. It was a deep red, bordered with gold swirls. Two crossed and rusted swords were nailed above the entrance. He unlocked it and ushered me inside.

The interior was spare and clean. Niles sat down on his bed, leaving me the one chair. He extracted a pack of cigarettes from his shirt pocket, shook two from the box, and handed one to me. We smoked in silence for a while. Then he began talking again, as if there had been no interruption.

"Pete wanted glammer. He was always hangin' around whenever anyone was practicin' an act. Tryin' to get 'em to teach 'im some tricks. Once in a while, someone would feel sorry for 'im and try to show 'im somethin'. It was never any good. Pete was an accident waiting to happen. He'd stab himself with my swords, get mauled by the cats. He singed his eyebrows off with the fire-eater's torch. Hell, the boy couldn't even juggle. He was a sad sack, what can I say.

"I think that's why he drank so much. 'I got no talent, Niles,' he used to say to me. He'd cry real tears sometimes, if he had enough likker in 'im. A grown man, forty-eight years old, carryin' on like a lovesick kid.

"You couldn't say nothin' to 'im. I tried. 'Talent, hell!' I'd say to 'im. 'So I can stick a bunch of blades down my craw. What do you need talent like that for? I'm just makin' a livin', same as you,' I'd say. Didn't make no nevermind."

Evening was falling fast. Niles hadn't yet turned on any lights inside the trailer. Purple twilight filled the little room, and our cigarettes glowed in the semidark.

"One night," he continued after a pause, "I found him by the tiger's cage, just starin'. 'What are you doin', old boy?' I ast him. It spooked me a little, the way he was lookin' at 'em. And he started talkin' about this lady from his hometown. She kilt herself one night, climbin' over the fence at the zoo to get to the tigers. It was in all the papers the next day, it was all anyone could talk about. 'Now, that's a magnificent death there, Niles,' he said to me.

"A magnificent death, that's how he put it. I told 'im to quit talkin' shit. But he kept right on like I wasn't even there. 'I could settle for a magnificent death' is what he said next. He said, 'That would make everything come out even, even if there wasn't nothin' in my life to ever write home about.'

"I looked real hard into his face. He sounded drunk but I knew he wasn't. You spend twenty some years around a man and you know things like that. I couldn't think of what to say."

Niles shook another cigarette from the pack, squinted at it, and lit it with the first. "I remember at that time we were in the state of Louisiana. New Orleans. Finally I told him to come on and let's get a plate of fried catfish. He loved them things. I said I'd treat him."

Niles stopped here. Silence settled into the small space. I waited for him to resume the tale, but he didn't. After what seemed an interminable length of time, I spoke gently into the near-dark. "The tattoo?"

He looked at me as if he'd forgotten I was there. Then he rose and switched on the light.

"Just about everybody in the circus has got tattoos," Niles said. He peeled off his wool sweater and stood before me in a sleeveless undershirt. His arms were heavily illustrated, mostly with circus motifs. There were leopards, elephants, women bursting out of jungle-printed bikinis. Dancing bears cavorted on his forearm; above his elbow a puma leapt through a flaming hoop. When he turned slightly to the side, I glimpsed a girl behind one shoulder, dangling from a trapeze.

"And that's just my arms," he chuckled, pulling his sweater back on. "You'd be hard put to find a man without 'em, here. Not Pete though. Not for the longest time. Not till we was all lookin' at one of them trade magazines. There was a feature piece in there 'bout Darwin. Oh, that boy could draw.

"We was all sittin' around talkin about 'im. Arguin' about 'im: why he cost so much and why he always asks the same amount of money. Why he'll only work on clean skin. June—that's the makeup lady—she said every artist wants a blank canvas. She wanted to be an artist herself once. Way she talks, tryin' to sound so—" And he stopped, waiting for me to fill in the blank.

"Sophisticated?"

"Yeah, high-blown as she talks, you'd think she made it. Then Samson—that's the name the strongman takes—said Bullshit. Said,

That coon jus' understands the philosophy of our founding father: there's a sucker born every minute. If people get the idea that a tattoo from him is something not just anyone can have—well, that'll make 'em want one, all by itse'f.

"Well, just then Pete was crossin' through the tent. He heard Samson talkin' and he said, 'What can't everybody have?' So we showed him the magazine. He studied it for a spell, turnin' it around and around, squintin' at the designs, readin' all the print. Finally he looked up and around at all of us. His mouth was hangin' open, and jus' like in the cartoons, it was like a lightbulb went on over his head. 'I am the only one in this company who could get one of them designs,' he announces. He was all puffed up.

"We all sat there and didn't no one say a word. Then he started figurin'. 'I get paid this week,' he says, 'and if I ask for an advance I could do it before we go south again.'

"'What did I just say!' the strongman yelled. And you had to give it to 'im, seemed like he had it right."

Niles returned to the bed and stretched out on his back. He laced his hands and placed them under his head. "I went with 'im when he gone," he said, addressing the ceiling. "Hell, I was curious. To some, Darwin is kind of a celeberty.

"Y'know, I think I wanted Sam to be right. I wanted the man to be a scam. To tell you the truth, I was right jealous that he was goin' to do Pete and not me. When had Pete ever cared 'bout tattoos? I wanted to think he was throwin' four weeks' pay down a rat hole.

"But when we got to that boy's place, when we was standin' there in the same room with 'im, I knew he warn't no quack. You don't know, you can't know till you been there, what kind of power he got. No lie, lady. He look carved out of stone, like someone chiseled every joint and muscle in his body. And his eyes—he got the oldest eyes I ever seen. They don't hardly never blink. He look like he seen the creation of the world."

Niles fell silent. I found myself again on the edge of my seat, as I had been at Sadie's and Taylor's. It took all my restraint not to urge him on. I let him meditate on whatever had taken hold of him, knowing it would ultimately pay off.

Finally he said: "How come you ain't writin' this up? You got any of them teeny little mikes on you?"

"No," I said. "Oh, no. I never record. I just listen, and if I have to remember something complicated, I'll write it down."

"Well, what I'm 'bout to tell you, I don't want you writin' down nowhere."

I leaned forward. "You have my word of honor."

"I'll tell you what thought come into my head when I was standin' there in front of that man."

"I'll keep it off the record."

Niles threw an arm over his face, and when he spoke, his voice was muffled.

"Don't know how this thought come into my mind. I been in the same profession for twenty years and I ain't thought about it once. But it suddenly come to me that, my line of work bein' what it is, I could prob'ly give a man some head like no one else on this earth."

Nothing he said could have been less expected. Shock washed over me, followed by a wave of amusement. I caught my breath and held it, casting desperately about for the right thing to say. But then Niles took his arm away from his face and laughed. His laughter was deep and infectious; mine joined it easily, filling the trailer.

"Darwin let Pete talk his ear off," Niles said when he could speak again. "We hung around 'im all day, helping 'im thread pipes, and Pete must have been yammerin' nonstop for hours. His whole damn life story, which I've heard at least three times a year for the last twenty. I coulda finished ever' one of his sentences for 'im. But here was the thing. Darwin was payin' attention. It was the damnedest thing, for anyone who knew Pete, to watch someone watch him with that much—concentration.

"Oh, and he unravel't th' whole nine yards. The disappointments and the bad luck. How all he'd ever wanted was to be at the top of somethin', even if it was only for a moment's time. He spun out every act in the goddamn circus and how he'd failed at ever'thing he ever tried. Made my stomach hurt. But then, I was thinkin', someone's listenin' to him for once. An' it was almost worth the money just to see the effect that was havin' on 'im.

"Finally Darwin ast him was he ready. And Pete said he sure was. Darwin trussed him up a little bit, somethin' he likes to do, but it warn't no big production. Pete wasn't gonna fight it."

Niles sat up on the bed and removed one of his shoes. He rested his foot on his knee, its sole facing me.

"Darwin put ropes on the bottoms of both his feet," he said, tracing a line from his own heel to toe for emphasis. "Straight up the middle like that. When I say ropes, what I mean is wires. High wires, woven fine and tight. I don't know how he knew what a tightrope would even look like. But it was so real there on the arches of his feet, looked like 3-D.

"I carried Pete out of there on my back. He'd had an even grand on 'im, no more and no less. I had to pay for the damn cab ride back to the circus lot. He couldn't walk for four days. Didn't bother him none, though. He was like a man with a fever. Delirious-like.

"As soon as he could stand, nothin' could keep him away from that tightrope. Day and night, he was like a human basketball, he spent so much time fallin' into that net. But I hafta admit, though it ain't sayin' much, he took to the wire faster than anythin' else he'd ever taken the notion to try. He told me he would line up the rope drawn into his feet with the real rope beneath 'em. He say it warn't hard that way. He claimed he could *feel* the tattoos.

"Well, soon he could walk across all right. And then he wanted to be a daredevil. That's kind of the way anyone livin' with the circus is gonna think. Who wants to do anythin' that looks safe? One evenin' when we were gettin' ready to load out, Pete was up on the tightrope platform actin' goofy. No one had a thought about what he could be up to. But then, as soon as we cut down the nets, he walked out on the wire."

Niles slipped into one of his silences and I rode it out. A light rain was beginning, tapping on the roof. I could guess what was coming and it filled me with dread.

"I looked up at 'im," he said finally, "and I broke out in chills. I couldn't believe he would be as big a fool as that. I wanted to yell, but I was afraid of spookin' 'im. No one else treated it like it was anythin' wrong. They all started clappin' and cheerin'. Eggin' him on. Me, I couldn't move. Couldn't *breathe.* It was like somepin evil had me by the throat. But even in the middle of feelin' that way, I couldn't help but notice."

"Notice what?" I asked softly.

"Notice that Pete looked like a happy man."

The sky shuddered with lightning just outside the window.

"I was paralyzed before he fell and I was paralyzed after. Ever'body screamin', runnin' around like geeked chickins. I jus' stood there, chills runnin' up and down. He was dead on impact, that's the only thing I'se glad about. I won't tell you what he look like. I seen worse in my time, but they wasn't buddies."

Niles stood abruptly and went to the window. He stood looking out into the worsening night. Without turning around he said, "I was the one cleaned out his trailer, straightened out where his stuff should go. He didn't hardly have nothin', and no family to take what there was. We shared it out among the comp'ny, mostly. But . . ." He opened one of his kitchen drawers and withdrew a yellowing piece of tablet paper. "I found this tacked to the wall. Felt like keepin' it." He passed it to me.

It had been folded a single time. The shaky handwriting of a man I'd never known filled the top line. "*Walking the wire is living. The rest is just waiting,*" read the feathery script. Underneath, the quote was credited to Karl Wallenda.

The very next morning, Darwin's lawyer called without warning. I was still half-asleep. I picked up the phone without opening my eyes and cradled it clumsily against one ear.

"Hello," I murmured, making no effort to sound less drowsy than I felt.

"Ms. Walker?" A crisp, male voice.

"Speaking . . ."

"This is Darwin Godfrey's attorney."

Immediately I woke the rest of the way up. I bolted upright in bed, clutching the receiver with both hands.

"Yes?"

"If you still want to speak with my client, you can have an hour with him on Friday the seventeenth of this month. From eleven until noon. No cameras. No recording equipment. Is this a problem for you?"

"Not at all," I responded instantly, not caring what appointments I might have had in that slot. Anything else could be rescheduled, rearranged. . . .

"Please be in my office at ten-thirty sharp on the seventeenth. I'll take you over to the prison."

"Yes. Thank you. I'll be there."

"Though I have to tell you," the lawyer said, "if you really went to school with Mr. Godfrey, he doesn't remember you."

"No. He wouldn't," I said. "But maybe he will."

"Can people get tattoos in prison?" I asked a friend of mine who had been there.

"Sure," he said. "That's where I got all of mine. There's always a tattoo artist or two in the joint. They usually get paid in cigarettes."

I had done many interviews in prison before. I was familiar with the entrance process, each door locking like the past behind my back after I'd stepped through. The momentous sound of metal catching metal echoed around our footsteps. No one spoke on the way to the pressroom.

I was left alone there for some minutes before they brought him in. The enormity of what was about to happen put a tremor in my hands, in my knees. I'm going to get to talk with him, I thought. I'm going to be in the same room as him. He's going to look into me. The tremor spread up my limbs and I sat shivering, waiting.

The door opened and he stood at the threshold. He appeared taller, gaunter, with hollowed-out eyes burning from a rawboned face. Niles's words came back to me as I gazed up at him: "Them eyes look like they seen the creation of the world."

He had a rag tied around his head, and wore a dark blue prison uniform. His hands were cuffed in front of him.

A guard was just behind him. "Okay, my understanding is, you got an hour. So please conduct your interview accordingly. I'm just outside, so he isn't likely to try anything."

"I'm not worried about that," I snapped, chagrined.

He gestured vaguely, a kind of half-wave, as if to say no offense was intended. Then he withdrew, leaving us alone.

Darwin seated himself across from me. "Were you a friend of mine at Colfax?" he asked. Colfax had been my—our—elementary school. His voice was low, rich, and faintly amused, as if he suspected I'd made it up.

"Well, maybe not," I said. "But you were sure a friend of mine. At least on one afternoon."

He tilted his head and waited for me to explain.

"You saved my life, in fact," I said, only half in jest. "From a mob of girls wanting my blood."

When his face still registered no recognition, I started spinning out the story. He listened intently, nodding every now and then at some detail. He remembered Renee, he could see that very street corner like it was yesterday, but the event itself was hazy in his mind.

"Something fuzzy is kind of coming back now that you tell it," he said. "Seems like a dream, though. Were you a thin little child? Backpack too big for your back?"

"Sounds like me."

"Yeah, I can see it now. But fuzzy. Blurry, like a dream. It didn't seem right to me, a pack of near-grown girls on a baby's tail."

"Well, you saved that baby's tail."

He smiled, but his eyes never changed. They rested on me, serious and questioning.

"They wouldn't let me see you for a long time," I began. "So I talked to a few people you tattooed."

I paused to gauge his response. He regarded me with interest. If he minded my little research project, he wasn't showing it.

"A woman by the name of Sadie—though she was Sara when she came to you. And a kid called Taylor, and Niles from the Barnum and Bailey Circus."

When he still said nothing, I said, "They had some of the most extraordinary stories I've ever heard."

"I suppose most people do, when you take the time to hear them," he said neutrally.

"You changed their lives."

"Everyone changes everybody else's lives."

"The prophet is modest," I said, mocking a little. It was a mistake. He didn't move a muscle but I could see his careful face closing against me.

"You changed their lives *dramatically*," I tried again.

"They changed their own lives."

"Well, let's just say you marked their maps," I said stubbornly.

Darwin's gaze was patient. "When you were a child, did they ever stick some inkblots under your face?" he asked. "Ask you what they were? Maybe you saw a butterfly and someone else saw a Mack truck. Know what I'm saying to you? Maybe I put inkblots on folks's skin. They decided what to do with them."

"Those were pretty specific inkblots, as far as I could tell," I said.

He didn't respond, but sat still and watchful. I realized he was waiting me out. We locked eyes across the table and as we did, I knew he had me. Who could win a staring contest with Darwin? Less than a minute passed before I gave it to him.

"Will you put one on me, then? Please?" I asked in a rush. Oh, and this wasn't how I'd intended to ask; I'd wanted to make it humorous and ironic, with at least the trappings of self-possession.

His flat and immediate response indicated that he'd expected it. "If you know what you're asking, and I can only assume you do, you have at least twelve C-notes on your person right now, ten for me and two for that guard out there."

I nodded. In fact, I had a little more.

"We have less than thirty minutes. I can't do much in that time. What I give you wouldn't cost more than twenty bucks anywhere else."

"I don't care."

"Then let me tell you where I want you to take that thousand. I want you to give it to a woman in my building. Carmen Salazar." He considered a moment. "But I want you to wait until just when she's really gonna need it. That'll be about six months from now. Do you know where I live?"

I said that I did.

"Give me the two hundred for Jackson out there," he said. I fished it out of my purse and handed it to him. What are you doing?

I asked myself. You're a professional woman in a cutthroat line of work. You've taken over a decade to carve out your career. The last thing you need is a tattoo. What if he stamps the anarchy symbol in the middle of your forehead?

Darwin rose and stepped just outside the door. There was a brief conference with the guard, whispered negotiations. Then: "Let's go," he said to me. I rose wordlessly and followed the two men down several corridors.

We came to an empty shop room. Once we were inside, the guard locked the door. Darwin's handcuffs were removed. "I'm gonna put these on you, if it's all right," he said.

"You really think that's necessary?" I asked uncomfortably.

"Well, yes. I do think so. It's going to hurt."

I felt a stab of fear at this. "You're putting it somewhere really sensitive, you mean?"

"Right."

Heart pounding in my throat, I allowed him to lock my wrists behind my back. The guard provided another pair of cuffs, to secure me to a chair. At Darwin's direction, the chair was placed against a wall.

Darwin got his paraphernalia out of a drawer and began to get it ready.

"Not your everyday interview, eh?" the guard—Jackson—chuckled.

I tried to smile.

Darwin came over and put one hand under my chin. At his gentle but insistent pressure, the back of my head rested against the wall. "Don't move," he said softly. Accordingly I didn't answer or nod, but my eyes told him I wouldn't.

With his thumb he peeled down my lower lip.

Even as the white-hot darts shot into that tender flesh, I was overwhelmed by the perfection of his putting it there. My eyes filled and spilled over, from pain and also from gratitude. The tattoo would be concealed completely, would never be seen by anyone unless I chose to show it. Not by bosses, by doctors, or even by lovers. I leaned up and into it, tears falling, mouth bleeding. I hung at his hand like a fish from a hook. He did his work, oral and intimate, in silence, reeling me in. It took less than ten minutes.

When it was over, I knew to wait. I did not ask to see a mirror. I did not ask anything at all. I was released from my seat, handcuffs were replaced on guard's belt and inmate's wrists, and the three of us returned to the pressroom with a couple of minutes to spare.

The lawyer drove me home. "Get any good material?" he asked, and I told him I had. If he noticed my swollen lip, he didn't mention it.

Once inside my apartment, I went straight to the bedroom. I stood before the vanity and gingerly turned my lower lip inside out. The ink was black, the lines were clean, the word was three letters long.

SEE

I'm a writer, so he gave me a word. I like riddles so he left it without punctuation. It could be a question, and I've used it that way. I've told men who think they've seen every inch of me that I have a tattoo. They never believe it. I pull down my lip, revealing the underside.

"SEE?" it mocks them.

It mocks me too, because I'm the only one who *can't* see it, not the right way. It's backward in the mirror, and if I stretch it out and peer at it cross-eyed, it's upside down.

I went uptown into the projects a few days ago. It had been the six months Darwin had asked me to wait. I gave the thousand dollars to Carmen Salazar and held her while she wept for him. Later we sat in her kitchen and passed the afternoon, sipping tea, trading stories, laughing into each other's eyes, as two women will who love the same prisoner.

Before I left, I showed her my tattoo. She nodded her understanding. Darwin had received a life sentence, but so had I.

SEE. It could have been a question, it could have been a taunt. But she knew it, as I did, for the command it is, one that will take the rest of my life to carry out.

Grateful Acknowledgments are made to the following:

To my mother and father, who have always accepted my going where I have to go, for their love and open-mindedness;

To my brother, Eric, for his special friendship and sense of humor;

To all my friends for their consistent support and encouragement: you know who you are, and fortunately for me, I know who you are;

To Charles LaFave for his relay service;

To Jennifer Hengen and Jody Hotchkiss at Sterling Lord Literistic;

To Colin Dickerman at Grove Press;

To Dave Schleifer, who surprised me;

To Charlie Stone, for the use of his computer, and years of faith;

To Tom Griesel, for his photography, generosity, and sensitive vision;

And to the late Doris Jean Austin, who always encouraged me to be bad, bold, and true to myself; who was the best writing teacher I ever had, and my most important mentor.